# Winter's Malice

Belinda G. Buchanan

D1473079

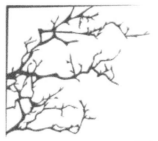

# Chapter 1

Liam Matthews felt his jaw tightening as he stood along the bank's edge watching the team of divers as they struggled to pull Hector Ramirez into the boat. The small craft tipped to the left and then abruptly righted itself, sending a fresh ripple of waves rolling across the water as Hector's bloated and mangled body was finally hoisted onboard. As the boat turned and headed for shore, the last rays of light slithered across the front of its bow and disappeared into a thicket of trees, signifying a bitter end to what had been a weeklong search for Weeping Rock's favorite son.

A fierce wind began to beat steadily down, transforming the ripples of water into rough whitecaps, which in turn caused the occupants of the boat—with the exception of Hector—to grasp onto its sides as it violently rocked back and forth.

Flipping up the collar of his coat, Liam scowled at the Channel 2 News helicopter as it passed overhead. Once word had gotten out that Hector's body had been located, it hadn't taken long for the media to converge upon their tiny town. Staring at the intrusive beast as it hovered above the water, Liam found himself hoping that the obtained footage would end up being too dark for them to use. Although he had nothing personal against reporting the fact that Hector had been recovered, he saw no need for an aerial view of the man's corpse to accompany it. Dropping to one knee, he grabbed hold of the front of the boat as it drew near and, after fastening his fingers around the edges of its aluminum frame, gave a hard tug, successfully beaching it upon the rain-swollen bank.

Gordon Stiles, who had been sitting by the bow, stood up first, giving Liam a full—and unexpected—view of Hector. Turning his head, Liam pressed the back of his wrist to his nose and lips as he stumbled to his feet.

"You all right, Sheriff?" asked Gordon.

Certain that more than words would come spilling out of his mouth if he opened it, Liam offered his deputy a stiff nod instead.

"Poor bastard," said Gordon, climbing out onto the bank. "Somebody sure fucked him up."

A flurry of movement on his right caused Liam to shift his attention to the top of the embankment—and sigh. The small group of curious onlookers initially crowded behind the yellow police tape had evolved into a frenzied horde of cell phone-clutching spectators who were fighting to get a front-row picture by using any means necessary, including, but not limited to, pushing, shoving, and throwing well-aimed elbows. Swallowing his irritation, along with everything else that had gathered in the back of his throat, Liam stepped to his left in order to block Hector from their line of sight, then taking his hand away from his lips, reluctantly coaxed his gaze back into the boat.

Stiles' words, although crude, were accurate, for even with the amount of decomp that was present, there was no denying the beating Hector had taken. Beneath his matted tangle of dark hair were bits and pieces of rotting flesh; brownish-green in color and putrid, they clung to a deep laceration that ran the length of his scalp. The lower part of Hector's jaw was crooked and slack, revealing a large gap where several of his teeth used to sit, and — what Liam could only guess was his nose, lay flattened against his face, which in retrospect, really didn't resemble a face at all. In fact, if it hadn't been for the one-inch symmetrical hole situated just below Hector's left brow that up until seven days ago had housed an inexpensive glass eye, he would have been unrecognizable.

"Looks like the son-of-a-bitch's luck finally ran out."

Knowing the gravelly voice coming from behind belonged to that of Bill Miller, Liam didn't bother turning around.

"Hey, Bill," called Gordon, giving him a wave. "How's it going?"

"How's it *goin'*?" Miller repeated. "I'm freezin' my goddamn balls off! That's how it's *goin'*!"

Gordon laughed and shook his head. "Aren't we all?" he replied, using his foot to steady the boat for the divers.

"Why the hell couldn't you have waited until the spring to have us search for him?"

"Because," said Gordon, nodding at the lake, "somewhere down there's a prized largemouth with my name on it, and I couldn't have Hector's smelly ass ruining my chances."

Miller let out a raspy snort. "I hear ya!"

As Liam bent down to retrieve the folded sheet beside him, he could feel the hairs on the back of his neck beginning to bristle over his deputy's easy-going banter with Miller, and—finding the exchange between them to be as disrespectful as it was disturbing—gave him a look that told him so as he tossed him the covering.

Still grinning, Gordon handed the sheet to one of the men in the boat and promptly returned his attention to Miller. "Besides," he said, gesturing at the chopper, "it's been so long since you've gotten any, I figured that putting your ugly mug on the evening news might help."

"Shit ..." replied Miller, dragging the word out as he laughed.

"Let's go, Stiles," the diver behind him said in a weary voice.

Chuckling to himself, Gordon grabbed hold of the corner of the sheet. "On three." After giving the count, he helped the divers carry Hector up the steep embankment.

The helicopter followed suit and moved in for a closer shot, causing the crowd of spectators to momentarily scatter.

"You know, I've been captain of Search and Rescue for almost twenty years," said Miller, shouting to be heard over the high-pitched whine of its rotors, "and I ain't never seen such a commotion over a dead man in my life. The press is gonna have a goddamn field day with him."

Shielding his eyes from the grass and debris being flung his way, Liam did his best to ignore Miller's comments as Hector's remains were placed inside a body bag and loaded onto a stretcher. Deep down, however, he knew Miller was right; with tons of questions and very few answers, the media was going to be feeding off of this for weeks, piece by broken piece, and story by unsubstantiated story. It was a forgone conclusion that everything learned over the coming days, whether true or not, was going to be sensationalized to the point that the only thing Hector Ramirez would be remembered for was the way he'd died.

A rough slap between the shoulder blades interrupted Liam's thoughts.

"You got it from here, Matthews?"

Liam forced himself to turn around. "I think I can manage."

Miller leaned over and spat, sending an arc of brown saliva hurtling towards the ground. "You know, I always liked workin' with your old man."

An unintentional smile found its way onto Liam's lips. "Is that right?"

"Yeah." Wiping the dribble from his chin, Miller narrowed his eyes. "He knew what the hell he was doin'."

Drops of rain, cold and stinging, began to fall upon Liam's face, yet did nothing to diminish the searing heat that had encircled his cheeks.

"Harlan always had a sixth sense about these kinds of things," Miller continued, the buttons at the bottom of his coat straining against their slots as he widened his stance. "It's a damn shame what happened to him."

Jamming his hands in his pockets, Liam watched the helicopter's sleek red-and-white tail disappear into the shadows as it swung around and began heading north.

"Yep ..." Miller paused to let go of a heavy sigh. "A *damn* shame."

Finding himself floundering in the unyielding silence left behind in the chopper's wake, Liam was relieved to hear his radio fill with static.

"Sheriff, do you copy?"

"Go ahead, Enid."

"I've got people from news channels 2, 7, and 11 on the phone wanting to know when you're going to give a statement."

Liam glanced at the covey of news vans parked along the edge of the embankment and felt his relief leaving him. "Give me fifteen minutes."

"Copy that."

Lifting his ball cap, Miller eagerly began smoothing his reddish-blond comb-over. "You want me to handle it for you, Matthews? Because I know how to deal with these bloodsuckers. Trust me when I say that I'd be doing you a favor."

Seriously doubting that he had his best interests at heart, Liam shook his head. "Thanks, but I've got it," he replied, wishing that Miller would just go back inside his little command tent at the top of the hill.

Miller stopped primping and jerked his thumb towards the embankment. "This isn't your average run-of-the-mill interview, you know. It's gonna get picked up by every affiliate in the country, and if you don't know how to handle yourself, you'll come across sounding like a jackass."

"Are you speaking from experience, Bill?" asked Liam, clipping his radio back onto his belt.

The brazen smile Miller had been sporting faded.

A small sense of satisfaction crept onto Liam's face making him purse his lips in an effort to hide it. It was a gesture that did not go unnoticed by

Miller, whose dismantled grin quickly morphed into a straight line that stretched taut across his pudgy cheeks.

"Sheriff!"

Glancing over his shoulder, Liam saw his other deputy coming towards him, yet noting the urgency in his steps, turned and met him halfway. "What's wrong?"

"Yeah," chimed Miller, bumping against Liam's elbow as he caught up to him, "what's your hurry there, *son*?" Running his tongue along the inside of his cheek, Miller leaned forward and spat again.

A pool of rainwater spilled from the brim of Aaron Red Elk's hat as he looked at the wad of tobacco lying near the tip of his boot. Slowly lifting his head, he locked eyes with Miller.

"What's wrong?" repeated Liam, having no desire to run interference between them this time.

Uncurling the fist that he'd made with his right hand, Aaron shifted his gaze to Liam. "The victim's—"

An earsplitting shriek ripped through the trees, piercing the darkness around them.

"—wife is here," he finished.

Liam visibly shivered as another shriek, more volatile than the one before, tore through him. "I need you to take her down to the station—*now*," he said, feeling his apprehension increasing as the crowd began to part down the middle. "I'll be there as soon as I can."

Aaron turned and started up the muddy slope, his long and deliberate stride enabling him to reach the top of it in a matter of seconds—just in time to grab hold of Hector's wife, who was in the process of ducking under the police tape.

"Let me go!" she screamed. "I want to see him! Hector! Hector!" The woman's demands were drowned out by her wails as Aaron awkwardly tried to console her amidst a sea of cameras.

"Well, good luck solvin' this one," said Miller with a condescending laugh as he slapped Liam on the back once more. "You're sure as hell gonna need it."

Liam used the sleeve of his coat to wipe the rain off his face before extending a rigid hand. "Thanks for all your help, Bill," he said, hoping that the curtness in his voice would somehow be mistaken for sincerity. "And thank your men for me too. I know the weather's been rough on them these last few days."

"Don't think nothin' of it," Miller replied, wrapping a meaty paw around Liam's fingers. "Be sure and let me know if you need anything else now."

"I'll do that," he said, persuading his tongue to let go of the words.

Pulling a small tin from his pocket, Miller stuffed a fresh pinch of tobacco inside his left cheek and shouldered past him. "Come on, boys!" he barked. "Let's pack it up!"

Liam's breath came out in a heated rush, instantaneously transforming the air in front of him into a cloud of white, as he watched Miller trudge up the embankment.

"Hey, Sheriff!"

Liam turned and looked in the direction the voice had come from, but between the encroaching darkness and the rain that was rapidly turning into an icy mix, he couldn't see much of anything.

"Over here!"

Grabbing his flashlight from his coat, Liam moved it back and forth in a sweeping motion until the beam fell upon a diver standing in waist-deep water. "Did you find something?" he called, fighting to keep his teeth from chattering as he made his way along the bank.

The diver, whom Liam had overheard the other men in the rescue unit refer to as Rusty, nodded. "There's a car down there, about twenty yards from where we found the victim." He paused to remove his mask, leaving a deep crease behind in his freckled cheeks. "It looks like it's been down there a while," he said, squinting against the light.

Disappointment churned inside Liam. "That's not unusual," he replied, adjusting his grip on his flashlight as he straightened to go, "this entire area used to be a junkyard before it became a lake. There are lots of abandoned —"

"But, Sheriff" — Rusty shook his head emphatically, sending droplets of water flying from a close-cropped set of red locks — "this one's not abandoned."

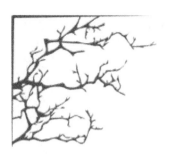

# Chapter 2

The tires on Olivia Matthews' car refused to respond to the brakes as she slowed to turn into the shopping center on her right. Gripping the steering wheel, she hurriedly cut it in the opposite direction, narrowly managing to miss the light pole looming in front of her, before aiming the car towards the empty space up ahead. Following several seconds of sliding, grinding, and jerking, the car's left front tire finally made contact with the concrete bumper, bringing her to a stop.

Letting out her breath, Olivia leaned across the seat and began to feel around in the darkness for her cell phone that she had thrown out of anger two blocks earlier. Retrieving it from the passenger-side floorboard, she sat up and pulled her keys from the ignition—only to discover that she'd parked in a handicapped zone. After a moment of deliberation, she grabbed her purse and flung open the door, justifying the infraction by pretending that she hadn't seen it.

Her black stilettos searched for traction as she race-walked across the frozen parking lot in a futile attempt to outrun the sleet that was pelting the top of her head. The wind accompanying it stung her eyes repeatedly, making it difficult to navigate the sidewalk, which had been littered with uneven — and rather useless — chunks of rock salt. Clutching the ends of her coat together, she stumbled over the pellets and quickly scissor-stepped around a white-haired man and his cane in her quest to reach the store's entrance.

The automatic doors of *Elmar's Drug Mart* slid open with a whoosh, welcoming her inside. With her feet now firmly on solid ground, and her path free of slow-moving octogenarians, Olivia's pace increased as she began making her way towards the counter in the back.

A cluster of heart-shaped foil balloons that — judging by their lack of helium — had exceeded their life expectancy by at least a week, bobbed sadly up and down as she breezed past, while dozens of cheaply made teddy bears, well-handled boxes of chocolates, and exorbitantly priced cards gushing false sentiments lay scattered across the shelves in front of her.

Reaching out, Olivia plucked a card from one of the slots, yet unconcerned with the words it held, stuffed it inside its matching envelope and continued on, the significance of the day having been made insignificant five minutes ago.

Hanging a right, she skirted around a large woman in pajama pants blocking the entire aisle with her cart, and a pimply-faced stock boy, who either didn't own a belt or had no idea what one was for.

With the pharmacy now in her sights, Olivia veered towards it only to notice her peripheral vision being inadvertently drawn to a giant, heavy-set man the next aisle over. Wearing a puffy green coat with a fur-lined hood, he stood in front of the magazine display rack looking at the current issue of *Cosmopolitan*. From this distance, she could just make out the image of a woman clad in red lingerie, as well as the man's index finger as it traced her body parts. Olivia shuddered at the intensity on the man's face as he repeated his movements over and over … and over.

An annoyingly snappy tune began to resonate from her purse, giving cause for the man to glance in her direction—where his distracted gaze instantly hardened upon meeting hers. Turning her head, Olivia pretended to be interested in the vast assortment of tampons on her right as she fumbled inside her purse for her phone. She didn't recognize the number that was flashing on the screen but swiped her thumb across it anyway in the hopes that talking to whoever was on the other end of it would help get rid of the blood that had pooled in her cheeks. "Hello?" she answered, resuming her pace.

"Olivia?"

"Yes?"

"It's Gary Castlen from corporate calling."

Her footsteps faltered.

"How are you?"

"I'm fine, Gary," she replied, scrambling to gather her thoughts. "And *you*?"

"I'm good. Hey, listen," he said, rushing his words, "I'm going to be in town tomorrow afternoon, and I'd like to meet with you in order to go over a few things."

Olivia's heart began to pound against her chest, causing her breath to come out in a jagged spurt.

"Are you still there?"

"What time tomorrow?" she murmured, tightening her fingers around her phone.

"Will two o'clock work for you?"

Half a dozen lies as to why it wouldn't ran through her mind, yet she found herself unable to divert any of them to her lips. "Two's fine," she heard herself say.

"All right then. Have a good evening."

Having no inclination to wish him the same, Olivia ended the call and tossed the phone back into her purse. With renewed anxiety, she finished making her way down the aisle and marched up to the counter. "Excuse me," she said, waving to get the clerk's attention.

"I'll be with you in just a sec," the girl replied, without bothering to look up.

Struggling to hang onto her last dregs of patience, Olivia stiffly shifted her gaze from the multiple piercings in the clerk's nose to the large black-and-white clock hanging beside the register. After watching the second-hand circle the twelve two and a half times, her fingertips began to curl inwards. "I'm in a bit of a rush," she said, leaning across the counter.

The clerk let out an audible sigh. "Picking up or dropping off?"

"Picking up."

"Name?"

"Matthews," Olivia replied, glancing around the store for the short brunette with the bubbly personality that usually waited on her.

The clerk entered her name into the computer and then tapped her nails against the counter. "It's going to be a few more minutes."

"I called these in on my lunch hour," Olivia said, straining to keep her voice pleasant.

The clerk cast a set of unapologetic, mascara-encrusted eyes at her. "We've been slammed this afternoon, so if you'll have a seat, I'll call you as soon as it's ready."

Turning from the counter, Olivia stalked over to the row of orange plastic chairs lining the wall. Taking the only seat available, she folded her arms against her chest and leaned back with a huff. As she sat there, mentally trying to transform the clerk's sloth-like movements into something more human, she became distinctly aware of the woman on her left who appeared to be staring at her.

Shifting in her chair, Olivia picked up a pamphlet off the table beside her and flipped it open. While pretending to read the arguments as to why she should be vaccinated against the influenza virus, she saw the woman lean over and pat the hand of the lady sitting next to her. "That's the one I was telling you about the other day."

The younger lady perked up and swept a narrowed gaze across the store. "Who?"

The woman pointed a crooked finger in Olivia's direction, which not only succeeded in garnering the younger lady's attention, but everyone seated around her as well.

Dropping the pamphlet on the table, Olivia rested her cheek against her knuckles in an effort to hide her face as the whispers commenced. After a few moments, she was relieved to see the clerk— and her sullen disposition—approaching the counter with a bag in hand.

The waiting area grew still as the girl bent down to speak into the microphone attached to the register. "Wyler?"

A collective groan sounded as a man wearing insulated coveralls got to his feet.

Olivia's cell phone went off again, sending a second wave of heat rolling across her face as everyone around her turned to look—because apparently, they had nothing better to do. Shoving her hand inside her purse, she shut off her phone and then crossed her legs in an attempt to alleviate the throbbing pain on her right side. When that failed to work, she tried taking a deep breath, yet before her lungs could fill to their capacity, a foul stench infiltrated her nostrils making her stop.

Glancing up, Olivia noticed that the man who had been fingering the *Cosmo* model had entered the waiting area. Clearing her throat, she casually turned her nose into the backs of her knuckles in an effort to keep the strong aroma of body odor, corn chips, and urine at bay as the man plopped himself down in the newly vacated seat on her right.

Whether it was the constant ache in her side, the fact that she'd skipped lunch, or the smells emanating from the creepy man, Olivia began to feel an excess of saliva building on her tongue. Seeking a distraction, she shifted her gaze to the front of the store where she watched beleaguered customers, armed with overpriced gallons of milk and toilet paper, hurry towards the exit. As the doors slid open, she saw that the sleet had changed to snow and had covered the parking lot in a dense landscape of white.

"Matthews?"

Catapulting herself out of the chair, Olivia gave a wide berth to the creepy man as she cut a hasty path to the register.

"Sign here," said the clerk, pushing a piece of paper across the counter.

Olivia scrawled her name on the receipt and then

dug her billfold out of her purse.

"That'll be forty-six dollars and twelve cents."

Upon hearing the total, Olivia checked the name printed on the sack and folded her lips. "This is for my father-in-law. You should have one for me as well—under Olivia Matthews."

The girl keyed in the information and shook her head. "I'm not showing anything."

Olivia's fingernails raked across the leather emblem on her billfold. "Are you sure you're spelling it right? Because the person I talked to on the phone told me it would be ready by five."

Another sigh, followed by more typing. "Here it is." The clerk paused to push her blue and purple bangs from her eyes. "But it has a hold on it."

"What does that mean?"

"Hey, Walt?" the girl called out, keeping her eyes locked on the computer screen. "Did you put a hold on a prescription for an Olivia Matthews?"

In the very back of the pharmacy, Olivia caught sight of a man hunched over a metal table; holding what resembled a butter knife, he stood there patiently raking clusters of pills across a small scale. When he had finished, he turned and started towards the front, his long arms dangling at his sides as he walked. Stopping short of the counter, he stooped to study the screen over the clerk's shoulder and then looked at Olivia. "I placed a hold on it because there are no refills left on your prescription."

Olivia's anger reignited, setting her tongue into motion. "Dr. Ellis told me that I could have a refill if I needed." Reaching inside her billfold, she yanked out her prescription and thrust it at him. "Here."

Adjusting his glasses, the man held the paper up. "This is the same one we have on file," he replied, handing it back to her, "and it expired three months ago."

Keenly aware of the quiet now surrounding her, Olivia crumpled the paper between her fingers and lowered her voice. "Jerry McCormick didn't have any issue filling this for me the last time I was here."

"I noticed that," the man answered, rubbing the edge of his jaw. "However, Mr. McCormick retired and —"

"Yes," snapped Olivia, "I'm aware."

The man's eyes flickered, giving a blip of life to their otherwise dull gray color. "As I was about to say," he began again, "I'm Walter Rafferty, *Elmar's* new pharmacist, and I'd like nothing more than to help you, Mrs. Matthews, but I can't do anything with an expired prescription."

"Then — call — Dr. — Ellis," she said, tapping her middle finger against the counter.

The pharmacist tilted his head. "I did, and he told me that he couldn't write you a new prescription without seeing you first."

The whispers resumed, causing the heat residing in Olivia's cheeks to spread to her extremities.

Seeming satisfied by her self-imposed reticence, Walter Rafferty offered her a curt nod. "Have a safe drive home, Mrs. Matthews."

Conscious of the air that had begun to noisily spill from her nostrils, Olivia held her breath as she watched him turn and walk away.

"Will this be all for you?" asked the clerk, her tone of indifference having been replaced with a smug cheeriness as she slid the valentine card into a sack.

Olivia remained silent as she swiped her credit card through the machine.

"Thank you for shopping *Elmar's*."

Grabbing the items off the counter, Olivia spun on her heels and started towards the exit, yet the main aisles had become crowded, causing her to bump into several shoppers in her endeavor to reach it.

"Olivia!"

She stopped mid-stride and turned, her eyes seeking a face to put with the voice. They were immediately drawn to the spindly blonde waving at her from the checkout. Muttering under her breath, Olivia half-heartedly returned the gesture and then grimaced as Debbie Blakeman left her place in the line and began hurrying towards her with open arms. "How are you?" the woman called out in an octave so shrill that several people turned to look.

"I'm fine, Debbie," Olivia answered, pulling herself out of her tight embrace. "And you?"

"Oh, you know me. I'm never one to complain but ..." She paused to toss her long wavy hair over her shoulder. "Rob, on the other hand, has caught that crud that's going around."

"Aww," replied Olivia, flicking her gaze towards the exit as she spoke, "that's too bad."

"I told him he just needed to stay home and rest, but according to him—he's dying," Debbie said, letting out an exaggerated sigh. "That's why I'm out on a night like this."

"Well, I hope he feels better soon," offered Olivia, glancing at the economy-size bottle of cough syrup and other provisions in the basket that hung from the crook of the woman's arm. "It was good seeing you—"

"So what brings you here? Is everything okay?" asked Debbie, her voice swimming with curiosity as she gestured at the white sack she was clutching.

"Just picking up a prescription for my father-in-law," she answered, taking a hopeful step towards the door, "and I'm running late, so—"

"You know, we've been missing you at church."

"I know," said Olivia, staring at the bottom of Debbie's pointy chin in order to avoid her prying eyes. "Things have just been crazy at work. We had a new computer system installed last month and it's been an absolute nightmare trying to do the changeover."

"Oh," replied Debbie, spreading her hand over her chest, "I'm *so* happy to hear that's all it is. We were afraid that after what happened ... well ...

that maybe you were feeling too embarrassed to come."

The smile Olivia had forged began to waver.

Debbie reached out and wrapped her long skeleton-like fingers around hers. "But I want you to know that no one's judging you for it," she continued, dropping her voice to a hissy whisper as several people walked past. "We've all done things we're not proud of, but the most important thing to remember is that the only forgiveness that matters is God's."

Jerking her hand out of Debbie's icy grasp, Olivia took a step backward. "I really need to go," she said, the words shaking from her lips. "Tell Rob hello for me."

# Chapter 3

"**D**o you like it?"

Alice Malloy stared solemnly at the diamond bracelet as it lay upon a slender bed of black velvet. "I love it."

"Really?"

She looked across the table at Michael and nodded. "It's beautiful."

Keeping his eyes locked on hers, Michael leaned back in his chair and picked up his glass. "I don't think you like it."

"Well, you're wrong, as usual," she said, conjuring up a smile that was as stiff as it was broad. "I'm just surprised, that's all."

"You're surprised that I got you something nice for your birthday?"

"That's not what I meant."

"No?" Tilting his glass, Michael paused to drain it of its contents before continuing. "What did you mean, then?"

Alice's mind fumbled as she searched for an answer.

"Well?"

"It doesn't matter," she replied, disliking his tone.

A waiter with dark, curly hair and frazzled appearance approached the table. "Are we ready to order?"

"Do you know what you want, Alice?" asked Michael.

She didn't, but upon hearing the impatience in his voice, pointed to something on the menu she couldn't pronounce. "I'll have this."

The waiter leaned over to see. "Excellent choice. And for you, sir?"

"I'll have the same," Michael replied, snapping the menu closed without looking at it.

"Very good," said the waiter. "Is there anything I can get you while we're preparing your order?"

Alice gave him a meager smile. "No, thank—"

"I'll have another scotch and water."

Alice glanced at Michael as he handed the waiter his empty glass. He didn't seem at all concerned with the fact that he was on call this evening.

"I'll have a fresh one brought out to you right away," the waiter promised, the cuff of his sleeve sliding past his knuckles as he paused to collect their menus before scurrying over to the next table.

"Christ," muttered Michael, watching him go, "I'm glad I called ahead for a reservation."

"What made you pick *Isidoros*?" Alice asked, jumping at the chance to change the subject.

"I don't know. I just thought it'd be a nice change of pace. You like Greek food, don't you?"

"I've never had it."

"Yes, you have," Michael said, looking back at her. "We had it that time we went to San Francisco."

"*San Francisco*?"

"It was three years ago, remember? I had to attend a medical conference, and you went with me."

Alice gave him a blank stare.

"It was our fourth date," he prompted, his irritation with her coming out in the form of a heavy sigh, "and we ate at that Greek restaurant near the Embarcadero."

Alice shook her head as her mind began to translate the muddled version of his memory into fact. "It wasn't San Francisco, it was *San Diego*. It was our *fifth* date — and it was *Thai*."

Michael's complexion darkened.

"But I'm always up for trying new things," she added, rushing to undo the damage.

Silence followed her words.

Reaching for her glass, Alice pressed it to her lips and took a long sip. As the wine washed over her tongue, she found herself wishing that they'd just stayed home.

"Would you like me to help you put it on?"

"Hmm?" she said, swallowing.

Michael pointed at the box.

Deciding it would be in her best interest to let him, she set her glass down and held out her wrist.

With nimble fingers becoming of a surgeon, he fastened the clasp on the bracelet and smiled. "What do you think?"

"I think it's beautiful," she said, holding it next to the candlelight.

"You know, you're good at a lot of things, but lying isn't one of them."

Alice dropped her arm. "You seem determined to pick a fight."

"Do I?"

"Yes," she said, snapping the box closed.

"Well, maybe that's because I didn't go through the trouble of rearranging my entire schedule just so you could sit across the table and sulk over the fact that you didn't get what you wanted."

The dull ache that had been nesting in Alice's heart turned to resentment. "You are unbelievable," she said, leaning forward, "in that you would intentionally start an argument just to avoid discussing the real reason—"

"Dr. Edmunds!"

Alice looked over to see a big, bald man with an equally big grin walking towards their table.

Pushing his chair back, Michael slowly got to his feet. "Yes?"

"John Corbin," said the man. "Remember me?"

"Of course," Michael replied, extending his hand. "How are you?"

"I've never felt better," he said, tapping his fingers against the left side of his chest.

The anger that had fallen across Michael's face began to recede. "Well, I'm glad to hear it."

"Since my bypass, I feel twenty years younger, and it's all thanks to you ..."

Alice watched the corners of Michael's mouth turn upwards as he listened to Mr. Corbin going on. After a few seconds, Michael glanced over at her and smiled, his dark-brown eyes piercing hers. Uncertain if the gesture was a preternatural instinct, or just a pathetic attempt to get her to participate in the avalanche of accolades being heaped upon him, she untethered her steely gaze from his and stood up.

"You're a miracle worker, Dr. Edmunds. That's for damn sure—"

"Mr. Corbin," interrupted Michael, "let me introduce my—um ... this is ..."

"Alice Malloy," she said, feeling her throat beginning to burn.

Mr. Corbin bowed in her direction. "It's nice to meet you, little lady. You know, you've got yourself one hell of a doctor here," he said, slapping Michael enthusiastically on his shoulder. "Why, I'd even go so far as to say he's the best cardiovascular surgeon in all of Rapid City."

"Yes, I know," she said in a perky voice. "He reminds me of that all the time." Grabbing her purse from the back of the chair, she stepped around Michael, whose smile was now reminiscent of a scowl, and set off for the ladies' room.

With her vision growing blurrier by the second, Alice hurried past a row of faux marble statues that were missing the lower halves of their arms and legs and shoved open the bathroom door. After a quick check under the stalls revealed there to be no shoes, she tossed her purse on the vanity and bowed her head, the sudden tilt of it giving her tears nowhere to go but down. She should never have allowed herself to believe the fantasy she'd created in her mind in regard to what this evening — which also happened to be the most romantic night of the year — was going to bring. Embarrassment, coupled with a rather large dose of humility surged inside her, increasing her body's output of tears.

Approaching footsteps sounded outside the door, making her jerk her head up mid-sob. Drawing a shaky breath, she wet a paper towel and dabbed at her eyes in an effort to remove the black smudges that had gathered underneath them. As the door swung open, she gave a polite nod to the woman materializing behind her reflection.

The woman walked past her and disappeared into the stall without so much as giving her a glance.

Staring into the mirror, Alice took a moment to adjust the olive-green straps of her dress and sighed; she had spent eighty dollars, as well as four hours of her life picking it out, yet Michael hadn't even noticed. Tossing the napkin into the wastebasket, she turned and walked out the door, but—being in no hurry to get back to the man-child waiting for her—took her time winding her way around the cluster of tables. However, when there were no more steps to take, and contact was imminent, she was grateful to find that the bald man had gone and their food had arrived.

"I'm sorry about that," said Michael, sliding her chair out for her.

"It's fine."

Returning to his own seat, he paused to tug at the sleeve of his blazer and cleared his throat. "I'm also sorry for my behavior earlier."

"It's fine," she repeated, wanting to move on.

Michael reached across the table and took her hand in his. "I know that you were expecting a ring tonight."

Startled by his words, Alice gave him a hopeful look.

"I'm sorry," he said tenderly, "but I'm just not ready."

Pulling her hand away, she grasped her fork and began poking at the food on her plate.

"Aren't you going to say anything?"

Alice knew that accepting his apology, regardless of how lame it was, also meant acknowledging the fact that she had indeed been expecting a proposal. Feeling as if she'd made enough concessions this evening, she chose to remain silent.

An exasperated sigh fell from Michael's lips. "You know that I'm still hemorrhaging money because of my ex-wife and that *asshole* attorney of hers."

Alice's face flushed as she cut her eyes to the surrounding tables.

"You take that, and combine it with the overhead of my practice ... and it's just not the right time to be getting married."

"And just when exactly *would* be the right time, Michael?"

"Look," he said, rubbing his temple, "you know how much Bethany despises you."

"I have a pretty good idea, yes," Alice replied, running the tines of her fork through the heart of the lasagnay-looking thing adorning her plate.

"I'd be afraid that she'd sue me for full custody if we got married."

"I doubt that," said Alice with a laugh. "It would seriously hamper her trips to Mexico, not to mention her cruises in the Mediterranean."

Michael set his drink down hard, rocking the table. "Do you think me losing my kids is some sort of joke?"

"No," she chirped, undeterred by his little tantrum, "but I think the drama you've fabricated over it is."

The tips of his knuckles turned white as he balled his fingers into a fist. "You don't know that woman the way I do," he said in a low voice. "Trust me when I tell you that she would do it just to spite me."

"So what are you suggesting we do?" Alice prodded, curious to hear where he was going with this.

He smoothed his tie against his shirt and shrugged. "I think we should wait a little longer. That would give her some time to adjust to us being together."

"It's been three years, Michael."

"I know that—"

"*And* she's remarried."

"I know—"

"She's moved on with her life."

"Alice—"

"Why can't we do the same?"

Michael's eyebrows took a downward turn. "I just told you why."

"No, you didn't. You offered me excuses."

"How is everything?"

Alice looked up to find the waiter and his ill-fitting shirt hovering over her. "Fine, thanks."

"Is there anything else I—"

"We're good," said Michael, dismissing him with a wave of his hand.

As the waiter slunk away, Alice shoved her loaded fork into her mouth. Lamb, eggplant, and a hint of nutmeg fell across her tongue, flooding it with a surprising flavor.

"Believe it or not," Michael said, "this isn't how I wanted things to go tonight. And I also want you to know that just because our relationship isn't moving as fast as you'd like it to, doesn't mean that I don't love you because I do. I absolutely adore you."

Alice kept her eyes on her plate. There were lots of things she could have said, but knowing that none of them would be conducive to her cause, picked up her wine glass instead and took a large sip, ushering her half-formed sentences to the back of her throat.

"Listen," he said, settling into his chair, "I've got the whole weekend off, and I promise, come Saturday, we'll talk seriously about marriage. Okay?"

Doubting the validity of his pledge, but too tired all of a sudden to argue the point, Alice felt herself nod.

The lines etched in Michael's face visibly relaxed. "Have I told you how beautiful you look tonight?"

"No," she replied, hiding her irritation as she played along.

"Well," he said, staring into her eyes, "you're simply stunning in that dress."

Her state of annoyance was immediately uprooted. "Thank you, Michael," she said, smiling as a familiar warmth began to flow through her.

He gestured at her chest with his fork. "It really shows off your cleavage."

Alice's smile crumbled. Finishing the contents of her glass in one swallow, she signaled the waiter for another.

"You're wrong about our fifth date, though," Michael stated. "It wasn't in San Diego."

"Yes, it was," she said, finding herself eager to unleash her rekindled wrath—regardless of the topic—upon him.

Michael gave her an amused look. "I happen to know for a fact that it wasn't."

"Really?" she countered. "You're *really* going to sit there and tell me that we didn't go there on our fifth date?" This coming from a man who couldn't even remember the year he was born.

"Technically," Michael said, wagging a finger at her, "our fifth date was when we took Claire to the carnival at the Central States Fair."

Alice felt her lips folding in on themselves.

"I'll take your silence as confirmation that I'm right," he said, flashing her a triumphant grin.

"I had completely forgotten about that," she replied sheepishly.

"Not me," said Michael, tapping the side of his head. "It's permanently wedged in there."

"I'm sure it is," she said, recalling what had happened that night. "You learned your lesson the hard way."

"Hey, I was just trying to score a few brownie points with your daughter."

"Letting her eat all the hot dogs she wanted and then taking her on the Gyro ride was not the smartest thing you could have done," Alice chided, refusing to let go of her anger.

"Well, I know that *now*, but how was I to know *then* that it was going to cause her to throw up all over me?"

The image of hot dog chunks splattered down the front of Michael's white cashmere sweater flashed before Alice, causing her to erupt into laughter.

"I'm glad you find it so funny," he grumbled.

Still giggling, she wiped at her eyes. "I wish you could have seen your face when you climbed out of that ride."

Michael's lips finally relented, allowing a rough chuckle to come tumbling out of them, and as they sat laughing over the events of that night from so long ago, Alice found herself wishing that this moment could last forever.

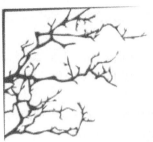

# Chapter 4

The garage door descended slowly from above, sealing Liam in a quiet cold as he sat down on the steps to take off his boots. A weary sigh fell from his lips as he tugged at the wet and worn laces. What had started out promising to be a long afternoon had spilled over into the night, and with the weather being what it was, he seriously doubted that he was going to make it through the next hour without being called.

Setting his boots aside, he placed his elbows on his knees and bowed his head. The body of Hector Ramirez — or what was left of it — was on its way to the medical examiner's office in Rapid City, while a second victim — of unknown circumstances and origin — was sitting behind the wheel of a submerged vehicle at the bottom of Crow's Foot Lake. Liam's shoulders slumped forward. The list of what he needed to do next was as long as it was uncertain, and now, thanks to Rusty, the overeager diver, it had spiraled out of control.

Trying to summon a moment of clarity, Liam closed his eyes and breathed in, yet his mind continued to race, grabbing hold of every stray thought he had in regard to Hector and entangling them to the point that he couldn't think straight.

Further adding to his frustration was the fact that he'd just spent the last two hours at the station talking with Hector's wife, which had proven to be nothing but a waste of time, as what little information he'd managed to get out of her was the same exact information she'd given him over the phone six days ago—only with more tears.

Decidedly giving up, Liam raised his head and ran a stiff set of fingers through his hair. As he began wiping away the grit that had accumulated in the corners of his eyes, his attention was drawn to the half dozen red roses lying on the step beside him. Suddenly remembering he had more important things than Hector to take care of at the moment, he pushed his jumbled thoughts on him to the side and got to his feet.

Grasping the bouquet, he held it up to the light for a quick inspection and felt his face contort. In his haste to get home, he'd failed to notice that most of the petals on the buds were either missing or wilted. Tightening his grip around their stems, he went to chuck them in the garbage but—upon realizing he had nothing else to offer—ripped off the orange sticker from *Bucky's Mini-Mart* instead and hurried back up the steps. As he paused on the narrow landing to take a steadying breath, he was grateful to find that the fragrance of the roses was still strong—even if they did contain the slightest whiff of fried chicken.

Walking inside, he could hear the TV blaring in the next room.

"... the twenty-five-year-old seemed unstoppable, tying Ken Baxter's record for home runs in his rookie season with the Orlando Pythons. He would go on to be named the National League's MVP, as well as win the Silver Slugger and Gold Glove Award, making him part of only a handful of players in Major League history to ever win all three awards in the same season. But just four years later, during the Pythons opening game against the Braves, Ramirez suffered a career-ending injury in the bottom of the third inning when he was struck in the eye by a shard of wood from teammate Drew Jackson's shattered bat ..."

Placing the pathetic arrangement on the dryer, Liam pushed the door to the garage closed.

"... in the spotlight again with his highly publicized marriage to former model and reality TV star Kiki Grey. Later that same year, Ramirez signed a multi-million dollar contract with NBSN, where he became a sportscaster for Monday night baseball. Yet this past September, following a heated argument with fellow sportscaster Don Green during a live broadcast, NBSN released a statement to the press that Ramirez had been let go for undisclosed reasons."

Warming his hands with his breath, Liam unbuttoned his coat and jerked his arms out of the sleeves.

"… during a recent interview, Ramirez opened up about his struggles with opioid addiction—"

The news anchor's voice cut off, surrounding Liam in a welcomed silence. A moment later, however, he heard the familiar sound of aluminum hitting hardwood and stifled a sigh.

"I was beginnin' to wonder about you."

Liam slung his coat over one of the nickel-brushed hooks fastened to the wall beside him before turning around. "I had a stop to make."

His father let go of the handle on his walker long enough to gesture at the door. "How're the roads?"

"Slick," Liam answered, squeezing past him. As he headed into the kitchen, the clanking noise followed, heightening his irritation.

"I saw you on the news earlier talkin' about Ramirez."

Knowing that beneath his father's seemingly innocent comment lurked an abundance of questions, all of which were locked, loaded, and ready to fire, Liam remained quiet as he pulled a glass from the cabinet above him.

"Well? Don't you wanna know what I thought about it?"

"Not particularly."

"The statement you made was misleadin' and your answers were vague."

The tips of Liam's fingers turned white as he held the glass under the faucet. "That was my intent."

"It was your *intent* to sound like you didn't know what you were doin'?"

The headache that had been plaguing Liam on and off throughout the afternoon returned. Not helping matters was his father's breath, which in spite of the distance between them managed to hit the side of his face repeatedly—and reeked of coffee and cigarettes.

"Was his cause of death clear?"

"Pretty clear," Liam mumbled, pressing the glass to his lips.

"So I'm guessin' it was no accident?"

Liam took several swallows of the water in the hopes that his refusal to answer would put an end to his father's interrogation.

"Well? Was it?"

Trying not to provoke the pain that was spooling up behind his eyes, Liam carefully shook his head.

His father smacked the counter with the palm of his hand. "I knew it," he crowed. "Isn't that what I've been tellin' you all along?"

Seeing no point in encouraging him, Liam wiped the water from his lips and focused his efforts on finding aspirin.

"Why didn't you tell the reporters that instead of sayin' you were gonna wait on the autopsy results?"

"Because," said Liam, rifling through the drawer in front of him, "keeping the media in the dark makes it easier for me to do my job."

"You talked to Ramirez's *wife*, didn't you?"

Liam stopped and looked back at his father. Taking in a sharp breath, he started to ask him how he knew that, but after determining that doing so would only serve to prolong their discussion, promptly closed his mouth.

"Well — did ya?"

"What's your point?" he asked, pushing the drawer shut.

"My point is what's to keep *her* from tellin' the press he was murdered? Did you stop to think about that? She's probably already talked to 'em, which means the only thing you've managed to accomplish is to come across soundin' like a jackass."

Liam's irritation turned to anger as it became clear to him just exactly who it was his father had been speaking to. "It's been a long day, Dad," he said, rubbing his forehead, "and I don't feel like doing this right now."

"Doin' what? Talkin' to me?" His father gave him a hurt look. "I was just tryin' to help."

"No," said Liam, arching his eyebrow, "you weren't."

A reddish hue enveloped his father's face, highlighting the crescent-shaped scar embedded in his left cheek. "Fine!" he snapped. "You know me so well, what was I gonna say next?"

"Dad—"

"Go on," he said, flicking his hand at him, "tell me."

Liam leaned against the counter and folded his arms. His father had a rather annoying way of forcing an unwanted conversation into continuing by turning it into an argument. "Have you eaten?" he asked, being in no mood to engage him.

His father rested his elbows on his walker, reducing his six-and-a-half-foot frame to that of an ordinary man. "Of course I've eaten. It's ten freakin' o'clock!"

Sweeping his gaze along the scarred butcher block in search of confirmation, Liam spotted the soggy remnants of a hot dog bun doused in ketchup by the stove. "What about your meds?" he asked, setting the plate in the sink. "Did you take them?"

"*You're* the mind reader. You tell *me*."

The sigh Liam had been holding onto came tumbling out.

"Well?"

A shrill ring began to bounce off the walls of the tiny kitchen, bringing an end to their standoff.

Pulling his cell from his pocket, Liam swiped his thumb across the screen and held it to his ear. "What'd you find out, Aaron?"

"I just got off the phone with Miller. He confirmed that he and his men would be back first thing in the morning to begin hooking the cables up to the car."

Liam groaned inwardly at the thought of having to see Miller again. "How long are we talking?" he asked, wishing that Orand County had enough money to fund their own Search and Rescue Unit.

"He said that if the current wasn't too strong, they'd probably have it out in three to four hours."

"What about—" Feeling the side of his cheek growing warm again, Liam cut his eyes to the right and saw that his father had closed the gap between them. Turning away, Liam stalked over to the farthest corner of the kitchen and lowered his voice. "What about the tow truck?"

"Everyone I called is tied up right now, as you can imagine, but *Murphy's* said they'd try to have one out there by ten. That should give Miller and his men enough time to get set up."

"All right, thanks," replied Liam, scratching the side of his neck. "Are you headed home?"

"I just walked in the door—"

An excited squeal penetrated Liam's ear, causing him to instinctively tilt his head away from the phone.

"*Pȟapa!*"

"*Hau, mičhiŋkši,*" Aaron said in a muffled voice.

"Who are you talking to, *Pȟapa*?"

"My boss."

"Can *I* talk to him?"

43

There was a rustling noise followed by several seconds of shallow breathing.

"Hi, Sheriff Wiam."

Liam felt a smile cross his lips. "Hi, Caleb."

"Did you put any bad men in jail today?"

"Not today," he answered, giving him a soft laugh.

"Why?"

"All right," Aaron interjected, his voice strong again, "time for bed. Go with your *iná*."

"Can you wead me a story, *P̌hapa*?"

"If you hurry."

"Well," said Liam, listening to the patter of Caleb's feet as they scurried across the floor, "it sounds like you've got things to do. I'll talk to you in the morning."

"Have a good night, Sheriff."

"Thanks," replied Liam, although he found himself doubting his night was going to go anything like his deputy's.

"So, what's the make of the car?"

Feeling his smile evaporate, Liam took the time to slip his phone back into his pocket before turning around. "What car?"

The Y-shaped vein residing in his father's temple began to bulge outwards. "Just because I'm retired doesn't mean I don't know what the hell's goin' on in this town!"

"I never said that you didn't," exclaimed Liam, matching his father's tone as he resumed his search for aspirin. After a moment, he spied a small bottle in the back of the cabinet.

"So, what's the make?"

"It was too dark down there to tell," Liam replied, fumbling with the cap.

"Is the victim male or female?"

"I don't know."

"What do you mean, you don't know? Are their body parts missin' or somethin'?"

"Dad" — Liam slammed the bottle on the counter sending the pills flying — "I can't do this right now!"

His father's chin jutted out, creating a hard line along the edge of his jaw, which combined with the ketchup stain on his shirt, made him look like a pouty five-year-old. Pivoting on his good leg, he swung his walker around and began limping away.

"Where're you going?"

"To bed!"

Refusing to apologize, Liam rolled the bottle cap between his thumb and forefinger as he watched his father hobble across the living room floor. It wasn't long, however, before he began to waver on his resolve. "Goodnight," he called in a contrite tone. "I think I'll turn in myself."

His father let out a disgruntled laugh. "With the mood that wife of yours is in," he said, maneuvering his walker around the edge of the sofa, "I wouldn't if I were you."

Liam's gaze involuntarily shifted to the hall. Feeling his anger giving way to trepidation, he tossed the cap on the counter and started towards the laundry room.

"And don't think those half-dead flowers you dragged home are gonna help matters either."

Liam stopped in his tracks.

"Where the hell did you get those anyway? Off someone's grave?"

"You've made your point."

"Because I tell you what," his father continued, "a man would have to be plum crazy to think he could get away with—"

"Yep—got it," said Liam, waving him off as he returned to the kitchen. "I'd have to be crazy—"

"Thinkin' those would actually work."

"All right. Thanks for the advi—"

"Because if *I'd* ever come home …"

Throwing his head back, Liam rolled his eyes.

"… carryin' somethin' like that to your momma, I wouldn't have lived to tell the tale."

"Are you done?" asked Liam, staring at the water stains on the ceiling.

The door next to the TV slammed shut, rattling the pictures on the wall.

Letting his hands settle on his hips, Liam cast a longing glance at the roses as they lay in a crumpled heap on the dryer. When that failed to magically transform them, he turned around and began rummaging through the lower cabinets in the hopes of finding a suitable replacement. After several moments of searching to no avail, he reluctantly straightened and once more started for the laundry room, yet as he walked past the microwave, something caught his eye. There, hiding in plain sight on the counter sat an unopened bottle of wine. Sensing that his luck had changed, he picked it up and began wiping the traces of dust from its label with his thumb.

"You shouldn't encourage her, you know."

A prickling heat swarmed Liam's cheeks. "I thought you were going to bed," he said, returning the bottle to the counter.

"I forgot my paper."

Liam impatiently shifted his feet as he waited for his father to retrieve the newspaper off the arm of the recliner. When he was at long last turned and headed back to the den, Liam reached up and pulled two glasses from the cabinet on his right.

"You only need one of those."

Setting the glasses down hard, Liam gripped the edge of the counter. "*Goodnight*, Dad."

His father remained where he was, his usually transparent expression unreadable. "You better hurry," he finally said, gesturing at the darkened hallway. "She's already got a good head start on you."

Unable to keep his gaze steady, Liam cast it to the floor.

Muttering something inaudible, his father picked up his walker and shuffled into the den.

Having no desire to be left alone with his thoughts, which were now surprisingly clear, Liam left the bottle on the counter and walked out of the kitchen.

The light coming from underneath the bedroom door cut a perfectly straight line across his socks as he stood in the hallway trying to steel himself for the impending argument that lay just beyond it. After drawing a miserable breath, he forced himself to twist the knob and stepped inside.

Olivia was sitting at the foot of their bed, staring at something only she could see.

Closing the door behind him, he reluctantly started towards her.

It was an action that caused her posture to stiffen.

"I'm sorry about tonight," he said, stopping just short of where she was, "but it was unavoidable."

"I understand," she said, getting to her feet.

Certain that she didn't, Liam waited for the rest of it as he watched her swaying back and forth.

The bottom of Olivia's silk blouse brushed against her panties as she gave him a sloppy, condescending glare. "Pulling a dead body from the lake trumps anniversaries."

And there it was.

"Come to think of it," she continued, the amber-colored liquid sloshing around in her glass as she spoke, "so does taking care of one's father-in-law."

Refusing to allow himself to be baited into having yet another meaningless argument with her, Liam concentrated on trying to salvage the remains of the evening instead. "You know, it's supposed to be nice this weekend," he began, "and I was thinking that we could drive up to Rapid City on Sunday and make a whole day of it. How does that sound?"

She responded by raising the glass to her lips and sucking down its contents. When she was finished, she lowered her arm and aimed a pair of unfocused eyes in his direction. "Don't make promises you can't keep."

Walking around the bed, Liam removed his radio and holster from his belt. "Olivia," he said in a tired voice as he placed them on the nightstand, "please don't be mad at me. I told you that I was sorry and that I'd make it up to you."

"Oh my God," she yelled, turning on him, "you are so *fucking* conceited! Do you really think that this is about you not taking me out on our anniversary?"

Liam's arms defensively shot out from his sides. "Well, what else am I supposed to think?"

"Just in case you haven't noticed," she said, tapping him on his chest, "I've got a lot of *shit* going on in my life too, and being stuck in this crappy house with your father every single night—while you're out playing *sheriff*—isn't helping matters!"

Liam glanced at the door.

"What's the matter? Are you afraid he's going to hear us?" She laughed and shook her head. "He's probably on the other side of it right now *listening*." Her left eyebrow suddenly darted upwards, dragging her top lip with it. "I know," she exclaimed, "why don't we find out?"

"Olivia—"

"Hey, Harlan?" she called, brushing past him. "Are you—"

Reaching out, Liam caught her by the wrist and spun her around. "Stop it."

"Don't you want to know?" she asked in a playful manner while trying to wriggle out of his grasp.

"What I *want*," he said, holding her firmly in place, "is for you to stop acting like a child and grow the hell up."

Olivia narrowed her eyes at him until they were just two small slits of darkness. "Screw you!" she said in a fiery whisper.

Realizing he'd just done exactly what he'd promised himself he wouldn't, Liam let her go and sat down on the edge of the bed.

Silence, awkward and uncompromising, filled the space between them.

Having an overwhelming desire to hold her in his arms, Liam reached out for her—gently this time—and drew her close. "I know these past few months have been hard on you," he said, straddling her bare legs with his knees, "but it won't be like this forever. Things will get better."

Olivia's face filled with a profound sadness as she gazed down at him. "Things are never going to get better."

Liam rested his forehead against the soft part of her belly and breathed in, letting her scent wash over him. "They will," he whispered. "I promise."

"No," she said, stroking the back of his hair, "they won't. They'll just plateau, only we won't know the difference — just like every other fucking thing in our marriage."

"Olivia ..."

Pulling away from him, she stumbled across the floor and picked up a half-empty bottle of bourbon off the top of their dresser.

"I think you've had enough," he said, standing up.

"Well, that's always been your problem, hasn't it?" she replied, tightening her grip on the bottle as he reached for it.

"*What* has?" he asked.

Pressing against him, she slowly ran the tip of her fingernail along his bottom lip. "You think too much."

A series of beeps sounded, making him flinch.

"County to Sheriff Matthews. Do you copy?"

Olivia's cheeks spread outwards as a pretentious smile slithered between them. "You better answer, *Sheriff*," she said, pulling the bottle out of his grasp.

Stepping around her, Liam snatched his radio off the nightstand. "Go ahead, County," he replied, rubbing a hand over his mouth to stop its tingling.

"We've got a report of a Signal 1 ... accident with injuries involving an SUV and a moose on Bow Mar Road."

"Oh, dear," murmured Olivia, her disheveled bangs falling across her eyes as she refilled her glass. "I hope the poor moose is okay."

The radio beneath Liam's knuckles shook as he jammed his thumb against the button on the side of it. "I'm on my way." Grabbing his holster, he turned and stormed out the door.

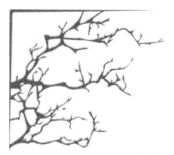

# Chapter 5

The harshness of Michael's words carried into the bedroom, making Alice feel sorry for the nurse on the other end of his phone. Pushing the door closed so she wouldn't have to listen, she dug her own phone out of her purse and swiped her thumb across its screen. Disappointed to learn that she had no messages, she pressed the small avatar of her daughter and sat down on the bed to take off her pumps.

It rang once and immediately rolled to voice mail.

Having done this enough times to know that meant she had declined the call, Alice pursed her lips as she waited for the beep. "Hi, Claire. I just wanted to let you know that Michael and I are home and to tell you that I miss you," she said, rubbing the ball of her foot. "Anyway, be good for

Mackenzie's mom, and I'll be by to pick you up in the morning. Love you." As she hung up, she heard the jingle of Michael's keys and glanced over her shoulder. "Are you going in?"

He came around the bed and tossed his phone on the nightstand. "I don't know yet," he mumbled, jerking his tie through his collar.

Alice stood and kicked her shoes to the corner of the room. "Well hopefully, you won't have to," she said, trying to lighten his mood. As she leaned over the bed to turn down the comforter, she suddenly felt Michael's master of ceremonies pressing into the back of her thighs. Caught off balance, she tried to straighten, but he held her tightly from behind, pinning her legs against the edge of the mattress.

"I want you," he murmured, kissing the side of her neck in a fervent manner as he unzipped her dress and pulled it from her shoulders.

Alice let out a contented sigh as Michael's fingers began touching her in all the places she liked. Turning around, she skillfully rid him of his pants and briefs before falling backward with him onto the bed. Parting her lips with his tongue, Michael yanked her panties down and shoved himself hard inside her, making her gasp. He then raised himself up on his elbows and started to thrust, pushing her across the mattress with each labored grunt.

Not wanting to miss the train, Alice frantically began moving her hips beneath him in an effort to catch up, but upon realizing he was already halfway down the tracks, arched her back, knowing that it would help speed things along on her end if he paid attention to her breasts. He obliged, and as his tongue eagerly roamed across them, she started to sense the moment on the horizon. Closing her eyes, she let out a soft moan in anticipation, yet before it could swallow her, she felt Michael's enthusiasm beginning to wane.

Wrapping her arms and legs around his torso, Alice did everything she could to encourage him as he readjusted himself and started again, but as his breath grew ragged, it soon became clear that it was a lost cause.

"I'm sorry," he panted, collapsing on the bed beside her.

"It's all right," she said, hiding her disappointment behind a sympathetic smile.

"No." Michael sat up and swung his legs over the bed. "It's *not* all right."

Wanting to assure him that it was, she reached out and tenderly wiped a trickle of sweat from the side of his face, but upon feeling the bone in his jaw hardening beneath her fingertips, withdrew her hand.

He turned to look at her. "This is all your fault," he said in a low voice.

Alice stared at him, dumbfounded.

"It's not like I don't have enough on my plate," he yelled, getting to his feet, "without you constantly bitching about us getting married!"

Tears, burning and unwanted, began to roll down Alice's cheeks.

"None of this," he continued, jabbing a pointed finger in her direction, "would've happened if you'd just taken the damn bracelet and been happy!"

Michael's cell phone went off, bringing an end to his tirade.

As he stomped across the floor to answer it, Alice shoved the tangle of covers out of her way and hurried into the bathroom. Shutting the door, she wet a washcloth and pressed it against her mouth in an effort to keep her sobs from materializing.

A few moments later, a soft but impatient knock sounded. "Sweetheart?" called Michael.

Ignoring him, she began wiping at her tears, but upon hearing the knob turn, dropped the cloth in the sink and spun around. Having no desire to talk to him — let alone do so naked — she placed her foot against the door as it opened, stopping it midway. The light coming from behind her fell across Michael's face, enabling her to see that his anger was still largely there.

"That was the hospital. I have to go in."

"Fine," she replied, pushing on the door.

"Alice — wait," he said, wrapping his fingers around the edge of it to keep it from closing.

She stopped and looked at him expectantly.

"I didn't mean any of those things I said."

"Then why did you say them?" she asked, trying to contain her tears.

The muscle in Michael's jaw twitched. "I just wanted to give you a nice birthday, but nothing went the way I'd planned for it to ... and now I've gone and screwed it all up, haven't I?" He shook his head and gave a miserable-sounding sigh. "That's the story of my life."

As Alice forced the lump that had gathered in her throat back down her esophagus, she found herself trying to determine if he was apologizing or looking for sympathy.

"It's all right," she said, deciding that whatever the reason, he was going to make this about himself regardless.

Michael leaned in and kissed her on the forehead. "You're too good for me."

Surrounded by his aftershave and the tenderness of his words, Alice breathed in, letting herself be engulfed by both.

He suddenly pulled back and fixed a cold, narrowed gaze upon her. "At least you *think* you are, anyway."

Alice's chin flattened.

Turning from her, Michael grabbed his coat off the chair in the bedroom and disappeared into the shadows.

Waiting until she heard the low hum of the garage door, Alice walked out of the bathroom and flung herself onto the bed. Burying her face in her pillow, the satin fabric beneath her lips grew wet as her cries, some silent, some not, came rushing out.

THE TOW TRUCK'S YELLOW and orange lights swept across the snow-covered branches of the trees, while the flashers on the red SUV tethered behind it blinked sadly at Liam — a steady stream of green coolant spewing out from underneath its buckled frame as it slowly rolled away.

Opening the door to his pickup, Liam set the rifle in the front seat and dragged a wind-bitten knuckle across his eyelids in an attempt to erase the image of what he had done, yet the sound of an approaching vehicle made him stop.

"Sorry I'm late. I came upon an accident on the way over."

Flexing his fingers against the numbing cold, Liam turned and started across the road.

A plume of smoke wafted out of the driver's side window as Gordon Stiles lowered it the rest of the way. "I met the ambulance at the curve. Anybody hurt?"

"The driver's got a pretty good cut on his forehead from the airbag," replied Liam, resting his hand on the door, "but nothing life-threatening."

Stiles jerked a thumb over his shoulder and grinned. "Looks like I missed all the fun."

Liam glanced at the moose lying sprawled in the middle of the road. The wind swirled around it, ruffling the thick brown fur along its distended belly, while spatters of blood, containing bits of flesh and bone, glistened in the snow beside its head. Judging by its size, he guessed it to be a calf, only two or three years of age at the most.

"How the hell do you think it got here?"

"I have no idea," Liam answered, scratching the side of his jaw. Although moose sightings in South Dakota were rare, they weren't unheard of, yet it was unusual to encounter one this far west of the Missouri.

"You want me to call Cooper?"

Liam shook his head. Despite the fact that Finley Cooper was known as the local roadkill connoisseur, Liam also knew that he normally rejected the ones that had been hit broadside, citing that it tainted the meat — and waiting out here for him in the frigid cold, only to have him refuse to take it, wasn't something that he wanted to do right now. "Do you have a rope?" he asked, returning his attention to Gordon.

"Yeah, got one in the back."

"Turn your truck around," he instructed. "We'll tie onto its legs and drag it off into the ditch. When we're done, I'll put in a call over to Hughes at Fish and Game. He knows a guy who'll process it for the food bank."

Tossing his cigarette out the window, Gordon cut the steering wheel to the left and gunned the engine.

As Liam began walking towards the carcass, his radio emitted a series of beeps.

"Sheriff? Do you copy?"

"Go ahead, Aaron."

"You need to head out Highway 44. We've got a situation over on Mill Lane."

"What kind of situation?" asked Liam, watching his shadow grow long as the headlights of Gordon's truck came up behind him.

He was answered by a burst of static.

Bringing the radio closer to his lips, Liam repeated the question.

Silence.

"Red Elk? Do you—"

"You need to get out here as soon as possible, Sheriff," Aaron blurted, "we've got a signal 15."

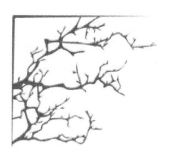

# Chapter 6

Liam's heart hammered relentlessly against his chest, making his sternum ache as he sped down the twisting, winding road. Sparsely littered with tin roof shanties and dilapidated mobile homes that sat far back and purposefully out of sight, Mill Lane ran east to west in a roundabout sort of way and was a good twenty miles from Weeping Rock.

Long branches, heavy from the sleet and snow, appeared in front of his windshield as he slid sideways around a curve, causing him to involuntarily duck as their icicle-like fingers scraped across the cab of his truck. As the road straightened, he was relieved to see the red and blue lights of Aaron's Silverado parked at the bottom of a steep driveway.

Taking his foot off the accelerator, Liam pulled in behind it and could just make out the image of a woman standing on the front steps of a run-down trailer, yet there was no sign of his deputy. Grabbing his flashlight from the console, he climbed out of his seat and hurried across the yard. "Ma'am," he said, giving her a quick tip of his hat as he drew near.

The woman took the cigarette out of her mouth and pointed. "Back there."

Changing direction, Liam headed around the left side of the trailer where an obstacle course of wrecked cars and broken appliances greeted him. As he began weaving his way through the piles of junk, he noticed a narrow beam of light zigzagging across the snow a few yards ahead of him.

"This way," called Aaron, motioning at Liam with his flashlight.

Shoving a mattress out of his path, Liam stumbled over a rusty propane tank and busted hose reel before catching up to him — but a snarling growl, coupled with the sound of thundering feet, brought him to an abrupt halt. Whirling around, he saw a large Rottweiler charging towards him and instinctively began scrambling backward — nearly losing his footing in the process — as he unsnapped his holster.

The dog left the ground as it lunged at him — slamming its massive paws against a chain-link fence concealed by the darkness.

Straightening up from the defensive stance he had taken, Liam wiped the embarrassment from his face and looked over at his deputy. "You could have *told* me he was in a pen."

Aaron pointed to a small clearing in the trees. "There," he said, resuming his pace.

As Liam turned to follow, the dog ran alongside him, its spiked collar clanging against the fence as it tried repeatedly to bite his leg through the wire holes. Increasing his stride, Liam hurried past the pen and fell into step with Aaron. "Who called it in?" he asked, having learned over the years to never assume the obvious.

"The lady in the trailer. She said she heard her dog barking, followed by what sounded like someone screaming. She was on her way to look out her back door when she heard a gunshot."

"Did she see anything?"

Aaron stopped and gestured at the ground in front of him. "Just the victim. That's when she called 9-1-1."

Taking in an unnecessary breath, Liam struggled to hold the flashlight steady as he knelt over the girl's body. Dressed in a purple hoodie, her right arm was pinned beneath her stomach while the other lay stretched out in front of her. Her fingers were spread wide apart as they clutched at the snow, enabling him to see a triad of stars, one large and two small, tattooed in dark-blue ink along the webbing between her thumb and forefinger.

"Best I can tell," said Aaron, standing at rigid attention on the other side of her, "it looks like she took a .22 to the back of the head."

Forcing his gaze upwards, Liam could see trace amounts of blood present in both nostrils as well as the corner of her mouth. Her eyes were open and bore a clouded look of terror, while long strands of coppery-brown hair, matted with leaves and snow, clung to the side of her face. It was a face that he quickly came to realize was far too young to be called anything other than a child.

Adjusting the beam on his flashlight, he let it travel the length of her body. Noting that the backs of both her legs were streaked with blood, he gestured at the bottom of the girl's hoodie as it lay across her bare thighs. "Is she wearing any underwear?"

There was a moment of silence as Aaron stooped to look, followed by the sound of him clearing his throat. "No."

Liam's jaw began to ache. "Is Abrams on his way?"

"I talked to him a few minutes ago."

"*And?*"

Aaron ran a gloved finger over his eyebrow and shrugged. "He told me he'll get here when he gets here."

Balling his hand into a fist, Liam got to his feet. Chet Abrams was a local rancher who pulled double-duty as coroner for Orand County; a crotchety old man who had no use for people, it was no secret that he'd only campaigned for the job because it came with free health insurance, and yet, in spite of his admission, had run unopposed for the last eight years.

Grudgingly accepting the fact that there was nothing else he could do with the victim until Abrams decided to show up, Liam focused his attention on other matters. "Do you know how far back these go?" he asked, nodding at the girl's blood-spattered footprints.

Aaron turned his flashlight towards the area of woods lining the edge of the property. "At least to there," he said, letting the light come to rest upon a fallen tree lying atop a small ridge. "But there's another set of footprints about ten yards to your left."

Making his way over to where Aaron had pointed, Liam examined the second set of tracks; twice as big and spaced far apart, they veered towards the girl's but never intercepted them, stopping instead just outside the clearing. He could see that some of the tracks were distorted, while others were unusually long, telling him that their owner had doubled back.

"Sheriff!"

Straightening, he saw Aaron waving his arms at him as he stood on the other side of the fallen tree. "Did you find something?" he shouted.

Dropping his hands, Aaron began moving his flashlight in wide, sweeping arcs across the snow.

Filled with a sense of dread, Liam's legs shook as he sprinted up the incline. As the ground beneath his feet began to level out, he noticed that

Aaron's cheeks had been drained of their inherent redness and were now a sickening shade of gray. "What's wrong?"

He stopped swinging his flashlight and aimed the beam at the ground.

Saliva, mixed with bile, swarmed Liam's throat, making him cough. A dark, bloody sac containing what looked to be an organ of some sort lay at his deputy's feet; about eight inches in diameter, it was covered in a thin, mucous-like substance and had what could only be described as an intestine attached to the top of it. Liam swallowed hard and shook his head, trying to make sense of what he was seeing. "What is it?"

Aaron's lips quivered as they fell open. "Afterbirth."

A deafening roar sounded between Liam's ears as he looked back at the girl and her blood-soaked legs. Gripping his flashlight, he forced himself to get control of his emotions before turning around. "I'll take these," he said, gesturing at the footprints in front of him as he stepped over the rotting trunk. "You take the others."

"Got it," replied Aaron, brushing past him.

"And call the fire department," he yelled over his shoulder. "Tell them to send every available man they've got!"

"Red Elk to County. Do you copy?"

"This is County. Go ahead ..."

The voices behind Liam grew distant as he ran after the bloody footprints ascending into the darkness. Layers of dead brush and razor-sharp briers grabbed at his pants, causing his steps to become as increasingly uneven as his breath as he scrambled up the rugged, bramble-infested hill in front of him. His eyes, straining to see beyond the realm of his flashlight, darted frantically from side to side as they searched the unforgiving landscape for anything that didn't belong, yet the farther up he went, the fiercer the wind became, making the task increasingly difficult.

Grabbing hold of a tree limb, Liam pulled himself the rest of the way up the hill, only to find that the girl's tracks had vanished. As he swept his flashlight across the white terrain in a desperate attempt to pick them up again, he came to realize that he was standing along the edge of a narrow bluff. Cautiously peering over its side, he noticed that along with it being a good fifty-foot drop nearly straight down, it was covered in the same prickly shrubs that were sticking out of the snow behind him. Thinking that the girl would have had as tough a time climbing up it as he was about to have going down it, he began to wonder if she'd come this way at all.

As he turned to get his bearings, a low rumbling sound drew his attention towards the bottom of the bluff. Discerning that Highway 81 was at the base of it, Liam placed all his weight on his left leg and started down, using the low-hanging branches in front of him for balance. He'd only gone a few yards, however, when the smell of burning wood made him stop.

Looking through the tangle of tree limbs on his right, he could see tiny specks of light in the distance; isolated and veiled in a foggy mist, they dotted the hillside.

Liam grabbed his radio from his belt. "Stiles, do you copy?"

The instrument crackled in the crisp night air, causing the icicles dangling above him to vibrate.

"Go ahead, Sheriff."

"Get out to Mill Lane," he commanded, resuming his descent. "I need you to search the properties that back up to the woods on the east side, including the trash cans."

A burst of static sounded.

"Copy that, but what am I looking for?"

Liam drew a jagged breath. "A newborn. Possibly one to three hours old."

Several seconds of silence passed before Gordon's voice came through the receiver. "10-4," he replied. "I'm on my way."

Liam returned the radio to his belt and leaned forward to take hold of the next tree branch. Water, ice, and shreds of bark came off in his palm as the limb snapped in half, sending him headfirst down the craggy hillside. Blindly reaching out to anything to grab hold of, his hand caught on something leafy and dense; closing his fingers around it, he managed to turn himself upright, but the sheer momentum of which he was traveling jerked his hand farther along the foliage of the bush, slicing his palm open on one of its barbed-like thorns. Releasing his grip, he slid the rest of the way down the slope on his back — until his legs collided with the guardrail, bringing him to an abrupt and painful stop.

Rolling onto his side, Liam grasped the steel post in front of him and slowly got to his knees. Wiping the warmth that was trickling down his cheek against the collar of his coat, he dug his flashlight out of the snow and held it in front of him. After blinking to clear his vision, he saw a fresh set of tire tracks stretched across the desolate highway, yet there were no footprints or markings of any kind to indicate that the girl had been this way.

The fever-pitched yips of coyotes sounded in the distance, making him shiver. "God," he prayed in a rushed whisper as he pulled himself to his feet, "please help me find this baby."

"Sheriff, this is Red Elk. Do you copy?"

"Did you find anything?"

"Negative. I've lost sight of the tracks."

Liam pressed the radio against his temple and closed his eyes.

"I'm going to head down to the highway and check out the truck stop."

Jerking his head up at Aaron's words, Liam saw an orange glow hovering above the line of scraggly boxelders that ran parallel with the highway.

"There's a chance she got a ride from one of the —"

"I'm already down here," said Liam, climbing over the guardrail. "I'll take a look."

"Copy that," Aaron replied. "I'll turn back and head west."

The faint wail of a single siren could be heard as Liam started across the road. "Be sure and search the area along the creek," he said, knowing the abandoned gristmill that sat perched on the hill beside it had become a haven for transients and crack addicts alike. "And check the barn at Ben Reynolds' place."

"10-4."

Liam's knees sank beneath the drifting snow, chilling his legs to the bone as he forged a path through the line of boxelders. Planted more than half a century ago to commemorate the new highway that promised to bring commerce and industry to Orand County, they were now nothing more than a dying barricade standing between him and the truck stop. After stumbling over countless broken limbs and branches, the partially lit sign for *Ike's* finally came into view.

A row of sleeping semis sat parked at an angle below it, their engines emitting a low but steady hum as plumes of thick gray smoke swirled from the tops of blackened exhaust stacks. Approaching the first truck from the rear, Liam knocked on the driver's side door. "Orand County Sheriff!" he said, and then quickly took three steps back. Most truck drivers carried, and Liam knew from experience that standing where they could see you *and* your hands helped to keep the situation from escalating — especially when startling them from a deep sleep.

The cab's interior light came on, illuminating a pale and bearded face.

"Sheriff," Liam repeated, holding up his badge. "I need to ask you a few questions."

Giving him a wary nod, the man opened the door and climbed down.

"I'm looking for an infant. Have you seen anyone with a baby or heard any screams or crying?"

"Naw," replied the man, jumping from the step onto the pavement.

"Have you seen or heard anything unusual at all?"

The man pushed a mop of hair from his eyes and shook his head. "Just you bangin' on my door."

"How long have you been here?"

"Well — *hell*," he said, scratching his backside, "I don't know. What time is it?"

Liam scowled as he pulled back the sleeve of his coat. "A quarter to eleven."

"Then about a half-hour, I guess."

Liam glanced towards the rear of the trailer. With just over thirty minutes having passed since he'd gotten the initial call from Aaron, and the fact that the tire tracks behind the semi hadn't been completely covered by the snow, told him the guy was telling the truth.

"Sheriff, do you copy?"

"Go ahead."

"Negative on the mill," said Aaron. "I'm heading over to Ben Reynolds' place now."

"Copy that."

"Did someone take a baby?"

Liam returned his attention to the truck driver, whose bleary eyes were now alert and sober. "That's what we're trying to find out."

"Uh, Sheriff?"

"Yeah?" he said, putting his radio away.

"Do you need a Band-Aid or … somethin'?"

"*What*?"

"You're … uh …" The man paused to gesture at Liam's head. "Bleedin'."

"I'm fine," he snapped, turning to go.

"Wait! Can I help you search?"

Liam's first inclination was to tell him that he couldn't, but with time running out, he knew he needed all the help he could get. He pointed towards a small building. "Look in the bathrooms and check the showers. If you find it, don't do anything," he said, accenting his last words. "Just come get me."

"You got it, Sheriff!" Leaning inside the cab of his truck, the driver pulled a long-handled flashlight out from underneath the seat and started across the parking lot.

Hurrying over to the next semi, Liam noticed that its tire tracks were still visible, as were those of the remaining two semis on the other side of it. Reaching up, he banged on the door. "Orand

County Sheriff!" he yelled, repeating the same actions as before, yet as he stepped back found his gaze being drawn to the space between the cab of the truck and the trailer. Peering through it, he could see a small light shining in the distance; two rectangular sticks, one crossing over the other, lit up the surrounding darkness like a beacon.

Sprinting towards the light, Liam felt his anger giving way to a fragile hope as he scrambled up a set of rickety steps that led to a door mounted on the far left side of a trailer. Finding it locked, he started to look for another way in but stopped when he noticed the spatters of blood across its threshold. Raising his foot, he brought it down hard against the door, tearing the top from its hinges.

Slipping inside, Liam's eyes followed the beam of his flashlight as it swept over the interior of the converted trailer. On his right, rows of metal chairs sat on either side of a narrow aisle, giving him only one direction in which to go. The floorboards beneath his feet creaked, sending their echoes ricocheting off the paneled walls like cracks of thunder.

As he continued making his way down the aisle, drops of blood, heavier and darker than what he'd seen outside, appeared before him, quickening his breath—and pace. The trail ended at the base of a wooden podium. Coming around its side, Liam saw that it was hollow in back and had a coat stuffed inside the bottom of it. Dropping to his knees, he reached in and gave a gentle tug on the sleeve. It tumbled out of the pulpit with ease, revealing a small, still body.

Gathering the infant in his arms, Liam held him close as he watched and listened for signs of life. "Red Elk," he said, fumbling with his radio, "do you copy?"

Static filled the trailer, electrifying the air around him.

"Go ahead, Sheriff."

"I found him—but he's not breathing," he said, fighting to keep his voice level. "Have the FD meet me at the truck stop."

"10-4."

Heavy footsteps sounded outside the trailer, causing Liam to move his hand to his Glock. A moment later, the truck driver from before appeared in the open doorway. "Did you find it?" he wheezed, shining his flashlight in Liam's eyes.

"Sir, I need you to wait outside," replied Liam, placing the baby on the floor. "This is a possible crime scene."

"Oh, *shit* ..." The man clasped his hands on top of his head and took a step forward. "Is it breathin'?" he asked, craning his neck in an attempt to see.

Liam pointed at the door. "If you want to help," he shouted, unable to stop his cheeks from becoming wet as he tilted the baby's head back, "go outside and wait for the fire department!"

Disappointment swarmed the truck driver's face as he turned and reluctantly made his way out of the trailer.

Leaning over, Liam covered the baby's tiny mouth and nose with his own and gave two short breaths, then finding the center of his chest, gently swept the umbilical cord that had been tied with a dirty shoestring out of the way and started compressions. As he counted under his breath, the tears that had been collecting at the bottom of his chin dropped in rapid succession onto the back of his hand.

The scream of an approaching siren was of little comfort to him as he frantically bent down to push another round of air into the baby's lungs. "God, please," he prayed, yet before he could expel his second breath, his shoulders began to shake, wrenching a despondent sob from deep within him.

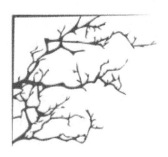

# Chapter 7

Squinting at the light overhead, Olivia clumsily drew back the shower curtain and reached inside. Accepting the fact that the water hitting her wrist was as hot as it was going to get, she reluctantly slipped out of her wrinkled blouse and panties and stepped into the tub—the movements of which sent a jarring pain trouncing through her head.

Leaning against the plastic surround, she held her breath as she waited for the agony to subside, but the lukewarm drops pelting her skin made her feel as if she were slowly being stoned to death. Staring at the water as it lapped at her ankles, she began to wish she'd run a bath instead, yet the thought of submerging herself in something permanently stained with rust and grime wasn't all that appealing.

As the bottoms of her toes scraped across the pink sandpapery butterflies, she found herself yearning for her old tub, along with the apartment it sat nestled in. Located on the other side of town and only minutes from the highway that led to Rapid City, the unit was cramped and overpriced, but what it'd lacked in terms of space, it had made up for with other things, such as hot water and non-leaking ceilings.

A wobbly smile pushed its way onto Olivia's lips. Inside those stark white walls of apartment 5B lingered the cyclonic memories of where she and Liam had started their lives together. It was full of firsts for them: their first kiss, their first time making love, their first fight ... their first everything. And it was where, on rigid knee, two days before Valentine's Day, he'd proposed.

Olivia tilted her head back, letting the water trickle down her throat. In spite of the promises they'd made to one another at the courthouse that day, their marriage was in shambles, the disarray of it comparable to most of the rooms in this godforsaken house, with the reasons why being as difficult to comprehend ... as they were to accept.

A wave of nausea washed over her, adding a sense of despair to her already miserable state. Clenching her fingers, she waited for it to pass, but the bile inside her continued to churn. Spinning the handle to the left, she jerked the curtain back and stumbled out of the tub—only to find Liam's tall and slender frame hunched over the sink.

Refusing to hurl in front of him on the grounds of vanity, and what was left of her pride, Olivia grabbed the towel beside her and pressed it to her nose and mouth. Closing her eyes, she concentrated on taking slow, measured breaths while letting the towel's clean, cottony smell infiltrate her nostrils.

"Are you all right?"

Her eyes snapped open to find Liam staring at her. Thinking she heard the slightest hint of concern in his voice, she managed a small nod.

In the suffocating quiet that followed, Olivia fought the urge to shiver as she waited for him to leave, yet he remained standing where he was. It was then that she realized the towel she was holding against her mouth hung straight down, leaving her left breast, along with most everything else, exposed. Adjusting her grip, she saw the subtle movement in his eyes as they took it all in. Desiring him to come closer, her mind began foraging for the words, but before her hungover brain could string together an intelligible sentence, he turned from the sink and walked out.

Letting the towel fall from her fingertips, she made her way over to the gold-veined mirror mounted above the sink and solemnly gazed at the image before her. Through the cracks of her eyelids, she could just make out a set of thin coral lips and flushed cheekbones that stood out against an otherwise colorless backdrop of flesh; holding them in place was a stoic jawline, the harshness of it a stark contrast to the trembling chin sitting below it.

As the tears began to spill down her face, the remnants of last night, which had crested midway up her throat, began to fluctuate. Dropping to her knees, Olivia leaned over the toilet and — as quietly as she could — heaved into the bowl. When she had finished, she felt along the floor for her discarded towel and dragged it across her lips. Using the seat as leverage to push herself up, she then pulled her arms through her robe and opened the drawer in front of her; after swallowing three aspirin and a breath mint, she hurriedly finger-combed her wet hair and went in search of her husband.

She found him sitting at the foot of their bed putting on his socks. As she drew closer, she noticed an ugly one-inch gash on the left side of his forehead being held together by two butterfly strips. "My God, Liam," she said, sweeping his light-brown locks out of the way to inspect it. "What happened?"

He moved his head back and out of her reach. "I cut it."

Pretending that his actions just now hadn't hurt her, she lowered her hand and sat down beside him. "What time did you get home?"

"Around four."

She tucked a strand of hair behind her ear for the sole purpose of letting her shoulder touch his. "I didn't hear you come in."

"No," he said, getting to his feet, "I'm sure you didn't."

Olivia bit down on the inside of her cheek as she watched him snatch his shirt off the bed and turn away. Having no wish to spend the next two days tiptoeing around his anger, her gaze aimlessly wandered the room in search of anything that would offset it. Spying the valentine card she'd bought last night at *Elmar's*, she eagerly got up and retrieved it off the dresser. Pressing the card to her chest, she took a deep breath and spun around. "Happy anniversary," she said in the most chipper voice she could find.

Silence.

"Aren't you going to look?" she pleaded.

More silence.

"Liam?"

Sighing, he stopped buttoning his shirt and glanced over his shoulder.

She held out the card and tilted it from side to side. "Happy anniversary," she repeated. To her surprise, he reached out and took it, sending a wave of goosebumps rolling across her flesh as his fingers grazed hers. Sliding the card from the envelope, he flipped it open and began to read. Preparing to kiss and make up, Olivia hurriedly licked the dryness from her lips and moved closer.

Liam tossed the card on the unmade bed and brushed past her.

"*What?*" she asked, following on his heels.

He stopped in the doorway and turned around. "It probably would've meant more if you'd written something in it—like your *name*."

Olivia glanced at the card as it lay face down on the rumpled comforter. A vague memory surfaced of her taking it out of the sack after Liam had left last night; it had occurred somewhere between feeling remorse for the terrible things she'd said to him ... and passing out.

Pushing away her embarrassment, she returned her attention to the doorway to find it empty. Partially formed excuses mixed with half-truths swirled inside her like a tempest as she started after him. Upon reaching the hallway, however, her footsteps stumbled to a halt.

Her father-in-law was in the kitchen, his irritatingly boisterous voice unusually low as he stood talking to Liam. Knowing that their conversation most likely had everything to do with her, Olivia retreated into the shadows.

"Was she a local?" asked Harlan, scratching one of his unruly sideburns.

"I don't know. She didn't have any ID on her."

"Probably a runaway," Harlan stated. "Let me make some calls. I'll see what I can find out."

"I'd rather you didn't," said Liam, reaching for the pot of coffee beside him.

"Why the hell not? Don't you wanna find the son-of-a-bitch who killed her?"

Liam cast his eyes downward as he filled his thermos, enabling Olivia to see the fatigue in his face. "That has nothing to do with it."

"What then? Don't you want my help?"

"Not on this."

"No?"

"No."

Clinging to the darkness in the hallway, Olivia watched her father-in-law pick up his walker and limp closer to Liam. "Well, tell me somethin'," he said, slamming the front legs of it down on the linoleum. "Just exactly how many murders have you solved durin' the four months you've been sheriff?"

"Look," said Liam, shoving the coffee pot back on its burner, "I need a minute to figure out how I want to handle this, and I'm not sure that getting the town in an uproar is the best way. We've got enough going on as it is."

"I'm just gonna make some calls," Harlan retorted, his voice back up to its annoying level. "Not sound a goddamn alarm."

Liam rubbed the back of his neck and sighed. "If you really want to help, you can look into the other matter."

A broad smile began to form on Harlan's lips.

"*Not* Hector Ramirez, Dad," said Liam, shaking his head. "The *other* matter."

"*What* other matter?"

"The one sitting at the bottom of the lake."

"That's nothin' but busywork," Harlan grumbled, waving a dismissive hand in the air. "Let Runnin' Deer handle it."

Liam's expression darkened as he screwed the lid onto his thermos. "Aaron's got enough to do," he finally said. "I'm leaving in five minutes — with or without you."

"But —"

"*Five minutes.*"

Swinging his walker around, Harlan began hobbling towards the den, his slow-moving gait, and sour disposition reminding Olivia of an angry turtle trying to cross a busy intersection. She was so caught up in watching him that she didn't notice Liam heading in her direction — until it was too late. His sock-clad feet collided with her bare toes as he rounded the corner, stopping him cold.

"Did you want something?" she asked, feeling the heat flood her face.

"I think it'd be best if I took you to work," he said in a clipped tone. "The main roads are clear, but the side roads are still covered."

Olivia mulled over the offer, yet the thought of having to spend the next half hour sitting beside her father-in-law and his unfiltered mouth made her shake her head. "I can manage."

A pinging noise sounded between them.

"Are you sure?" he asked, pulling out his phone.

As he swiped his thumb across it, Olivia saw a deep cut on the inside of his hand that ran the length of his palm. Figuring it would be pointless to ask him about it, she answered his question with a nod ... then upon realizing he hadn't seen it, followed it up with a verbal affirmation.

"I might be running late this afternoon, so you need to be ready to go when I come by to pick you up. It's a thirty-minute drive to Crawford, and then another ten after that to the courthouse."

Olivia's heart began to beat erratically, sending the blood it was pumping slamming into her right temple as the memory of what the day entailed materialized from the foggy, bourbon-soaked recesses of her brain.

"We also need to allow a few minutes to talk with Dwayne before going inside —"

"There's no need for us to ride together," she said. "I'll meet you there."

He looked up from his phone. "Are you sure?"

Having heard that question twice in the last twenty seconds, Olivia realized that she wasn't sure of anything, except for her ability to constantly upset him. Wanting his forgiveness over anything else at the moment, she forced herself to look into his eyes. "Liam, I'm —"

"I'm ready!" yelled Harlan, emerging from the den. "Where the hell are ya?"

Liam glanced towards the living room. "I'm coming!" he shouted, then drawing an impatient breath, turned back to Olivia. "What were you going to say?"

Knowing that any explanation regarding her behavior last night would undoubtedly be lost on him because of his hurry to leave, she dropped her outstretched hand and let the hastily built apology die on her tongue. "It can wait," she replied, shaking her head.

Liam eyed her closely as he put his phone away. "I'll meet you outside the courthouse at three forty-five."

Uncertain if he was repeating himself for her sake or his, she gave him another compliant nod.

"Be careful on the way in."

"I will," she said, glancing at the clock in the kitchen, then with nothing left to say, mumbled a feeble goodbye.

Clearing his throat, Liam bent down and placed a small kiss on the right side of her cheek; it was startling, and warm … and left her wanting to reciprocate. Wrapping her arms around his shoulders, she turned her lips into his, yet upon feeling their indifference for her stopped and drew back.

"I'll see you this afternoon," he said, looking in any direction but hers as he turned away.

Fighting the sting of tears, Olivia slumped against the wall, purposefully removing herself from the line of sight of her father-in-law, who'd witnessed the entire exchange, and escaped to the safety of her bedroom.

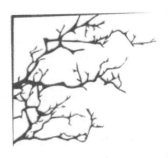

# Chapter 8

Even though Liam had parked right outside the station, his usual ten-second walk to the front door had evolved into an agonizingly cold crawl, as he had to force himself to stay a step behind his father who'd developed a bad habit of shuffling his feet since the accident. Not helping matters was the fact that while listening to the news on the drive over, he'd learned that his carefully worded statement regarding Hector Ramirez had been ignored in favor of his widow, who'd given an interview implying that he'd been murdered—lighting up the radio's phone lines, and eliciting a smug 'I told you so' from his father.

The bitter wind sliced across Liam's face and ears, making him long for the shelter of his Stetson, which had been lost during his tumble down the embankment last night.

"You go on in," said his father, leaning against the railing as he reached into the pocket of his coat. "I'll be along in a minute."

Liam pressed his lips together.

"Don't give me that look."

"And what look would that be?" asked Liam, tilting his head. "The look that says, 'I've got a million things to do today but can't get started on them because I've got to stand out here and wait on you while you have a smoke'?"

"Well, you won't let me do it in your truck and you won't let me do it in *there*," countered his father, gesturing at the station with a crumpled pack of Marlboros. "So where the hell else am I supposed to do it?"

"Fine," replied Liam, checking his watch. "Just hurry up."

His father waved him away. "I told you to go on," he said, cupping his hands around his lighter. "I'm not a goddamned invalid, you know."

Gritting his teeth, Liam grabbed the handle on the door. "Watch your step when you come in," he said, pointing at the clump of ice in front of his father's feet.

"I always do," he snapped. "I haven't fallen yet, have I—"

Slamming the door, Liam walked inside the station, where he was instantly greeted by the smell of burnt coffee and cigarette smoke.

"Mornin', Sheriff."

Holding onto his sigh, Liam hung his coat on one of the wooden pegs and turned to look at Enid Willoughby. "Any messages?"

"Seven so far," she replied, keeping her eyes on her newspaper.

"But I've always parked there."

"Yes, ma'am."

"I've been parking in that exact same spot for twenty years."

Making his way over to the counter, Liam's gaze was drawn to the conversation that was taking place on his left. Gordon Stiles was leaning back in his chair, impatiently tapping his foot against the floor as he listened to the woman across from him carrying on. Though Liam couldn't see her face, he recognized her voice, and not wanting any part of it, swiftly shifted his attention back to Enid, who was still reading her newspaper. "Can I see the messages?" he prompted.

"They're where they always are," she replied, licking the tip of her thumb before turning the page.

Letting go of his sigh, Liam reached over the counter and pulled the slips of paper out of the mouth of a green plastic frog with googly eyes. "Anything from the M.E.'s office?" he asked, trying to decipher her scrawled handwriting.

"Nope."

"What about Cam Peterson?"

Enid shook her head. "But this came yesterday afternoon for you," she said, holding up an envelope.

Turning it over, Liam saw that it was from the county commission office.

"… and in all those years, I've never been told I couldn't."

"I understand, ma'am," Gordon said, rolling his pen between his fingers, "but *Bowman's* has the right to reserve that parking space for his customers."

"Now you listen to me." The woman sat forward in her chair, making it creak. "Archie Bowman is just doing this out of spite because I called the health department on him. That so-called *deli* of his is crawling with roaches. You wanna do something? Do something about *that* instead of writing me tickets."

Stiles shot Liam a beleaguered look.

Pretending he hadn't seen him, he started towards his office.

"Oh, and Hector Ramirez's wife called."

Liam turned back to Enid. "What did she want?"

"I dunno. She just said that she needed to talk to you."

A familiar pain began to resonate between his shoulder blades. "Call her back and tell her that I can meet her here at ten."

"I can't do that."

"Why not?"

"She said that the roads are too bad for her to drive into town," Enid replied, the cigarette fastened between her lips bobbing up and down as she spoke. "She wants you to come out to her house."

Liam walked back to the counter and leaned in close. "Is there anything else you want to tell me about the conversation you had with her?"

"No, that's pretty much it."

"Where's Aaron?" he asked, rubbing his jaw.

"He's working an accident over on Valley Station Road. A car went off the side."

"When he's done, have him meet me at Ramirez's house."

"You got it."

"And, Enid?" he said, drawing his head back from the smoke that was pouring out of her nostrils.

"Yeah?"

"We talked about this."

She lowered the corner of the paper and peered up at him through her cheaters. "Talked about what?"

He gestured at the cigarette.

Enid shrugged. "Yeah, we talked about it," she said in a tone that sounded as unapologetic as it did defiant.

"This is a public building," stated Liam, reciting the words that he'd said to her countless times over the last four months. "You can't smoke in here." The cowbell behind him clanged, diverting what little attention he had of Enid's to the door, and as the sound of his father's walker hitting the tile floor echoed behind him, he watched the apathetic expression on her face change to indignation.

"Uh ... mornin', Enid."

Stamping out her cigarette, she stood up and marched over to the coffee machine.

"Hey, Harlan," called Gordon. "How the heck are you?"

Liam saw his father reluctantly shift his gaze to his former deputy. "I can't complain."

Getting to his feet, Gordon anxiously gestured at the woman sitting across from him. "You know Sadie McGee, don't you?"

"Of course I know her," he replied. "Hell, we go way back, don't we?"

"That's right," said the woman, her considerable girth unfolding around her as she rose from the chair.

"And I might add," his father said with a wink, "that you're lookin' prettier than ever."

"Oh, be careful now ..." Sadie McGee paused to touch the frizzy nap of curls that sat in a tight cluster on the top of her head. "You know what they say about flattery, Sheriff."

Resting his elbow on the counter, Liam waited for his father to remind her that he no longer held that title—but instead, listened to him let out a crusty laugh while cutting his eyes towards Enid, who remained at the coffee machine sprinkling what must have been her fifth packet of sugar into her *I love my Yorkie* mug.

"So what brings you by, darlin'?" his father asked in a voice that was ten times louder than it needed to be.

"Well, I was just explaining to your deputy here," said Sadie, pointing an accusatory finger at Gordon, "that I've been parking at the corner of Second and Maple five days a week for the last ten years and never had any problems until the city put in that turning lane ..."

The telephone rang drawing everyone's attention — except for Sadie, who went right on repeating the whole sordid story regarding her lost parking spaces, the cockroaches in Archie Bowman's deli, and her duty as a citizen to report them.

"... place is unsanitary ..."

Leaning across his desk, Gordon eagerly snatched up the receiver. "Sheriff's Office."

"Business isn't what it used to be here, you know. And if I were to go and park my car in front of *my* store, it would take away a spot from the handful of customers that I do get ..."

"Hey, Bill," said Gordon, switching the phone to his other ear. "Are you guys on your way?"

"Now you know me well enough to know that I get along with just about everybody," Sadie continued, "but I'm drawing the line with Archie Bowman. You're going to have to do something about this situation, Harlan, because I simply can't afford to pay these parking tickets that your deputies keep putting on my windshield."

"I'll tell you what," his father said, putting an arm across Sadie's shoulder. "You just throw away those tickets. And don't you worry none about ole Archie. I'll talk to him."

The messages in Liam's hand crumpled between his fingers.

A broad smile dug into Sadie's cheeks, bolstering their plumpness. "I knew I could count on you to make things right, Sheriff."

"Don't think nothin' of it," his father replied, pointing her towards the exit.

Pushing himself away from the counter, Liam hurried to get the door for her. "Have a nice day."

The woman stopped and arched a pencil-drawn eyebrow at him. "You could stand to take a few lessons from your daddy on runnin' this town, you know."

Taking in a deep breath, Liam managed a polite nod. "Yes, ma'am." Pulling the door closed behind her, he gave his father a sidelong glance as he turned and stalked into his office.

Tossing the messages aside, he sat down at his desk and eagerly tore open the envelope from the county commission office. Liam only had to read the first two sentences below the letterhead, however, to see that his request to fill the deputy position, left vacant after the board of county commissioners had appointed him sheriff last November, had been denied.

Stuffing the letter back inside its envelope, Liam shoved it in the bottom drawer of his desk and reached for his thermos—only to realize he'd forgotten to bring it in. Not wanting to tread back out into the cold for it, he grabbed the folder in front of him instead and flipped it open. Looking at Hector Ramirez's file had become a part of his morning ritual, and even though he could recite the information it held verbatim, he was, unfortunately, no closer to uncovering the truth now about what had happened than he was a week ago.

The only fact he knew for certain was that the last time anyone saw Hector was when he was leaving the high school last Tuesday after practice. Liam propped his fist against his head as he stared at the file's worn pages. Despite having interviewed everyone at the school that had anything to do with Hector, his whereabouts from six o'clock that night until nine the next morning—when his glass eye was discovered by a jogger along the bluff overlooking Crow's Foot Lake—remained unknown.

Adding to the mystery was Hector's Jeep; his 2016 white Wrangler was found two days later parked at a substation some thirty miles away, and although it had been wiped clean of prints, various drug paraphernalia, including several needles and a nickel bag containing trace amounts of heroin were recovered from the console. Thirty dollars in cash and a cell phone charger were also recovered—but no phone.

"Hey, what the hell did you do with my fish?"

"I put it in the storage room," Liam answered, without bothering to look up.

"Well I hope you took the time to put it in a box or somethin' before you just tossed it in there," his father grumbled. "Do you know how much I paid to have that thing mounted?"

Closing Hector's file, Liam leaned back in his chair. "Why did you tell Sadie McGee to throw her tickets away?"

"To get her out of my hair. Why the hell else?" he said, coming in the rest of the way. "Besides, we're only talkin' what, twenty bucks?"

"Try a hundred."

His father cleared his throat and shrugged. "I think the town will survive."

"Are you going to talk to Archie Bowman?"

"Why would I do that?" he asked with a laugh.

"Because you told her you would."

"Why're you gettin' your panties in such a wad over a bunch of parkin' tickets?"

Liam got up and shut the door, rattling the metal blinds attached to it. "It's not just the parking tickets, Dad. It's *everything* you do, *every* time you come here. There are certain rules and procedures that have to be followed, and when you tell someone it's all right to ignore them, it just makes it that much harder on me and my deputies."

"They're *my* deputies," his father said, easing himself into a chair. "Well … at least *one* of 'em is, anyway."

"Don't go changing the subject."

His father scratched the side of his face, generating a sandpaper-like sound as the tips of his fingers moved across his unshaven jaw. "Look," he finally said, picking a file up from the corner of the desk, "this isn't New York City—or even Rapid City. It's Weepin' Rock."

Liam reached over and snatched the file out of his father's hands. "I know that."

"No, I don't think you do. Because if you did, you'd know that people in this town just wanna be able to pay their rent, put food on their table, and hope to have enough money left over at the end of the week for a beer or two. They've got enough worries without you following along behind them like Barney Fife, writin' *tickets* and citin' *ordinances*."

A loud knock sounded on the other side of the door.

"*What?*" yelled Liam, keeping his eyes on his father.

Stiles poked his head inside. "Bill Miller called. His men are getting ready to go down and start hooking up the cables."

His father sat forward and wrapped his fingers around his walker. "Let me have your keys, Gordo," he said, pulling himself to his feet. "I'll get the truck warmed up."

"Uh ..." Gordon turned sideways in order to keep the right front leg of the walker from coming down on his foot. "They're in the ignition."

Liam stepped in front of the doorway, blocking his father. "The plan is for you to stay here. Once the car's out of the water, Stiles will call the plate number in, along with any other details regarding the victim, and you can take it from there."

"That's *your* plan," said his father, motioning for him to get out of his way. "Not mine."

"If he wants to come along, Sheriff, I don't have a problem with it."

"Did you hear that?" his father said to him, jerking his head towards Gordon. "He said he doesn't have a problem with it."

"The car's on the north side of the lake," Liam argued. "It's physically impossible for you to get down there—"

"Hey, Sheriff?" Enid's nasally voice carried through the doorway and scraped across the back of Liam's neck. "Cal Mobley called and said that two men just robbed his store."

A look of excitement engulfed his father's face, bringing a clarity to it that Liam hadn't seen in months. But then, just as quickly as it had come, it disappeared, swallowed whole by the four aluminum legs in front of him that now defined his life.

"You want me to take it, Sheriff?"

Liam's gaze stumbled over to Gordon.

"No," he said, the word coming out softer than he'd intended as he turned away, "I've got it. You take care of Miller."

"You know," said Gordon, following him out of the office, "Miller's probably gonna have his tent set up at the top of the embankment like he did yesterday."

"What's your point?"

"Well, I figure I can put Harlan inside it. That way he could still be in on the action, and it'd give him and Miller a chance to talk about their glory days. When we're done, I'll bring him back here to the station."

A bitter taste swarmed Liam's mouth. When it came to Gordon's relationship with his father, he had stopped trying to understand it years ago, as it only served to stir up feelings of confusion, hurt, and jealousy—especially when compared to the man's obvious disregard for *him*.

Stiles scratched the grayish-black stubble dotting the underside of his throat and gave him a crooked smile. "So, what do you say, *Sheriff*?"

Grabbing his coat, Liam shoved open the door and started down the steps. "Do what you want," he called over his shoulder, knowing that if he stayed any longer, he would end up saying something he would most likely regret.

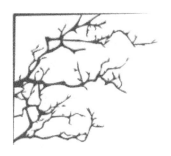

# Chapter 9

"It was a twenty-six piece set, valued at over six hundred dollars. They're forged from steel and micro-alloy, and I'm the only one that sold it this side of the Black Hills. I bought it off a guy up in Pierre who—"

"So besides the set of wrenches," said Liam, trying to speed things along as he stood in the middle of Cal Mobley's hardware store, "is there anything else missing?"

Mobley ran his tongue across a snarl of crooked teeth as he made his way over to the next aisle. "They took four Stihl chainsaws and a torque wrench, all still in their cases," he said, stooping down to show him.

Looking past the mouse droppings, Liam saw the dusty outlines of where the cases had sat. "Anything else?"

The man straightened, but his withered shoulders remained in a hunched position beneath the straps of his Carhartt's as his clouded blue eyes searched the cluttered shelves in front of him. "No," he finally said, scratching the tuft of hair that was sprouting out of his right ear, "I think that's it."

Tucking his pen in the pocket of his shirt, Liam lowered his clipboard and walked to the back of the store, the pungent aroma of oil, rubber, and paint thinner converging upon him as he knelt to inspect the padlock lying on the floor.

"They used bolt cutters to get in," said Mobley, pressing his hip against the corner of the counter beside him. "You see how it's severed in the middle there? That's because—"

"You said that the men were still inside when you pulled up?"

"That's right," Mobley replied, reaching behind the counter. "But they took off runnin' when they saw me comin' through the front door with *this*."

Standing, Liam placed his hand on the barrel of the 12-gauge shotgun that Mobley was proudly holding and carefully pointed it in the opposite direction as his chest. "Which way did they go?"

Mobley kicked the lock to the side and went through the open door. "That way," he said, extending his left arm. "They climbed over the fence and drove off."

The cold infiltrated Liam's lungs, making him shiver as he stepped into the alley.

"You know, those sons-of-bitches are just lucky I couldn't get a shot off. Once, I hit a coon that'd been killin' my chickens — right smack between the eyes," explained Mobley, pausing to press his index finger to the area just above the bridge of his nose for effect. "Nailed him from twenty —"

"Did you get a good look at them?"

"The *coon*?"

Liam drew a heavy breath. "The men who robbed you."

The excited expression Mobley had been wearing slid down into the crevices of his face, leaving it blank. "No," he said, shaking his head. "I don't see too well anymore. Got cataracts in both eyes."

"Could you tell what kind of vehicle they were driving?"

"Nope."

"Color?"

"Nope. But one of them had a hurt leg or somethin'."

"What makes you say that?"

"Looked to me like he was draggin' it behind him as he ran out of the store."

Turning from Mobley, Liam focused his attention on the chain-link fence that stretched between the buildings in the back of the alley. Just beyond it sat Glenn Avenue; situated near the railroad tracks, it held four-blocks of duplexes that over the last few years had become a thorn in Weeping Rock's side. Built by the city nearly two decades ago as affordable housing for the less fortunate, they were now nothing more than a dwelling for degenerate lowlifes, crackheads, and the Colter brothers. In and out of juvie since they were teens, Frank and Jesse Colter had rap sheets a mile long, and included everything from petty theft, to aggravated battery, to assault with a deadly weapon.

Mobley cleared his throat, the guttural sound of it reminiscent of machine-gun fire, and spit the outcome in the snow beside him. "Yes, sir. Those guys were damn lucky ..."

Continuing to stare at the fence, Liam involuntarily ran his thumb over the scar that cut through the middle of his left eyebrow. Last April, he'd gone to serve an arrest warrant on Frank, the older of the two brothers. Refusing to come with them peacefully—and higher than a kite—it had taken all of Liam's, his father's, and Gordon's strengths combined to subdue him, and by the time they'd gotten the cuffs around his wrists, they couldn't tell whose blood was whose. Three months later, Frank was back on the street.

"...gotten here ten seconds sooner, they would've been in a world of hurt—"

"Sheriff, do you copy?"

"Go ahead, Enid."

"The M.E.'s office in Rapid City called."

"What'd they say?" he asked, walking out of earshot of Mobley.

"Dr. Fuller's gonna be performing the autopsy on Ramirez this afternoon."

"*When* this afternoon?"

"They didn't say."

Liam tossed his head back, allowing a barrage of silent obscenities to escape his lips. When he was finished, he held his radio up. "I need you to call them back and get me a specific time."

There was a long pause, followed by the sound of Enid sighing. "Copy that."

"So, you got any idea who killed Ramirez?"

Liam turned to find Mobley standing nowhere near the spot he'd left him.

"Well, do you?"

"We're working on it," Liam answered. As he spoke, he noticed a large camera mounted on the brick above the door; long and sleek, its lens was pointed at the alley.

"My son-in-law bought that for me after the last time I got broken into. Do you remember when that happened? You were a deputy back then. My front window got smashed and someone stole —"

"I remember," said Liam, wishing Mobley had told him about the camera fifteen stories ago. "Can you pull up the footage?"

"Oh, it ain't a real camera. It's one of those fake ones."

Liam's newfound optimism died before it could draw its first breath.

"Had you fooled though, didn't it?" said Mobley, grinning. "Too bad it didn't work on those guys that robbed me. I guess they were just smart enough to know the difference."

The wind picked up, strafing Liam's cheeks. "You can stop by the sheriff's office for a copy of the report tomorrow. In the meantime, if you should think of anything else," he said, handing him one of his cards, "give us a call."

"Wait." Mobley's grin faded. "Aren't you gonna go after the ones who did this?"

Although the probability was high that the items taken from Mobley's store were now in the possession of the Colter brothers, Liam couldn't spare the time *or* manpower to pursue it right now. "Without a description, there isn't much we can do," he said, clipping his radio back to his belt, "but we'll send a list of the items that were stolen to the area pawnshops."

"So in other words, no."

"As I said, without a—"

"You know," said Mobley, resting the butt of his shotgun on his thigh, "I figured now that you were sheriff you might be more useful." Crumpling the card in his hand, he threw it at Liam's feet. "Guess I was wrong."

Liam's tongue gravitated to the roof of his mouth, preventing his reply from making an exit. Over the years, he'd learned not to take what victims said personally, yet this seemed to be more than just an emotionally charged rant.

Enid's voice crackled around his waist. "Got an answer for you, Sheriff."

Reaching for his radio, Liam turned and started for his truck, leaving Mobley and his disgruntled face behind.

GLANCING AT THE CLOCK on his dash, Liam was glad to see Aaron's truck already in Hector Ramirez's driveway when he pulled in. "Thanks for meeting me," he said, opening his door.

Aaron shook his head. "It beats spending the morning with Bill Miller."

As Liam came around the front of his Silverado, he watched his deputy struggle to stifle a yawn before doing the same.

"What are we doing here?"

"Ramirez's wife called the station and said she needed to talk to us."

Aaron's left eyebrow disappeared beneath the brim of his hat. "*Us?*"

"You know what I mean," Liam snapped.

The right corner of Aaron's mouth twitched. "I *do* know what you mean. So, do you want me to record her coming onto you with my bodycam? Oh—wait," he said, feeling behind the small medicine bag that lay against his chest, "I forgot. We don't have one of those."

Liam's scowl deepened.

"I'll tell you what," Aaron continued, patting the pocket of his coat. "I'll just use my phone. Maybe she won't notice."

"I'm glad you find this so funny."

"You have no idea," Aaron said with a laugh, his dark, shoulder-length hair whipping about his face as they started up the drive.

Surrounded by tall oak trees and pines, Hector's property, which sat near the highway, was peaceful and serene, yet Liam felt the one-and-a-half-story white brick home with faded green shutters and sagging carport was an ill fit for someone who'd earned over sixty million in their career.

"Have you heard anything from the M.E.'s office?"

"Fuller's doing the autopsy later this afternoon," answered Liam, returning his attention to Aaron.

"Well, here's hoping he'll give you something you can use."

Liam rubbed the back of his neck, trying to force the tension from it. "Unfortunately, I'll be in Crawford by then."

Aaron gave him a puzzled look. "Oh," he finally said, his face taking on a somber expression as he dropped his gaze to the ground, "I forgot that was today."

The snow crunched beneath their boots, amplifying the silence that had surrounded them.

"So, how's the head?" Aaron asked, still looking down.

Eager to move past the discomfort his words had brought, Liam smiled and let out a small chuckle. "Sore."

"I bet it is," said Aaron, yet the laugh accompanying his reply sounded to Liam to be as forced as his own. As they walked on, Aaron cleared his throat. "Do you want me to go see Fuller in your place?"

Even though Liam had wanted to be present for the autopsy, in reality, he knew nothing earth-shattering was going to come of it. "I think it'd be best if you searched the area where the girl was found, while there's still enough daylight to do so."

"I'll head over there as soon as we're done here."

As they made their way across the yard, Liam warily eyed the black van that was sitting in front of the carport.

"I hope you're ready for your close-up," Aaron mused.

Liam's shoulders stiffened as he climbed the steps to the porch. "I'm not giving another statement."

"That's not a news van," said Aaron, pointing out the red and gold lettering on the side of it. "That's LRTV, the Atlanta network that produces *Here Comes Kiki*. They're right in the middle of filming the fifth season."

Liam stopped and looked at his deputy.

Aaron gave him an innocent shrug. "*What?*"

A creaking noise and a barking dog drew both men's attention to the door. A few seconds later,

Kiki Grey appeared. "Sheriff Matthews," she said, dabbing at her eyes with a tissue.

Liam raised his hand to tip his hat only to grasp at the chilly air around him. Clumsily running his fingers through his hair instead, he offered her an awkward nod. "Ma'am."

"Come in," she said, widening the door.

As she turned away, Liam couldn't help noticing that she wasn't wearing anything underneath her silk robe. Hanging back, he motioned at Aaron to go first.

Removing his hat with a smirk, Aaron gave him an exaggerated wink and stepped inside.

As Liam trailed after him, he found himself hoping that this wasn't going to end up being another waste of time—yet his aspirations were immediately dashed at the sight of the film crew standing in the foyer. Before he could protest, a rhythmic melody on steel drums began to play.

Kiki held up her finger. "I'm sorry. I'll just be a minute." Pulling out her phone, she made sure she was facing the camera before swiping the screen. "Bonnie, hi. ... Thank you. ... Can I call you back? The sheriff is here and I really need to speak with him. ... All right, talk to you in a few." Hanging up, she turned her watery eyes to Liam. "Can I take your coat?" she asked, touching his arm in the same troubling manner as she had last night at the station.

"No, thank you," he replied, glancing at the boom mic hovering above his head. "I'm good."

"You can take mine."

Kiki's gaze unceremoniously shifted to Aaron and the broad grin that was plastered on his face. With reserved politeness, she took his offered coat and led the both of them into the living room, where several tripods with bright lights, a snarling Pomeranian, and a man with a camera on his shoulder were waiting. "Please have a seat," she said, tossing Aaron's coat on the chair beside her.

"Before we proceed any further," said Liam, keeping his eye on the dog as he walked around the sofa, "I'm going to need you to stop filming."

Kiki turned around and gave him a knowing smile. "This isn't live, Sheriff." She glanced at the man standing next to her. "Tell him, Tristan."

Removing his headphones, the man stepped forward. "That's right, Sheriff, and as producer for the show, I can assure you that this episode we're shooting won't air until next week. Now, I just need you to pretend like we're not here and talk to Kiki like you normally would." He snapped his fingers at the cameraman. "Close in on the sheriff and be sure and get a shot of the deputy."

Recognizing Tristan—and his man bun—as a part of Kiki's entourage that he had refused entrance into the station last night, Liam began shaking his head. "I don't care when it airs," he said, shoving the camera out of his face. "I'm still going to need you to stop."

The edge of Tristan's stubble-lined jaw grew more pronounced as a crimson hue spread across it. Reaching up to adjust his glasses, he narrowed his eyes at Liam before looking back at Kiki. "I told you he wouldn't go for it."

"Give us a few minutes," she said, wadding the tissue between her fingers.

Tristan's lips disappeared inside his mouth, drawing the skin around them tight. "Fine," he said, dropping his clipboard on the coffee table. "Come on, guys. I guess we're taking a break."

The television crew, consisting of six men and two women, shut off the lights, cameras, and sound equipment before aimlessly shuffling out of the living room with Tristan in tow. "If you need me, Ki," he said, glaring at Liam from the foyer, "I'll be in the van going over the footage from last night."

As the door slammed closed, Aaron nudged Liam in the ribs. "Looks like you've got some competition," he sang under his breath.

Moving out of his deputy's reach, Liam waited for Kiki to sit down in the chair across from him before taking a seat on the far end of the leather sofa, which incited another low growl from the dog.

"Ollie, hush!" Kiki's highlighted tresses fell across the dog's snout as she bent over to pick it up, making it sneeze. "I'm sorry," she said, glancing apologetically at Liam. "But this whole ordeal has been upsetting to him."

"The dog or Tristan?"

A silky laugh came from deep within her sun-kissed throat. "So," she said, crossing her legs, "a sense of humor lurks behind that serious face of yours after all."

The sound of steel drums resonated beneath Ollie's front paws.

"Oh," exclaimed Kiki, peering down at her phone, "I'm sorry, but I really, really need to take this."

Checking his watch, Liam let out an anxious breath.

"Kristoff, hi. … Thank you," Kiki said, pressing the tissue to her nose. "I know. … I just can't believe it. …"

Settling back against the cushion, Liam let his gaze follow along behind Aaron, who was wandering about the living room studying the giant pictures it held of Hector. Tucked inside rich mahogany frames, each live-action photo depicted Hector doing what he did best. The first one was of him standing at the plate; sporting his signature goatee and the cool blue and white colors of the Orlando Pythons, his left knee was bent in, his upper body twisted at the waist, and his elbows locked in front of him as his powerhouse swing connected on a pitch. Another captured him diving in the outfield; suspended in the air like a bird in flight, his face bore a look of gritty determination as his outstretched glove closed around the ball. The last one was of him sliding feet first into home amidst a cloud of red dirt and cheering fans.

"I appreciate your concern," said Kiki. "No, the meeting's been pushed back to next week …"

Liam's gaze impatiently drifted past Aaron and over to the fireplace on his right; taking up nearly half the wall, its gaping mouth, stained black from years of soot and creosote, was surrounded by smooth red bricks that were stacked floor to ceiling. Several trophies sat along the top of its distressed oak mantle, while a giant flat-screen TV hung in shameful silence above them. A well-stocked wet bar, complete with a backlit counter and cowhide stools, stood on the opposite side of the room, rounding out the man cave-shrine Hector had made for himself. It was no match for the rest of the house, which was stark in comparison.

Scratching the side of his head, Liam glanced behind him. Due to the possibility of exigent circumstances, he had done a search of Hector's home early on in the investigation, and although he hadn't found anything unusual, he had noticed that it lacked certain items consistent with having a wife — and with the exception of the film equipment and a sweater-wearing dog, today was no different.

"Thank you for calling. ... I will. ... Ciao, Kristoff." Placing the phone on the table beside her, Kiki wiped at her eyes and sighed. "I'm sorry, but it's been like this all morning."

Liam sat forward. "Did you live here part-time with your husband, ma'am?" he asked, feeling the need to talk fast in case her phone rang again.

"Call me Kiki," she replied, flipping her golden hair over her shoulder. "And no, I didn't. Yesterday was the first time I'd ever set foot in this place."

Aaron turned from the wet bar. "Why's that?"

"Because my life is in Atlanta," she said, keeping her shimmering gaze locked on Liam. "I have my show, my family, my clothing line—it's all there." She shook her head definitively. "The plan was for Hector to fly home for the holidays and over summer vacation."

"And did he?"

She cut her eyes to Aaron. "Yes," she said, the word snapping from her tongue like a rubber band before returning her attention to Liam. "As I was saying, Sheriff—"

"When?"

Her lips flattened. "When what?"

Aaron rested his elbow on top of the bar. "When did he last fly home?"

The pale blush covering her cheeks began to glow a deep red as she took in a sharp breath. "Over Christmas."

"It must have been hard trying to carry on a long-distance relation—"

"You know what?" she said, holding up her hands. "Let me just save us all some time here and answer the question that you're both alluding to. When the cameras weren't rolling and the paparazzi wasn't stalking us, Hector and I had what you would call an open marriage, and before you ask—no, it wasn't always that way, but between his drugs and his inability to keep his pants zipped around anything with a vajayjay, that's what it became." Shoving Ollie off her lap,

Kiki stood up from the chair and reached inside the purse that was sitting by her feet.

Liam got up from the sofa as she began walking towards him.

"Here," she said, thrusting a crinkled newspaper in his hands. "I bought this in the gift shop at the Atlanta airport yesterday before boarding the plane."

Unfolding the paper, Liam found a photo of a grinning Hector, whose good eye appeared to be just as glassy as his other one, cozied up next to a dark-haired female. The accompanying article talked about the fact that he had been reported missing before hinting that his marriage to Kiki was floundering. The title under the photo read, "Trouble in Paradise?" along with the caption, 'This past December, Hector Ramirez was seen dining with swimsuit model Tara Harmon in the back of a trendy restaurant in Midtown Atlanta.'

Kiki tapped the picture with her fingernail. "Hector was so high that night he didn't even notice the paparazzi tailing him."

Liam handed the paper back to her. "Why did you continue to stay married to him?" he asked, folding his arms against his chest.

She looked at him as if he were stupid. "Because it would've been bad for business. We were a power couple. A brand. Those two things *combined* made money—and thanks to a slew of idiotically bad investments on Hector's part, we needed every single cent we could get!" Throwing the paper on the table, she placed her hands on her hips and took a step closer. "Does that answer your question, Sheriff?"

Unfazed by her revelation, Liam stared down at her, trying to determine if her lack of empathy for her husband was real ... or simply a defense mechanism. Considering the fact that the tears she'd been so eloquently shedding moments ago were no longer visible, he guessed it to be the former.

"Oh ..." The corners of her eyes crinkled as she tilted her head. "You thought I was going to say it was because I loved him, didn't you? That's so sweet," she said, running her fingers along his wrist. "Old fashioned, but sweet."

Uncrossing his arms, Liam let them drop to his sides.

A ripple of darkness rolled over her face, causing her newly formed smile to fluctuate. "Since we're on the subject of Hector," she said, turning away, "when will his body be released? There are a ton of preparations I have to make for his funeral, which is going to be aired exclusively on *Here Comes Kiki*." Returning to her chair, she patted her lap for Ollie and gave Liam a look that was as cold as it was expectant.

Liam listened to Ollie's toenails click across the hardwood as he obeyed her command. "Probably in the next day or so," he replied, figuring that telling her the truth would only serve to delay the autopsy, as the last thing Dr. Fuller needed was

Kiki and her film crew camped outside his office. "I'll check with the medical examiner and have someone from his staff call you."

Seeming satisfied with his answer, Kiki placed her elbows on the wide, curved arms of the chair and leaned back, creating a slight gap in her robe.

Doing his best to ignore the delicate mound of flesh that was now peeking out of it, Liam's eyes darted to Aaron—who was standing behind the bar running a cigar underneath his nose. Shifting in his seat, Liam cleared his throat. "Ms. Grey," he finally said, fighting to keep his attention on her face, "what was it that you wanted to speak to me about?"

She raised a slender brow at him. "That was it," she replied in a clipped tone. "So, if you have no more *pressing* questions, I need to get back to taping my show that Tristan and the crew drove all the way here for."

Liam's teeth came together hard, making an audible crunch.

Kiki tucked Ollie under her arm. "Let me show you to the—"

"We can show ourselves out," said Liam. Tossing Aaron his coat, he walked around the sofa and out the front door, dragging his anger with him.

"So you'll have the coroner person call me?"

Liam stopped and turned. Kiki was standing behind him on the porch, her dark-green eyes boring into his. "Yes, ma'am," he said, forcing himself to unclench his jaw long enough to answer her.

"Thank you," she said, flicking her gaze to the cut on his forehead where it hovered for several seconds, seemingly more out of curiosity than concern, before returning to his face. "Have a nice day, Sheriff."

Jogging down the steps, Liam blew out his breath as he started across the yard.

"Don't worry," said Aaron, catching up to him, "I forgive you."

"For what?"

"For crushing my dreams. I was *this* close," he quipped, pressing his index finger against his thumb, "to becoming a reality TV star."

Not in the mood for his deputy's humor, Liam gave him an irritated sigh as he pulled on the handle of his truck.

Aaron leaned against the door, blocking him. "It wasn't a complete waste of time, you know."

"How do you figure?" he grumbled.

"Because while Kiki was busy showing you her … assets," Aaron said, pausing to steal a glance towards the house. "I found these on the other side of the wet bar."

Liam looked down at the book of matches his deputy was holding and let go of the handle. They were from *Greer's,* a hole in the wall bar on the west side of town that was known for its brawls, back-room prostitutes — and nickel bags of heroin.

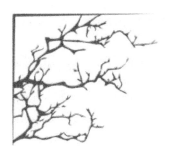

# Chapter 10

The sputtering purr of the tow truck's engine thrummed in Harlan's ears as he stood watching the divers from his dismal vantage point at the top of the embankment. Holding onto the side of the small rescue boat, chunks of ice drifted past the men as they took turns disappearing beneath the water, their sleek black hoods making them look like hapless sea lions bobbing for fish.

Shifting his weight to his other leg, Harlan pressed the tip of his boot up against one of the steel posts sticking out of the ground in front of him. A battered guardrail was affixed to the side of it, its misshapen form winding its way around a hairpin curve in the road that had come to be known as Bloody Bend. Before the barrier had been erected by the county a decade ago, a number of reckless drivers—mostly teenagers—had failed to correctly navigate the curve and had ended up in the lake. Despite its nickname, however, there hadn't been any fatalities, as the vehicles had all managed to land on a small sandbar a few yards out from shore, enabling their occupants to swim to safety.

Harlan scratched the back of his head and sighed. During his twenty plus-years as sheriff, anytime a wreck had occurred here, half the town had turned out to see it, which was why it was somewhat inconceivable to him that a car could make it past the sandbar and sink without anyone knowing about it.

"*Goddamn*, this wind stings like a mother!"

Harlan turned to look at Bill Miller, who had emerged from his tent.

"Don't you wanna come back inside?" asked Miller, rubbing his hands together. "It's a hell of a lot warmer."

"Nah," he replied, digging in his pocket for his cigarettes. "I'm good."

Crossing his arms, Miller tucked his fingers underneath the armpits of his coat and spit over the side of the guardrail. "You know, this weather reminds me of that time Lester Wilson was ice fishin' over at Goose Hollow. Do you remember? His buddies talked him into streakin' across the ice, but Lester was so drunk, he got his boxers tangled around his ankles and fell into his own hole!" Miller paused to let out a loud, emphysemay-sounding laugh. "I've seen a lot of things in my life ..."

Harlan hid his fatigue behind a small grin as he lit the tip of his cigarette. For the past two hours, his conversation with Miller had been mostly one-sided, consisting of tales and accounts that he had absolutely no recollection of, and with each passing story, he could feel the weariness inside him — which seemed to be ever-present as of late — beginning to grow.

"... didn't know a pecker could turn that color!"

A dark-green F250, missing its tailgate, pulled up alongside them and came to a hard stop, sending a spray of mud flying out from underneath its front tires.

Miller mumbled something under his breath as the driver's side door creaked open.

"How's it goin', Chet?" asked Harlan, giving him a nod as he stepped out of the truck.

"Where's the body?" Abrams snapped.

Harlan took a long drag on his cigarette and pointed towards the lake. "Down there."

"*Where* down there?"

"Under the water."

Abram's gaze shifted from Harlan to the lake and then back to Harlan. "How much longer is this gonna take?" he demanded.

"Don't know," Harlan answered, relishing the fact that he couldn't speed things along in this instance. Chet Abrams may have been the coroner, but at the end of the day, he still worked for the county and deserved no better treatment than anyone else here did.

The purple spot in the middle of Abrams' bottom lip got bigger as the edges of his mouth disappeared inside a scruffy beard. "Why are you here, Harlan? I thought you were retired."

"I'm just helpin' out," he answered, feeling his chest swell with pride as he spoke the words.

"What's the matter? That son of yours not ready to cut the strings yet?"

Harlan's lungs deflated. "Three bodies in twenty-four hours is a lot for anyone to handle," he said, flicking his cigarette on the ground.

"I'm sure it is," Abrams replied in a tone that was as condescending as the expression on his face.

"Cap, do you copy?"

Miller, who had remained oddly quiet, jerked his hand to his radio. "Yeah? What is it, Rusty?"

"We're hooked up and ready to go."

"Stand by." Peering around Harlan, Miller waved to get the attention of the tow truck operator. "Start it up!"

Nodding, the man walked around the side of the truck and pulled one of the levers on the back of it. A whirring noise sounded and Harlan saw the winch attached to it begin to shudder as its cable — which had been lying slack on the ground for the past hour and a half — snapped to attention.

A rush of excitement surged through Harlan, sending his breath hurtling from his lips as the water began to roil. Moments later, the trunk of a car with a spoiler attached to it broke through the surface.

"Bring it up slow," Miller shouted.

"Ain't no fanfare today, is there?" remarked Abrams.

Harlan briefly glanced at the half-dozen or so spectators behind the caution tape and shook his head.

"You know why that is, don't you?"

Harlan kept his eyes on the lake. As the rest of the vehicle began to emerge, he could see that it was a Monte Carlo SS. It appeared to be black in color, but he couldn't tell for sure because of all the mud and silt covering it.

"It's because nobody gives a shit about *this* person," continued Abrams.

Ignoring his comment, Harlan tightened his grip on his walker as he watched the front tires, both of which were flat, carve a deep trail into the embankment as the winch struggled to pull the car—and all the water gushing out of it—up the slope, while Gordon Stiles and his two good legs followed along behind.

As it breached the top of the embankment, Miller held up his hands. "That's good! Go ahead and set it down!"

The operator let out the cable, lowering the car's rear tires to the ground.

Abrams and Miller took off around the tow truck at the same time, leaving Harlan in their wake. Abrams emerged from the other side of it first and immediately began barking orders at Miller's men. "Undo those straps so I can open the door!"

"They can't do that," said Miller, coming up behind him. "The damn thing will go slidin' back into the lake!"

"The hell it will," countered Abrams, pointing at the ground. "Look where it's sittin'!"

As Harlan listened to the two of them arguing over whose was bigger, he reached into his pocket for another cigarette. Flipping open his lighter, he saw Gordon come around the tow truck. "What'd you see?" he asked, waving him over.

Three beeps echoed between them.

"County to Stiles. Do you copy?"

Making a fist with his right hand, Gordon pressed it against his mouth and blew, warming his fingers. "The victim appears to be male," he replied, reaching for the mic that was clipped to his coat, "but that's about all I can tell you." Rolling his head towards his shoulder, he pressed the button on his mic. "Go ahead, County."

"We've got a Signal 1 over on …"

Quickly losing interest in his former deputy, Harlan shifted his attention back to the car. Ignoring the pain that was radiating from his hip, he flattened his arms against his walker in an attempt to better see what was happening. Unfortunately, the only thing he could make out was the back of Chet's scrawny ass as he leaned inside the car. Straightening himself up with a groan, Harlan saw movement down below and noticed the divers trudging up the embankment; carrying their tanks and fins, their chapped faces bore the look of utter exhaustion as they climbed over the guardrail and disappeared into the tent.

"I'm on my way," said Gordon. "ETA, ten minutes." Letting go of his mic, he gave Harlan an expectant look.

"Go on," he replied, shaking his head, "I'll catch a ride back with Miller."

"Check your phone," Stiles called over his shoulder. "I sent you a couple of pics of the car."

Harlan scowled. "You could've told me that first!" he yelled.

Gordon gave him a wave with the back of his hand. "You're *welcome!*"

Jerking his phone out of the fabric caddy that was tied to his walker, Harlan opened up his text messages. After a moment, the skeletal remains of a man in a tattered suit materialized. Enlarging it with his thumb and forefinger, he cupped his hand around the screen to block out the light and held it close. Amidst the decaying interior of the car, he could see strands of wet black hair clinging to a skull that was slumped over the dash, while the band of a gold watch, caked with mud and debris, hung from his left wrist bone, the fingers of which were still clutching the steering wheel.

Scrolling to the next picture, he saw a brown briefcase lying on its side on the floorboard behind the driver's seat. Upon hearing the sound of crunching gravel, Harlan lifted his head in time to see Chet Abrams walking past. Shoving his phone back into the caddy, he swung his walker around and hobbled after him. "Well?" he said, catching him at his truck.

Abrams stripped off his latex gloves and threw them on the ground. "He's dead. Been dead for a long time."

Harlan swallowed his sigh. "Are his injuries consistent with a crash?"

"Yeah," replied Abrams, tossing his clipboard on the seat of his truck. "The big crack in the windshield matches the big crack in his skull." Reaching inside his coveralls, he pulled a black wallet out of a small baggie and thrust it at Harlan. "Here. This should solve your case for you."

Closing his fingers around the billfold, Harlan eagerly flipped it open, where his gaze instinctively gravitated to the driver's license that was nestled behind the small plastic window. Licking his thumb, he quickly began wiping away the layers of silt — and felt his breath catch in his throat. "*Fuck me*," he whispered.

OLIVIA PLACED THREE more aspirin on her tongue and washed them down with the last of her coffee before turning her attention to the eighty-seven unread emails in her inbox, yet as she moved her finger across the mouse pad, the light emanating from the screen scorched her bloodshot eyes, intensifying the burning pain that was lurking behind them.

Swiveling in her chair, she cradled the left side of her head in her hand and began shuffling through the mound of paperwork on her desk instead. Choosing a stack of reports that required nothing more than her signature, she pushed everything else out of her way and reached for her pen. As she began scribbling her name at the bottom of the first document, the man's voice she'd been listening to on and off for the last twenty minutes — as it bled through the thin, glass-paneled walls of her office — said something that made her glance up.

Earl Hornaday, along with close to one-third of the men in Weeping Rock, were milling about the lobby, waiting to do the same thing they always did on the second Wednesday of the month, which was to write a check for cash against their social security deposits. While standing in line, they talked amongst themselves in their grammar-impaired English, which — along with using words like *ain't* and *ort* — included the inability to add the letter *g* to the end of any present participle as they discussed their farms, the weather, and their enlarged prostates.

This particular afternoon, however, the only topic of conversation was Hector Ramirez. A deep ache settled in Olivia's jaw as she listened to Hornaday loudly voicing his doubts over whether Liam and his sidekick Tonto were smart enough to catch Hector's killer, provoking a round of laughter from the other men. Gary Castlen's face suddenly appeared in Olivia's line of sight, causing the flaming mental daggers that had spawned from her eyes to surreptitiously fall to the floor before they could strike the back of Hornaday's unsuspecting head.

Tapping on the glass, Gary gave her a friendly wave before opening the door. "Good afternoon."

"Gary," she replied, tossing the bottle of aspirin back in the drawer.

"I know I'm a few minutes early," he said, glancing at the clock on her wall, "but would you mind if we went ahead with our meeting?"

"Not at all," she heard herself say, gesturing at the chair across from her desk.

Gary pushed the door the rest of the way open. "Why don't we go to the conference room?"

Although Olivia knew this was a tactic he liked to employ in order to keep her from having the home-field advantage, she found herself unable to come up with a logical reason to refuse him this time. Grabbing a note pad off her desk, she gave him a polite nod as she walked out the door.

As her heels clicked across the tile floor, Earl Hornaday turned around. Biting her tongue, Olivia kept her gaze in front of her as she strode past him and made her way into the conference room — where she was dismayed to find Tim Moseley, Gary's tag-a-long pansy from corporate, already seated at the table.

"Hi, Olivia," he said, looking up from his phone.

Ignoring him and his tinny voice because she could, she came around the other side of the table and sat down.

"Wow," exclaimed Gary, coming in behind her, "I was listening to the news about Hector Ramirez on the way down. Sounds like your husband's got his hands full."

"Yes, he does," she replied in a stiff tone.

"You know, a few years ago, I was in L.A. and saw Ramirez play against the Dodgers. Man, he had a hell of a swing. He hit two home runs that were nowhere even close to being caught." Taking the seat next to Moseley, Gary cast a sad smile at Olivia and shook his head. "What a waste of a life."

"I don't follow baseball."

"Well," said Gary, clearing his throat in the silence that followed, "let's get down to business, shall we?" Reaching inside his satchel, he pulled out a thick file and placed it in front of him. "As you know, there's been a lot of reorganization going on at corporate."

"This is the first I've heard of it," said Olivia.

"Really?" Gary shifted in his chair. "I thought you knew."

"No."

"Well, anyway," he said, talking faster than normal, "I've been going back and forth with upper management, and after careful consideration, we feel that your talents would better serve us in loan processing."

Feeling her emotions beginning to flail, Olivia sank her fingernails into her palms in order to keep them from surfacing.

"I understand this is short notice," he continued, "but I want you to realize—"

"Why?"

"Why …" Gary tilted his head like a cocker spaniel who hadn't understood his master's command.

Having been around him enough to know the gesture was nothing more than a means of stalling, Olivia drew a constricted breath and pressed her chest against the cold metal edge of the table. "Why am I being transferred?"

"Well, it's—"

"To loan processing, nonetheless," she finished.

"I know what you're thinking, Olivia."

Her attention shifted to Tim Moseley.

"You're thinking this is a demotion," he said, offering her a condescending smile, "but it's not. It's actually a lateral move."

Olivia's temper emerged, transforming her logical reply into a sarcastic spray of words. "I am the goddamned manager of this bank, and you're proposing to stick me in a cubicle—pushing papers—in Rapid City. So, tell me, *Tim*," she said, folding her hands together, "just how exactly do you figure that equals a lateral move?"

Moseley's Adam's apple bobbed up and down like a slide whistle, igniting his cheeks.

Olivia watched with grim satisfaction as his gaze floundered along the top of the table for several seconds before falling into his lap.

"It's a lateral move, Olivia," Gary replied, "because your salary will remain the same."

Having once read in an article that a person's IQ could drop as much as forty points when they were angry, Olivia sat back and smoothed her pants, then for added measure, counted to ten. When she had finished, she looked up at Gary. "That still doesn't answer my original question."

"Listen," he replied, running his fingers across the small patch of hair covering the top of his head, "in lieu of what happened last month, this is your only option."

Olivia stared at the hawk-like beak that served as Gary's nose; sharp and curved at the end, it cast a giant shadow across his thin lips. "In lieu of *what* happening last month?"

"Olivia—"

"*What*?" she demanded, wanting to hear him say it.

Gary leaned back in his chair and sighed.

With her eyes stinging, Olivia glanced at the paneled walls surrounding her. "I've done a good job of turning this branch around, Gary," she said, pressing her knuckles against the bottom of her chin to hide its trembling, "and you know as well as I do that I'm the best manager this bank has ever had."

"I'm not disputing that, Olivia. But getting arrested is something that—"

"It was *in* a different county—"

"—*that*," he continued, talking over her, "*Houdek Savings and Loan* has zero-tolerance for."

As a watery film fell across her eyes, Olivia focused her attention on Tim Moseley, who was still staring at his lap. "I haven't been convicted," she said in a half-whisper.

Gary shook his head. "*Houdek's* terms are carefully stated in the employee handbook. An arrest, regardless of the outcome, is grounds for immediate termination. Now, I've kept that from happening by recommending the transfer, and considering what the alternative would be," he said, pausing to turn his hand over, "I strongly suggest you take the offer."

Olivia kicked the chair out from underneath her, sending it sliding into the wall. Marching around the table, she grabbed hold of the silver knob mounted on the door and yanked it open, drawing the attention of Hornaday and several others who were still talking in the lobby.

"Olivia ..."

Glancing over her shoulder, she leveled a steely—albeit—blurred gaze at Gary. "You know what you can do with your offer."

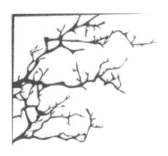

# Chapter 11

Clouds, gray and swollen, drifted aimlessly across the sky, surrounding Liam in intermittent pockets of darkness as he stood in the open field behind the truck stop. A set of tire tracks lay at his feet; wide and half-buried beneath the snow, they came right up alongside the edge of the pavement before looping their way back towards a gravel road.

Lifting his head, the muscles in his neck tensed as he stared at the crumbling silo in the distance. Long before Ike Nelson and his truck stop existed, this parcel of land plus all the acreage leading up to the highway had been part of a farm owned by Ezra Reynolds. Ezra's brother, Ben, had a farm just west of here, and together the two men had built the small access road between them in order to shuttle their shared equipment back and forth. It was something an outsider would know nothing about.

Liam ran the tip of his boot over the tracks and sighed. This was no random murder. It had been planned down to the very last detail ... but something had obviously gone wrong. Shoving his hands in his pockets, he turned and started back around the side of the makeshift chapel.

As he jogged up its wooden steps, he paused to glance at the giant cross sticking out of its roof; it was pitted, rusted, and not nearly as bright in the daylight, while the cables that held it in place vibrated from its constant hum.

Walking inside, Liam took a moment to study the partially open window on his left before making his way down the aisle. As he drew closer to the pulpit at the front of the trailer, he could see that the pool of blood near the base of it had soaked into the pine floorboards during the night, staining the planks a dark red. Tucked in the corner a few feet away were a blanket and pillow, while on the other side of the podium, pink panties tangled around black leggings lay next to a pair of bloodstained scissors.

Not finding anything under the blanket, hidden or otherwise, he turned his attention to the folding chairs that were facing the pulpit. Sitting in tight pairs on his left and single file on his right, they went five rows deep. Bloody palm prints graced the backs of several of them on both sides of the aisle, yet they remained perfectly aligned. That, combined with the fact that there was no interior lighting in the trailer, led Liam to believe that the girl had been familiar with her surroundings.

Having run out of things to look at, he solemnly pulled on a pair of latex gloves and knelt to inspect the girl's coat, but upon touching the sleeve, the sensation of him cradling the baby returned, making his throat ache. Struggling to shove the memory aside, he began turning every pocket the coat had inside out in the hopes of coming across something that would help him identify the girl — yet the only thing his search yielded was two crumpled up dollar bills and a packet of ketchup.

Tossing them on the floor, Liam rocked back on his heels and rubbed his eyes.

"Find anything?"

Jerking his head up, he saw Stiles watching him from the doorway. "What are you doing here?"

"I figured you might need a hand."

"You're supposed to be at Crow's Foot."

"The car's out of the water and the body's about to be bagged. There wasn't a whole lot left for me to do there." Stiles paused to yawn as he stepped over the drops of dried blood in the aisle. "Besides, I had to respond to a call."

"What about my —"

"Don't worry about Harlan," Stiles replied, coming to a stop on the other side of the girl's coat. "He's laughin' and talkin' it up with Miller, just like I said he would."

Liam got to his feet. "You were his ride back to the station," he said, feeling his anger rising.

"Miller's gonna take him home."

"That's not what we—"

"So," said Gordon, rubbing his hands together, "catch me up to speed here. What have you found?"

Liam stared blankly at his deputy, wondering if he was apathetic to his exasperation with him—or just oblivious to it. "Nothing that'll tell me her name," he finally said, gesturing at the spoils beside his boot.

Hitching up his pants, Gordon squatted in front of the blood-smeared coat and rested his elbows on his knees. "Not much to go on is there?" he grunted.

"Not in here, but I found some fresh tire tracks in the field around back. The snow's done a good job of covering them up, but you can still see that they come from—and lead to—the access road. I think they belong to whoever killed her."

"Makes sense," said Gordon, straightening. "It'd be hard to see anyone approaching from that direction, especially at night." He pointed at the window. "My guess is she heard it being pried open and ran."

Nodding in agreement, Liam's gaze drifted from the window to the door; still attached to the bottom of the jamb by its hinges, the rest of it lay in a twisted heap against the wall. A sense of sorrow washed over him as he stared at the shards of wood scattered across the floor. By taking the time to lock it behind her, the girl had used up precious seconds — she didn't have — in an effort to save her baby.

The alarm on Liam's phone went off, reigniting his anxiety. Dismissing it with a quick tap of his thumb, he turned back to Stiles. "I need you to go to the middle school as well as the high school and show her picture around. See if anyone recognizes her."

Gordon laughed under his breath. "Come on, *Sheriff*," he said, holding his hands out from his sides. "The girl had her kid in the chapel of a truck stop for Christ's sake. She was a runaway."

"Well, it's been my experience with runaways," countered Liam, crossing his arms, "that they generally pack a few items to take with them before running away, and aside from the clothes she was wearing, there's nothing else of hers here."

The loud rumble of a diesel engine sounded outside.

Making his way down the aisle, Liam peered through the open door and saw that a semi was in the process of squeezing itself and its fifty-three-foot trailer between his county-issued Silverado and the yellow-and-black police tape surrounding the chapel.

"This must be our guy," said Gordon, coming up behind him.

Stepping out onto the landing, Liam stripped off his gloves and crammed them into his pocket as he watched the tires on the rig roll to a stop.

"Have you had a chance to talk to anyone over at the diner?"

"Not yet," answered Liam, keeping his eyes locked on the semi.

"Well, if you don't care," Gordon continued, "I think I'll head on over and nose around a bit. The ketchup packet you found might've come from there. Maybe someone remembers seeing her."

Liam opened his mouth to answer but stopped when he heard the sound of retreating footsteps. Glancing over his shoulder, his lips folded in on themselves as he watched his deputy strutting across the parking lot towards the run-down eatery.

"Hey! Would someone mind telling me what the hell's going on?"

Sighing, Liam turned and hurried down the steps. "Good afternoon, sir," he said, ducking under the tape. "I'm Sheriff Matthews."

Glancing at Liam's extended hand, the man reached up to close the door of his cab. "Wayne Caffrey," he replied, leaving a set of clean fingerprints in the middle of a weathered and muddied decal that was cut in the shape of a cross, "but everyone calls me Rev."

With his hand still in the air, Liam used it to gesture at the chapel. "Is this yours?"

The man plucked a pair of aviator-style sunglasses from his face to reveal a set of steel-gray eyes that impulsively shifted from Liam to the chapel, and then back to Liam. "I believe my bein' here answers that question, doesn't it?" he said in a slow, southern drawl.

The alarm on Liam's phone went off again.

"You got somewhere else to be?"

"As a matter of fact, I do," he replied, shutting off the alarm. "So I would appreciate it if you could just answer my question with a yes or no."

Caffrey placed his sunglasses on top of his long, slicked-back mane, the silvery ends of which hung in stiff ringlets around the collar of a worn leather jacket, and gave a curt nod towards the trailer. "I'm the owner and pastor of *The Way, The Truth, and The Life Chapel*."

Pulling out his notepad, Liam flipped it open. "When was the last time you were here?"

"Yesterday afternoon. I hold prayer services every Tuesday and Wednesday. And I'm here most Saturd—"

"Do you keep it locked when you're gone?"

Caffrey folded his arms against his chest. "Yeah."

"Who all has a key?"

"Just me," answered Caffrey, using his thumb to pop the knuckles on his left hand.

"You sure about that?"

The stilted expression Caffrey was wearing darkened, highlighting the sharp edges of his cheekbones. "I said so, didn't I?"

"Where were you last night between the hours of nine and eleven, sir?" asked Liam, watching Caffrey's bloodshot eyes bounce back and forth in their sockets like a ping-pong ball.

"Deliverin' sixty pallets of chicken feed to *Sanford's Farm Supply* over in Sioux Falls."

"Can anyone verify that?"

"I've got a signed bill of lading showing the date and time of when they unloaded me," he said, unzipping his jacket.

"What are you hauling now?"

"Nothin'," he answered, handing him the document, "I'm empty."

"Would you mind showing me?"

"You got a warrant?"

Liam looked up from the bill of lading. "No," he said, feeling his patience leaving him, "but I can get one within the hour."

The bone beneath Caffrey's jaw shifted, nearly piercing the sallow skin in front of his right earlobe. "Well, I guess that would make you miss your appointment then ... wouldn't it?"

Keeping his gaze steady, Liam reached for his radio.

A crooked smile broke out across Caffrey's lips. "I was just givin' you a hard time, Sheriff. You can look if you want." Pivoting on his silver-tipped boots, he waved his arm through the air as if he were lobbing a baseball. "Come on."

Following him around to the back of the semi, Liam casually rested his fingers on his holster as he watched him lift the latch on the door and throw it open.

"So," Caffrey said, wiping his hands on his jeans, "now that we've established the fact that I'm not lyin', and you know *who* I am and *where* I've been, would you mind tellin' me what the hell's goin' on?"

Liam turned from the empty trailer. "When you were here yesterday, Mr. Caffrey, did you see—"

"Call me Rev."

Sighing, Liam rubbed the back of his neck. "Mr. Caffrey," he began again, "have you seen a girl with reddish-brown hair, about thirteen years of age, hanging around here?"

"Can't say that I have. Why?"

"She gave birth inside your chapel last night."

Caffrey shrugged. "And?"

The fingers on Liam's right hand curled inward. "And *what*?"

A deep laugh came from the back of Caffrey's throat as he shook his head. "Babies are born in unusual places every day, Sheriff," he said, gesturing at the chapel. "So there must be more to it than that if you're here."

"We found the girl's body in close proximity to the truck stop. She'd been murdered."

The sneer on Caffrey's face faded. "Well, that is unfortunate," he said in a somber tone. "You must be thinkin' I'm a real dick right about now. Please accept my apologies, Sheriff. After Sioux Falls, I took a load up to Fargo. I've been drivin' for eight hours straight, and I'm runnin' low on coffee *and* sleep." Caffrey's battleship-colored eyes stopped moving and slowly zeroed in on Liam's. "And from the looks of things ... so are you."

"Sheriff, do you copy?"

Putting some distance between himself and Caffrey, Liam unclipped his radio from his belt. "Go ahead, Aaron."

"I finished searching the area where the girl's body was found."

"Did you find anything?"

A burst of static sounded.

"Just your hat."

The wind skipped across the snow in front of Liam, engulfing him in a vortex of white. "I need you to knock on the doors of the surrounding houses," he said, struggling to keep the disappointment out of his voice, while at the same time straining to see Caffrey. "Maybe somebody heard something."

"Copy that," Aaron replied. "And the Rapid City PD called. They're sending Reed Maxwell over from forensics. He should be here sometime this afternoon."

"Make sure he dusts for prints outside the chapel's window," said Liam, settling his gaze upon Caffrey as the wind began to die down.

"10-4. Are you on your way to Crawford?"

"I'm leaving now," replied Liam, starting towards Caffrey.

"Well, good luck—in court, I mean."

"Thanks," Liam mumbled. "I'll talk to you later."

"Everything okay there, Sheriff?" asked Caffrey, pushing himself away from the fender of his truck. "Because you seem—"

"Thank you for your cooperation, Reverend," Liam said, thrusting the bill of lading at him.

Arching a wiry brow, Caffrey dipped his head in acknowledgment. "That's close enough ... I guess."

"If you should happen to remember anything regarding the girl," said Liam, turning to go, "give the sheriff's office a call."

"Wait—what about my chapel?"

"We're not ready to clear the scene just yet, but it shouldn't be more than a couple of days."

"A couple of days? What the hell am I supposed to do in the meantime? I can't very well lead men to Christ out here in the goddamn snow now, can I?"

"Have a good afternoon," said Liam, walking away.

"Yeah, you too," Caffrey called after him in a snarky tone. "Or—maybe I should say good luck in court!"

Liam stopped and looked back.

Another smile, this one thin and insolent, unfurled inside Caffrey's scraggly goatee. "The wind," he said, circling the air with his finger. "It has a tendency to carry things … like *words*."

With his cheeks burning, Liam climbed into his truck and slammed the door.

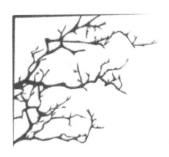

# Chapter 12

Liam swore under his breath as he paced the floor outside the courtroom. "Olivia, where are you?" he demanded, pressing the cell phone against his ear. "I need you to call me back—*now*."

"Any word?"

He turned to find Dwayne Ballard standing behind him. "No."

"We have to go," said Dwayne, tapping his watch. "I've stalled as long as I can."

"Let me try her one more time."

Dwayne shook his head, causing what little hair he had left on the top of it to flap about in the self-made breeze. "There *is* no more time, Liam. The judge is waiting."

Liam's panic began to rise. "What are you going to tell him?"

"I don't know," he whispered, motioning for him to hurry as he pulled on the handle of the door. "I'll think of something."

Finding Dwayne's lack of confidence discouraging, Liam stuck his phone in his pocket and reluctantly followed him inside.

The soles of his boots echoed off the marble tiles with each step he took, causing everyone on either side of him to turn and stare; haggard-looking women wearing snug-fitting sweaters and skintight leggings, sat next to boyish-looking men in button-down shirts, whose wrinkled collars were doing a poor job of hiding the tats emblazoned on their necks. Continuing down the aisle, Liam watched their faces, world-weary and indignant, fill with disdain as their eyes fell upon his badge.

"Where's your client, Mr. Ballard?"

Liam's attention shot to the front of the courtroom where Judge Elias Whitmore and his permanent scowl were waiting.

"My client has fallen ill, Your Honor," replied Dwayne, slipping behind the wooden table on the left side of the room.

"Is that so?"

Dwayne paused to adjust his glasses. "Yes, Your Honor. Her husband just got off the phone with her."

Whitmore's iron-like gaze shifted to Liam and dropped anchor. "Sheriff Matthews, is this true?"

"It is, Your Honor," replied Dwayne. "My client—"

"Hush, Mr. Ballard," said Whitmore, holding up a bony finger. "I want to hear it from her husband."

Liam stood perfectly still, fearing that any movement—no matter how small—would cause the earnest look that was perched precariously upon his face to go toppling to the floor.

"Sheriff Matthews?" Whitmore arched his unibrow, deepening the scowl between his eyes. "I'm waiting."

Liam's mouth twitched as he forced his lips to part. "It's true, Your Honor," he said, acutely aware of the murmuring that was taking place on his right.

"What's wrong with her?" asked Whitmore, peering at Liam over the front of his bench.

Liam drew a deep breath. "I don't know—"

"When Sheriff Matthews spoke with his wife," Dwayne interjected, "she told him that she was on her way to the emergency room in Rapid City."

"Your Honor ..." Phil Gibbons, Crawford County's longtime prosecutor, tossed his pen onto his legal pad and got to his feet. "This is nothing more than a pathetic display of theatrics by Mr. Ballard and his client in order to gain a continuance."

"My client *is* ill, Your Honor," insisted Dwayne, "and I can assure you that she is fully aware of the importance of this hearing, and would be here if she could."

Growing more and more uncomfortable with each word that tumbled out of Dwayne's mouth, Liam's gaze began to spiral downwards — only to become entangled with the deputy's that was seated next to Gibbons. Leaning back in his chair, Kyle Robinson eyed Liam with contempt as the two attorneys argued back and forth.

"Your Honor," continued Gibbons, "I find it highly unlikely that Mr. Ballard's client happened to become ill just moments before she was to appear in court."

"My client *is* — "

"All right, that's enough," Whitmore snapped, rubbing the creases in his forehead. "Mr. Ballard, I'm rescheduling the hearing for one week from today, and your client best be here, along with a note from the ER doctor that saw her."

"Yes, Your Honor," replied Dwayne, "and thank — "

"Next case," said Whitmore, banging his gavel.

Turning on his heels, Liam strode out of the courtroom.

"Sheriff, wait!" yelled Dwayne.

Picking up his pace, Liam edged his way past several people lined up outside the door of the DMV office and rounded the corner. A moment later, his attorney's stubby little legs appeared beside him. "I've got things to do, Dwayne," he said, starting down the steps.

Without warning, Dwayne cut in front of him and stopped. "Look," he wheezed, holding up his hands, "I know you're upset with me, but I had to say something."

"And that was the best you could come up with?"

"Under the circumstances," Dwayne replied, using his index finger to push his horn-rimmed glasses back up the bridge of his nose, "yes—that was the best I could come up with."

Liam sighed and stepped around him.

"Judge Whitmore doesn't like no shows," Dwayne called. "With him, you'd better be dead or—at the very least—dying."

A troubled weariness settled over Liam, bringing him to another stop. "It's getting late, Dwayne," he said, keeping his eyes on the exit below as he rested his hand on the wooden railing running along the wall. "I'll talk to you tomorr—"

"That's a shame about your wife, Matthews."

Glancing over his shoulder, Liam's gaze skipped across the top of Dwayne's head to find Kyle Robinson standing near the edge of the landing.

"I sure hope it's nothing serious," Robinson continued, pressing his holster against his leg as he started down the steps.

Returning his attention to Dwayne, Liam gave him a quick nod. "I'll talk to you tomorrow," he said, then, knowing nothing good could come from engaging Robinson in conversation, took the remaining stairs two at a time.

As he reached for the door, Robinson's hand shot out in front of him. "Where are you going in such a hurry?" he asked, grabbing hold of the push bar.

Liam turned from the door. "What do you want, Kyle?"

"I heard you pulled Ramirez out of Crow's Foot yesterday," he replied, eyeing him with the same disregard as before.

"That's right."

"So," he said, leaning in close, "I guess the real fun starts now, huh?"

Liam felt his jaw stiffening.

"And speaking of fun ..." Robinson lifted his eyebrows, pulling his upper lip tight against his nostrils. "Man, I bet it's really chappin' Harlan's ass that he can't be in the middle of all that." He shook his head and laughed. "Am I right?"

Liam shoved his boot against the kick plate of the door, wrenching the bar out of Robinson's grasp.

An unexpected blast of cold air tumbled inside, catching them both off-guard.

"You know," said Robinson, moving out of the wind's line of fire, "I never did like working for him."

"That was never a secret, Kyle," said Liam, struggling to keep his anger in check as he stepped out onto the sidewalk.

"I guess that's true," Robinson replied, catching up to him, "but let me tell you something you don't know. Being a deputy under Sheriff Davis is a hell of a lot more gratifying."

Ignoring him, Liam checked his phone to see if he'd missed a call from Olivia, then unable to shake his anxiety when he saw that he hadn't, tried her number again as he started for his truck.

"Don't you want to know why that is?" prompted Robinson, walking along beside him.

"No," said Liam, bringing the phone to his ear.

Robinson grabbed him around the wrist, stopping him in his tracks. "You see, here in Crawford County when I arrest someone and haul their ass off to jail—the next morning, they're still there. And you wanna know *why* they're still there?" he asked, tightening his grip. "Because my paperwork got filed like it was supposed to and the evidence I collected didn't mysteriously disappear."

Liam jerked his arm back with such force that Robinson had to take a step forward to keep his balance. "You don't know what you're talking about," he said in a low voice.

"Listen to yourself," Kyle retorted, fostering a grin that was as dark as his eyes. "You sound just like him."

Putting his phone away, Liam flicked his gaze towards the cars that were crawling up the street. There were many, many more things he could have said to Robinson, but knowing that getting into a pissing contest with him over his father would only serve to damage Olivia's case, forced his lips to remain closed.

"You know, I figured things would be different working for you," he said, "but you never gave me the chance to find out."

"The Orand County Sheriff's Office currently consists of only myself and two deputies," said Liam, unable to keep the words he'd been harboring for the past four months from leaving his tongue. "That's three of us to cover over seven hundred square miles. I needed someone I could depend on — someone who I knew would have my back."

Robinson's eyes flashed, short-circuiting his contrived smile. "And you think Red Elk is that *someone*?" He took a step closer to Liam, touching the tip of his boot with his own. "Well, tell me something, Matthews," he said, resting his hand on his Glock, "when it comes down to saving your life or a Lakota's ... who do you think he's gonna choose?"

Fighting the urge to knock the hat right off of Robinson's pointy little head, Liam turned and once more began walking in the direction of his truck.

"Are you runnin' home to check on your wife?" Robinson called after him in a voice loud enough to catch the attention of several passersby. "I'd start with the bars, first. Might save you some time — "

Spinning around, Liam grabbed Robinson by the front of his coat. "What the hell is your problem?" he asked, jerking him closer.

A series of beeps sounded between them.

"Any available unit. 10-54. 419 Circle Drive. Two male suspects …"

The grin returned to Kyle's lips as Liam lowered his hands. "Duty calls," he said, backing away. "See you around, Matthews."

As Liam watched him trot down the sidewalk towards his patrol car, he got the distinct feeling that the gathering onlookers were none too pleased with the aggression he'd just shown their deputy. Dropping his gaze, he cautiously weaved his way through the crowd before disappearing into the parking garage around the corner.

"GET OUT OF THE TRUCK, Olivia."

Staring at the rain-splattered windshield, Olivia folded her arms tighter against her as the bitter cold infiltrated the cab.

Liam gave an exasperated-sounding sigh. "Listen," he said, opening the door as wide as it would go, "I'm tired, and I just want to get this over with. So will you please get out?"

Olivia forced herself to look in his direction. The collar of his coat was flapping relentlessly in the wind, drawing her attention to his reddened cheeks and nose. "I still don't understand why we have to do this," she said, unable to summon any sympathy for his impending hypothermia.

"We've gone over this three times already," he countered. "I'm not going to do it a fourth."

She dug her fingernails into the pocket of the armrest. "In case you've forgotten, I lost my job today, so this is absolutely the last thing I feel like doing right now," she replied, pulling on the door.

Liam held it steadfast, refusing to let it close. "You *quit* your job—you didn't *lose* it. It was self-inflicted."

"Oh—my—God," she muttered, flinging her head against the back of the seat. "They expected me to drive seventy miles round trip every day, and they weren't even going to reimburse me for the mileage! They *wanted* me to qui—"

"We can talk about this on the way home," Liam said, leaning inside the cab of the truck. "But right now, we're walking into that ER." Wrapping his fingers around her arm, he yanked her out of the seat.

Olivia promptly fell against him but didn't know if it was due to the slippery pavement beneath her heels or the three shots of bourbon she'd had earlier. "No," she argued, pushing him away upon finding her footing, "we're not."

Liam's face darkened, highlighting the jagged scar that ran through his left eyebrow. "I lied in front of a judge for you today!" he yelled, slamming the door closed. "Do you have any idea how hard that was for me? Now—if you walk into that courtroom next week without a doctor's note,

Whitmore is going to throw you in jail for failure to appear!"

Olivia looked away as Liam's heartlessness caused an onslaught of tears to flood her eyes.

"Do you understand what I'm saying?" he shouted, stepping in her line of sight. "I can't *fix* this for you!"

A thin white mist swirled in front of Olivia as her breath rushed from her lips. Shoving Liam out of her way, she began an uneven march across the parking lot towards the sliding glass doors of Regional Hospital.

LIAM STARED AT THE set of numbers blinking beside acronyms he didn't understand on the monitor in front of him. After spending over an hour and a half in the waiting room, Olivia's name had finally been called, but rather than follow her back to a curtained cubicle, which would've undoubtedly involved more waiting — and glaring, he'd opted to remain behind. The constant feeling of disquiet churning inside him, combined with his inability to remain seated, had led him here.

But *here* wasn't where he wanted to be either.

A green line moved up and down in rapid succession across a black screen, giving off an indication of life that was otherwise nowhere to be seen. Wires, needles, and tubes covered most of the infant's body, while his tiny hands, wrapped in a loose-fitting gauze, lay motionless beside his head.

The fingers on Liam's right hand suddenly curled inward, stinging the open cut on his palm. Pushing through his tears last night, he'd fought hard to save this little boy who'd come into the world under such cruel circumstances, and yet, as he stood watching his chest move slowly up and down ... couldn't help wondering if the only thing he'd managed to do was prolong his suffering.

"Sheriff Matthews?"

Setting his jaw, he turned from the incubator to find a woman in blue scrubs standing behind him. "The nurse at the station told me I could —"

"It's okay," she said, giving him a friendly smile. "She told me you were back here."

Recognizing her as one of the nurses from last night, but unable to recall her name, Liam offered her a small nod instead. "How are you?"

She let out a deep sigh. "On my fourteenth hour of a twelve-hour shift," she replied, rolling her neck across her shoulders. "What about you? You're here awfully late."

"I was in the area and just wanted to see how he was doing."

The nurse's big brown eyes shuttled from Liam to the incubator. "He's tough, that one."

A surge of hope swelled inside Liam. "Does that mean he's going to be okay?"

"It means," she said, tossing her long black braid over her shoulder, "that we're being cautiously optimistic."

Having heard those words a thousand different times under a thousand different circumstances, Liam felt his hope beginning to slip away — because regardless of the confidence with which they were spoken, the outcome was always the same. "Do you know if anyone has called, or come by asking about him?" he said, rubbing his chin in an effort to hide his despair.

"I can check with the other nurses," she answered, closing her fingers over the ends of the stethoscope as it hung around her neck, "but I don't believe anyone has."

Liam's phone dinged, drawing his attention downward. "I need to go," he said, seeing that he'd missed a call from Olivia, as well as Aaron. "If anything changes, will you let me know?"

"Of course," she replied, stepping aside to let him pass. "Oh ... and, Sheriff?"

He stopped and turned.

"I did see in his chart that CPS was notified this afternoon, so I'm sure Loretta Boyd will be getting in touch with you."

Having no doubt that she would, Liam sighed inwardly as he made his way out of the NICU and down the corridor to the elevator. While waiting for it to arrive, he decided to make use of the time he had and call Aaron back.

"How did the hearing go?" he asked, answering on the first ring.

"It got rescheduled," replied Liam, not wanting to go into details.

"Did you get the pics I sent?"

"Hold on." Putting Aaron on speaker, Liam went into his text messages and pulled up the first picture. A dark, blurry object filled his screen. "What am I looking at?"

"After I finished canvassing the neighborhood — which was a complete bust by the way — I checked the area between the highway and boxelders and found a bloody print on the guardrail. Reed Maxwell arrived at the truck stop about an hour after you left, so I had him check it against the ones in the chapel."

"Is it a match to the girl's?" he asked, jabbing the button for the elevator again.

"Yeah. Maxwell's running her prints through AFIS for us now. Maybe we'll get lucky and she'll be in the system."

Doubting that was going to be the case, Liam scrolled to the next pic. "What's the second one of?"

"Her cell phone."

Liam's heart began to pound with excitement.

"It was half-buried in the snow by the guardrail," Aaron said. "I'm guessing she either dropped it or it fell out of the pocket of her hoodie when she was running."

The elevator chimed, announcing its arrival.

"What'd you find on it?" asked Liam, lowering his voice as an orderly walked past.

"Nothing yet. I used the charger in my truck but it still won't turn on. It got pretty wet."

The beating of Liam's heart slowed to a lethargic pace.

"I removed the SIM card and battery," Aaron continued, "and with any luck, it'll be dried out and working by tomorrow afternoon."

Liam rubbed his forehead, wishing he could share in his deputy's enthusiasm. "All right," he finally said, stepping onto the elevator, "I'll talk to you in the morning."

"Have a good one, Sheriff."

As the doors slid shut, Liam's phone dinged again. Knowing that it was Olivia, he leaned wearily against the paneled wall and closed his eyes.

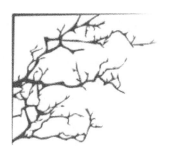

# Chapter 13

*T*races of darkness slithered along the walls of the hospital room, devouring the squares of sunlight one by one until there were none left. As the afternoon became cloaked in the shadows, breath, jagged and moist, fell across the backs of Liam's knuckles. Reaching up, he tenderly brushed a strand of hair from Olivia's face, all the while wishing he could take away her pain.

"I just need one more push, Olivia."

Liam shifted his focus to Dr. Brendan Ellis, who was sitting at the foot of the bed with his shoulders wedged between Olivia's raised thighs. Two nurses stood on either side of him, and although their faces were hidden behind their masks, Liam saw that their eyes bore the same solemn look as his own.

Olivia squeezed his hand, drawing him back. Slipping his arm around her shoulders, he helped her sit up, just as he had the past nine times and held her tight. Clenching her teeth, her fingers began to tremble as they intertwined with his, setting off a chain reaction throughout the rest of her body.

"Okay – stop," said Dr. Ellis.

Liam's own breathing grew erratic as he watched the flurry of activity taking place below Olivia's knees. The nurses worked in quiet unison alongside Ellis, seeming to anticipate his needs before he asked. The nurse to his right handed him several instruments off the tray beside her, while the one on his left, a tall, thin woman with amber-colored eyes, readied a blanket – and for just the briefest of moments, Liam held onto the hope that Ellis had been wrong about everything.

Silence, sharp and deafening, began to fill every corner of the tiny room.

Feeling Olivia's fingers tearing themselves from his, Liam looked back at her. Her beautiful face, pale and reflecting the exhaustion of the past twenty-four hours, was contorted and streaked with tears. At a loss for words, he cupped her chin in his hand and kissed her on the cheek as the nurse with the amber eyes approached them.

"Mrs. Matthews?" she said in a soft voice. "Would you like to hold your son?"

Waving her away, Olivia's shoulders began to shake as a breathless sob fell from her lips. Hugging her tight, Liam buried his face in the folds of her hair as the rims of his eyelids began to grow wet. From the blurred edges of his peripheral vision, he saw that the nurse remained by the bed. Straightening, he nodded at the woman through his tears and held out his arms.

Wrapped in a blue blanket, Daniel Christopher Matthews had a fine layering of dark hair, chubby cheeks, *and Olivia's button nose. He was absolutely perfect in every way. Cradling his son in the crook of his elbow, Liam bent down and pressed a quivering mouth to his lifeless gray forehead. "Daddy loves you," he whispered.*

Liam woke to the sound of his chest heaving. Sitting up, he swung his legs over the side of the bed and dropped his head in his hands.

"What's wrong?"

He used his palms to wipe his cheeks before glancing over his shoulder. In the early morning light, he saw that Olivia's eyes and face were etched with concern as she stared at him. Taking in a shallow breath, he shook his head. "Nothing."

The strap of her nightgown fell down around her arm as she slipped her hand underneath her pillow. "I'm sorry I woke you," he said, reaching out to caress the area of skin below it.

She flinched at his touch.

Moving his gaze upwards, Liam saw her concern for him fading as her anger from last night returned. Having no desire to rehash something that could never be rectified, he snatched his pants up from off the floor and walked out.

The linoleum in the kitchen was freezing beneath his bare feet as he filled the coffeemaker with water. After dumping the grounds into the filter, he made his way into the living room, where he paused to adjust the thermostat on the wall before flopping down onto the couch. As the old furnace groaned to life, he leaned back against the worn cushion and closed his eyes. The dream followed, and in his awakened state, he could feel his veins flooding with grief as it began to replay itself in his mind.

A creaking noise sounded to his right, accompanied by a heavy clank and a thump; the latter two continued, one after the other, across the living room floor. Keeping his eyes closed, Liam remained still.

Something hard nudged his knee. Twice.

"*What?*"

"How'd the hearing go yesterday?"

"It didn't," answered Liam, repositioning his neck on the cushion.

"What do you mean?"

"We got a continuance."

"How in the hell did you manage that?"

Stuffing his dream back inside the hole it had come from, Liam opened his eyes. His father was peering down at him, his spine nothing but a rounded hump as he leaned against his walker. "It doesn't matter," he said, casually reaching up to brush away a stray tear that had caught on his eyelash.

His father gave him a curious look before swinging his walker around. "Where were the two of you last night? The house was empty when Miller dropped me off," he stated, easing himself down onto the cushion beside him.

Taking notice of the pained expression on his father's face, Liam quickly came to regret his decision of letting him accompany Gordon to

Crow's Foot yesterday. Sitting forward, he let the bottoms of his feet rest on the edge of the coffee table. "I had to take Olivia to the ER," he said, picking up the remote for the television.

"Is she all right?"

"She's fine."

"Well, if she's fine, why the hell did you take her?"

"It's a long story."

"It always *is* with that wife of yours."

Hearing the coffeemaker beep, Liam stared darkly into the kitchen, hoping that his father's backhanded comment would be the end of the discussion.

"So she pretended to be sick in order to get a continuance, huh? Whose dumbass idea was that? All that's gonna do is just delay the — "

Liam slammed the remote against the coffee table and got to his feet. "You know what? We wouldn't be worrying about a continuance at *all* if you hadn't managed to piss off every law enforcement official in the tri-county area!"

His father wrapped his hands around the grips of his walker and in one rough and clunky motion pulled himself up. "Don't you dare lay this on me just so you can feel better about believin' her when she whines about it not bein' her fault!" he yelled, stabbing a pointed finger towards the hallway. "Because the truth of the matter is, we wouldn't even be havin' this conversation, argument — or whatever the hell you wanna call it—if she hadn't been drivin' drunk that night!"

A drop of water, startling and cold, fell upon Liam's cheek. Knowing it hadn't come from him, he turned his attention towards the ceiling. The plaster above him was wet, telling him that the snow on the roof was melting. Retrieving a bucket from the hall closet, he returned to the living room—in all its miserable silence—and set it on the floor.

"Listen," his father said, the gruffness of his voice still present, but the level of it nowhere near where it had been a moment ago, "I'm not gonna try and pretend I understand everything that goes on between you two, because, honestly, I'm not sure you understand it either."

"What'd you find out about the victim in the car?" asked Liam, shoving the couch out of harm's way with his foot.

"Did you hear what I just said?"

Having learned the hard way that acknowledging his father meant the same thing as admitting he was right, Liam bent down to retrieve the remote and its battery cover from off the floor. As he straightened, he felt his father's hand come down on his left shoulder; it was as unwarranted as it was tender, and brought his emotions rocketing to the surface.

"Over the last few months," his father continued, "I've seen you build up a tolerance … a *dangerous* tolerance for her drinkin'. And it's high time you stopped."

"What goes on in my marriage is none of your concern," Liam said, moving his shoulder out of his reach, "and even if it was, you are the *last* person on earth I would take advice from."

His father's eyes narrowed as he returned his hand to his walker. "This has nothin' to do with me and Enid."

"No?"

"*No.*"

"Then why are you living in my house right now? Oh, that's right!" exclaimed Liam, snapping his fingers. "It's because Enid kicked you out."

His father gave him a wounded look.

Brushing aside his guilt, Liam started towards the kitchen only to stop as he neared the edge of the linoleum. "Olivia's not going into work today," he said, glancing back at his father, "so I want you to do your best not to bother her. And by that — I mean leave her alone."

The hurt expression on his father's face changed to resentment.

Figuring they'd inflicted enough damage on each other for one morning, Liam turned and started for the coffeemaker.

"I've got a name for you."

"A name for what?" he muttered, reaching up to pull a mug out of the cabinet.

"The victim in the car," said his father.

Setting the mug on the counter, Liam gave him an expectant look.

His father ran a weathered hand over his lips and shook his head. "You're not gonna like it."

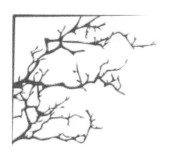

# Chapter 14

**A**lice hurriedly checked her hair and makeup in the rearview mirror as she waited for the light to change. "Did you remember your history binder?" she asked, reaching up to wipe a trace of lipstick from the corner of her mouth. After a moment, she dropped her hand and cut her eyes to the right. Less than a foot away, her daughter sat hunched over her cell phone, the glow from its screen making her face look like an alien entity whose only form of communication was through its thumbs. "*Claire?*"

"I *heard* you."

"Then why didn't you answer?"

A heavy sigh filled the front seat of the car, fogging up the passenger-side window. "It's in my backpack."

"What about your workbook?" asked Alice, remembering having seen it on the kitchen counter last night — as well as the six nights prior.

Silence.

"I think next time I'll just let my purse ride shotgun," Alice murmured, pressing on the accelerator.

"What's that supposed to mean?"

"Nothing," she said, imitating her daughter's sigh as she made a left onto Upper Pines Trace and pulled into the driveway at the end of the street. "Tell Mrs. Chen I'll be back to pick you up at eleven."

Claire glanced up from her phone. "Wait. Aren't you going to come in?"

Discerning that it would serve no purpose to remind her that this was the second time in the last ten minutes they'd had this conversation, Alice rested her arm on the steering wheel and shook her head. "I have a lot of errands to run."

"What's Michael got you doing for him today?" Claire asked. "Starching his underwear or picking up his dry cleaning?"

"If you must know," Alice replied with a tight-lipped smile, "I'm getting a mani-pedi and a facial."

Claire gave her a skeptical look.

"Go on," said Alice, shooing her out with her hand. "I'm going to be late."

"Fine, but what do you want me to tell Lily's mom about tomorrow night? She needs to know if you're coming."

"Tell her that I'll let her know when I pick you up."

"Honestly, Mom ..." Claire paused to flip her long ginger hair over her shoulder. "What's going to change between now and eleven?"

"I just need to check with Michael before I make any commitment."

"Of course you do."

Alice struggled to keep her smile upright. "I'll see you in a couple of hours."

Answering her with a roll of her eyes, Claire dragged her backpack across the seat and slammed the door.

As Alice watched her stomp away, she couldn't help but wonder where her happy, freckle-faced little girl, who used to play with toy ponies and had a laugh that was as infectious as it was endearing, had gone. Determined to prove to herself that she was still in there somewhere, Alice lowered the window. "Bye, sweetheart," she called out, "I love you!"

Claire's gait stiffened as she marched up the drive.

Slumping against the seat, Alice began backing down the driveway. As she turned her head to check for oncoming traffic, she saw that Nancy Chen had come out of the house and was standing on her wraparound porch; wearing an oversize sweater and a cream-colored pair of pants, she gave Alice a warm smile and enthusiastic wave.

Alice waved back and then promptly looked away, fearing that if she made eye contact with her she would motion for her to stop. Ignoring the yellow triangular sign warning motorists about children playing in the area, she shifted into drive and gunned the engine, making it to the entrance of the subdivision in seconds flat.

Although Alice genuinely liked Nancy Chen, over the last year and a half, she had slowly come to dread her monthly get-togethers with the other homeschool moms. They would always start out the same: low-key, friendly, and supportive, but after a few glasses of wine, the conversation would take a darkly competitive turn. So-and-So's husband had gotten a promotion, So-and-So's husband was doing this, and blah, blah, blah. Alice would sit there, quietly nibbling on her cheese cube, yet it wouldn't take long for someone to ask when she and Michael were going to get married, and regardless of how optimistic her answer was, her words would be met with *sure he is* glances and sarcastic whispers.

With Nancy Chen's house no longer in her rearview mirror, Alice shoved her and the rest of the moms to the back of her mind as she turned her attention to a more pressing matter. Michael had barely spoken to her over the last couple of days, and this morning had left the house without telling her goodbye. His actions, though juvenile, were intentional, and meant to let her know that he was still angry with her over what had happened the other night.

Making a sharp left, she sped up to avoid getting caught at the next light. As Michael's office building came into view, she saw several trucks with flashing lights stopped along the side of the street, while orange cones, splattered with dried tar, lined the entrance of the parking lot.

Having forgotten about the lot being repaved today, Alice scowled at the construction workers — who didn't appear to be doing a whole lot of anything — and went up another block before turning down a small alleyway that ran between the side of Michael's office and the medical supply store next door.

Spotting Michael's BMW, she carefully backed her car into the narrow space across from it and checked her face in the mirror once more. Satisfied with her appearance, she reached behind her seat for the insulated cooler she'd packed this morning. Placing the bag in her lap, she lightly ran her fingertips along its zipper and sighed. Reluctantly accepting the fact that the well-being of Michael's ego was more important than that of her own, she stepped out of her car and made her way around to the front of the building, hoping that her homemade frittatas and earnest apology would put an end to the tension between them.

Several people in the waiting area eyed her as she bypassed the receptionist's window and turned the knob of the coveted door that led to the examination rooms.

"Dr. Edmunds office. How may I help you?"

"Morning," Alice whispered, wiggling her fingers at Kristen, Michael's receptionist.

Kristen's eyes widened as she mouthed *hello* in return and smiled. "Lindsay? I don't think she's here yet," she said, switching the phone to her other ear as she glanced down the empty corridor behind her. "Can I take a message?"

Knowing that she had exactly eighteen minutes before Michael saw his first patient, Alice stooped to catch Kristen's gaze once more and pointed towards his office.

Kristen nodded and waved her on. "Yes," she said, returning her attention to the phone, "I'll have her call you as soon as she arrives ..."

Not missing her days as Michael's receptionist in the least, Alice started down the corridor that she and his nurses jokingly liked to refer to as Vanity Row, where displayed in a prominent manner along the wall, were countless certificates, diplomas, and newspaper clippings, as well as several pictures of him posing with state politicians and local celebrities.

Upon reaching the end of the framed exhibit, Alice took a moment to smooth her dress before opening the door to Michael's office. "Good morning, sweethear—" The bag of frittatas slipped through her fingers as her eyes went from the surprised look on Michael's face to the shorthaired brunette whose head was firmly wedged between his knees.

Michael leaped to his feet. "Alice," he said, fumbling to stuff his ego back inside his pants, "I can explain."

Knowing that the tears streaming down her cheeks were misleading, Alice struck out at the first thing she could find, sending the Tiffany-style Peacock torch lamp—the one that had been on backorder for six months—hurtling towards the floor, where its stained-glass shade shattered on impact.

"Alice—"

"Don't touch me!" she yelled, slapping at Michael's outstretched hands. As he lowered his arms, her gaze darted across the room to Lindsay, who had come out from underneath the desk and was now standing beside his chair, the expression on her face as sheepish as it was smug.

"Alice," Michael pleaded, "let me explain—"

"Don't," she said, shaking her head. "Just— don't." With her eyes and throat burning, she backed through the doorway and into several of Michael's nurses who had come out of the breakroom to see what the commotion was. Weaving her way through their colorful scrubs, the corridor became a blur as she hurried towards the exit.

"Alice," said Kristen, hanging up the phone, "what's wrong?"

Rushing past her, Alice flung open the door and was halfway across the waiting room when she heard Michael's footsteps closing in behind her.

"Alice, wait!" he said, catching her by the wrist.

"Let me go!"

"Listen to me," he said, pulling her close. "What you saw back there wasn't—" He stopped and glanced to the left.

Wiping her tears, Alice followed his gaze and saw that they had the unwavering attention of everyone in the waiting area. Looking back at him, she jerked her wrist out of his grasp. "Wasn't *what*?" she prompted.

Michael shook his head and swallowed. "That wasn't what it looked like," he said in a half-whisper.

Alice put the force of her entire body behind her hand as it fell across his face. "You know what? I may not be a doctor, but I'm pretty damn sure that wasn't a thermometer you were sticking in her mouth!"

A combination of gasps and snickers echoed throughout the room.

Michael stood there unmoving—except for the muscle in his jaw, which twitched repeatedly beneath a growing swath of red.

Pivoting on her heel, Alice turned and strode out the door.

"Alice!" called Michael, running after her.

"Fuck off!" she shouted, marching around the corner of the building. Upon reaching her car, she paused to retrieve her keys and saw Michael's reflection coming up behind her in the driver's side window. "I said, 'fuck off —'" The back of her neck suddenly snapped forward, sending her face slamming into the doorframe of her car. A breathless cry fell from her lips as a sharp pain sliced across her forehead.

"I don't care how upset you are with me!" he said, twisting her around to face him. "Don't you *ever* embarrass me like that again!" He slid his hand to her throat and squeezed. "Do you understand?"

Clawing at his fingertips, Alice frantically swept a distorted gaze across the deserted alleyway in search of help.

Michael shoved her up against the car. "*Answer me, goddamn it!*"

Alice managed a shaky nod as she forced herself to look into his eyes. Two unblinking orbs of darkness stared back at her.

"*Hey!*" yelled a man's voice.

Dropping his hand, Michael jerked his head over his shoulder.

Drawing an uneven breath, Alice saw that one of the construction workers was standing a few yards away, but her hopes of being saved were immediately crushed when she realized that he was yelling at another worker in order to be heard over the machinery and wasn't even looking in her direction.

Michael turned back to her. "We'll talk about what you *think* you saw when I get home," he said, the blackness in his eyes fading, "but right now, I've got patients to see — if I still *have* any, that is."

With her airway no longer blocked, Alice felt the adrenaline beginning to course through her body, yet it was too little too late and only served to heighten the trembling in her legs as she watched him walk away. Scrambling inside her car, her fingers fumbled along the edge of the door panel before finding the lock; having no desire to see if the wetness clinging to her cheeks was water or blood, she jammed the key into the ignition and started the engine. As she shifted into drive, she could see Michael smoothing his hair with his hands as he made his way towards the rear entrance of his office.

Alice's adrenaline, as well as her tears, began to ebb, allowing her anger to reseed itself. Gripping the steering wheel, she began to visualize running him down. She would trap his pudgy little body beneath her tires and then slowly roll over him, inflicting as much agony upon him as possible before the weight of her car squashed him like the cockroach that he was.

With her foot still on the brake, she stomped on the accelerator. The smell of smoke and burnt rubber quickly surrounded her as the rear tires on the car started to squeal.

Michael stopped in his tracks and spun around.

An unorthodox sense of glee began to swirl inside Alice as she let off the brake.

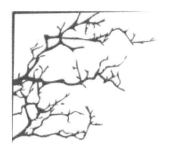

# Chapter 15

Liam tapped his fingers against the armrest of his truck as he waited for Olivia to answer her phone. Five rings later, his wife's unnaturally chipper voice began to flow into his ear. "Hi, I can't take your call right now, but please—"

Tossing the phone on the seat beside him, he made a right at the light and angled his truck into the first available parking space he could find. Leaning back against the headrest, he stared at the row of buildings in front of him as he tried to focus on the task at hand, yet his thoughts refused to leave Olivia. Picking up his cell once more, he slid his thumb across the screen, and after a moment of deliberation, tentatively pressed the number that was displayed just below hers.

"Hello?"

"Dad, it's Liam."

"I know that," he snapped. "Don't you think I know what your name flashin' on my screen means?"

Switching the phone to his other hand, Liam snatched his keys from the ignition. "Is Olivia home?"

"Yeah."

"Where is she?"

"Same place she's been holed up in all mornin'."

"Well, I need you to go check on her for me."

"You told me not to bother her."

"I *know* what I told you," said Liam, rolling his eyes as he climbed out of his truck, "but I need you to do it anyway."

"Well, how am I supposed to do that if I'm not allowed to—"

"Dad, I just need you to check on her!" he said, slamming the door.

Silence, obstinate and laced with heavy breathing, filtered through the phone.

Glancing at the darkening sky, Liam tenderly rubbed the cut on his forehead and sighed. "Please?"

"Fine, I'll check on her, but don't you go blamin' me if she gets mad over it!"

"Thanks, and tell her to call me when she gets a chance."

An inarticulate and profanity-filled reply followed his words.

Having no desire to ask his father to repeat it for the sake of clarity, Liam ended the call and started around his truck. A steady stream of water trickled past his boots as he neared the sidewalk, and he found himself hoping that the impending rain and above-freezing temperature would linger long enough for the remaining snow to melt. Over the past couple of days, it had been pushed to the curbs by plows and shovels, causing it to evolve into blackened mounds of frozen slush that lined the streets like trash ... and was something that Weeping Rock, a town dreary enough by its own rights, didn't need.

As the air around him began to grow damp, Liam trudged past Sadie McGee's consignment shop and half a dozen other forgettable stores before crossing the intersection.

"Hey, Matthews!"

Glancing over his shoulder, Liam saw a man in a knee-length black parka hurrying towards him, and—upon recognizing the exaggerated swagger beneath it as belonging to that of Cam Peterson—suppressed another sigh.

"Looks like we're about to get some rain, doesn't it?" he called.

"Looks like it," said Liam, continuing on.

Peterson caught up to him a few steps later. "I heard you were looking for me."

"I was. *Two* days ago."

"I've been busy putting out fires," Peterson replied in a defensive tone. "I'm assuming your wanting to talk to me has something to do with Ramirez?"

"It does."

"Are you close to making an arrest?"

Liam kept his eyes straight ahead. Even though he had been asked that question more times than he could count over the last forty-eight hours, he still found himself grappling for an answer that would imbue confidence in the citizens of Weeping Rock that he was capable of doing his job. "The investigation is ongoing," he finally said.

"What the hell does that mean?" Peterson scoffed.

The smell of freshly baked bread surrounded Liam as he walked past Archie Bowman's deli, making his mouth water in spite of the large C that had been posted in the shop's window by the health department.

"It means that the investigation is ongoing," he said again, wishing that he'd stayed in his truck another thirty seconds.

"Well, you need to hurry it up," grumbled Peterson, "because the phone in my office hasn't stopped ringing. Half the parents are demanding an answer and the other half are threatening to keep their kid home from school because they're worried about their safety."

Knowing Peterson's penchant for exaggeration, Liam guessed *half* meant one. "They don't have anything to worry about," he replied, refusing to give him the details he was so obviously fishing for.

"I know that," said Peterson in a flustered voice, "but have you ever tried explaining yourself to a parent?"

"On a daily basis," Liam said dryly.

"Then you of all people should know what I'm dealing with," he sputtered. "Hell, I'm even getting calls about it at home."

Considering the fact that Cam Peterson was only the acting school superintendent, having been selected by the school board during a special hearing to replace longtime superintendent Larry Dutton, who'd passed away last September after suffering a heart attack, Liam seriously doubted that was the case.

"Anyway … what was it you wanted to speak to me about?" he asked, making a big deal out of checking the time on his watch. "I've got about ten minutes before my next meeting."

Although Liam wasn't keen on questioning Peterson on a public sidewalk, he figured it was better than having him sucking up all the oxygen in his office. "How exactly did Hector Ramirez come to be the coach of the Prairie Dogs?"

"He called me up out of the blue and asked if he could."

"That's it?"

"Yeah." Peterson paused to tilt his head. "And you'd know that if you bothered to attend the board meetings once in a while."

The tip of Liam's tongue shoved itself against the inside of his left cheek. "Did he tell you why he wanted the job?"

"Eh ..." He waved his hand in the air. "It was some mumbo jumbo about him wanting to get back to his roots and be around people that liked him for who he was, not just because he was a celebrity. To be honest, I stopped listening after he told me he wanted the job."

Liam began shaking his head.

"Oh, come on now, Matthews. You know as well as I do that Hector's presence on our baseball field would've been a huge draw. The school would've made money hand over fist on ticket sales and concessions alone, and that would've benefited everybody."

Arriving at his destination, Liam stopped and gave him a curt nod. "Thanks for the information."

An amused look crossed Peterson's face. "You goin' in there to question a suspect?" he asked, gesturing at the door beside him.

"Something like that."

"Well, while you're in there doing your *interrogation*, be sure and tell Madge not to take too much off the top." Without warning, Peterson reached out and tousled Liam's hair. "You wanna look good for those TV cameras now."

Taking a step back, Liam flexed his hand in an effort to keep it from curling into a fist.

Peterson's lower jaw dropped open, allowing a deep, donkey-like laugh to come tumbling out of it.

"I'm just messing with you, Matthews," he said in between brays. "Don't look so serious."

Combing his hair with his fingers, Liam shoved open the door and stepped inside, leaving Peterson to hee-haw on the sidewalk by himself.

Several women, sitting underneath helmeted, archaic-looking hairdryers, glanced up as the door clanged shut behind him, the expressions on their faces teetering somewhere between boredom and curiosity.

The smell of perm-solution, hairspray, and other unpleasant odors permeated Liam's nostrils, making him reel in his breath as he made his way towards a small counter.

"Can I help you, Sheriff?"

Turning, Liam saw a lady with spiked black hair and sparkly cheeks eyeing him from across the room. "I need to speak with Madge Johnston," he said, watching her lather the hair of a woman whose neck was cradled in the curve of a large brown sink.

"Hey, Tonya?" said the lady, directing her attention to the slender girl next to her who was sweeping piles of hair into a dustpan. "Is Madge still here or has she left already?"

"Just a minute and I'll check," she replied.

As Liam waited for the girl to finish sweeping, he saw a set of curtains hanging from a doorway in the back of the salon begin to part down the middle; a moment later, an older woman wearing a navy-blue coat and red hoop earrings emerged.

"I'm leaving now, Jeanie," the woman said, digging a set of keys out of her purse as she hurried across the floor. "I'll be back in a …" Her words and steps faltered as her frenzied gaze fell upon Liam.

"Hello, Mrs. Johnston," he said, walking around the counter.

The woman's mouth, caked in a bright-pink lipstick, opened and closed several times but emitted no sound, making her appear as if she were stuttering in silence.

Coming to stand in front of her, Liam cleared his throat. "There's something I—"

"Who called you?" she asked in a sharp voice.

"Uh …" He paused to shake his head. "No one."

"Then why are you—you know what—never mind," she said, slinging her purse over her shoulder.

Feeling the weight of a dozen pairs of eyes on his back, he leaned in closer. "Is there a place we can talk in private?"

Mrs. Johnston gathered the ends of her coat together. "This isn't a good time," she said, rushing past him.

Liam scrambled to get the door for her. "It won't take long. I promise."

"I'm sorry," she said in a clipped tone, "but I have somewhere else to be."

"I just need a moment," Liam insisted, following her outside.

Mrs. Johnston stopped in the middle of the sidewalk and whirled around. "Who called you?"

"*No one*," he said again, finding it strange that she kept asking that question.

Narrowing her eyes, the woman searched Liam's face, bringing about an uncomfortableness in him that made him shift his feet. As the rain began to fall, she dropped her head and began marching towards an older-model Buick with mismatched tires.

"It's imperative that I speak with your daughter, ma'am," he called after her. "Do you know where she is?"

Mrs. Johnston's shoulders grew rigid. Clutching her keys in a tightly wound fist, she turned back to him. "Yeah," she said, the lines around her mouth deepening, "I know *exactly* where she is."

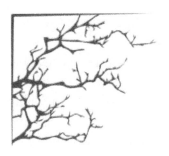

# Chapter 16

Alice chewed on her thumbnail as her gaze flitted back and forth between the clock on the wall and the stocky detective sitting across from her. Dressed in a tan button-down that was so thin she could see his undershirt, the bottom of his frayed polka-dotted tie rested upon the edge of the table as he wrote on the legal pad in front of him, while a wedding band, dull and scuffed, occupied the middle of his ring finger—the skin surrounding it pale and engorged.

"Is there anything else you'd like to add to your statement, Ms. Malloy?"

Her attention shifted from the gold-plated tourniquet to a set of buttonhole eyes that were brown, intense, and accusatory. "I wasn't aware that I was giving you one," she replied, arching her brow.

The detective leaned back in his chair, dragging his sad little tie with him. "Several witnesses told police that you and Dr. Edmunds were arguing in the waiting area outside his office when you assaulted him."

Alice stopped biting her broken nail. "Assaulted? Is that *your* word or theirs?" she countered. "Because I doubt that any of Michael's patients would use such a broad term when describing a bitch-slap."

The detective scratched the side of his jaw and gave a tired-sounding sigh. "What were the two of you arguing about?"

"Didn't your *witnesses* tell you? Or are you having trouble coming up with a fancy word for blow job?"

The detective's right eyelid twitched, which seemed to extend all the way down to his butt cheek. Taking a sip of coffee, he flipped to a clean page on his legal pad and smoothed the paper with his hand. "Let's jump forward a bit."

"Yes," said Alice, tilting her head, "let's."

"I want you to tell me what happened when you were pulling out of the parking lot in the alley."

The sarcasm dripping from the corners of Alice's mouth evaporated. "I think you've jumped a bit too far forw—"

"Was it your intent to kill Dr. Edmunds?"

Shifting in her chair, she summoned a listless laugh. "Of course not."

"He says the only reason he's still alive is because you ran into his *car* instead of him."

"Well, I suppose it's natural for him to think that," she mused. "The entire world *does* revolve around him, after all."

Laying his pen down, the detective pinched the bridge of his nose. "Ms. Malloy, I have a hundred other things that I have to do today, so I would appreciate it if you could just tell me what happened."

"I already told the arresting officer what happened, and I know that you know because you have a copy of the report right there," she said, pointing at the paper beside his beefy arm.

Without looking, the detective picked up the report and turned it over facedown. "Dr. Edmunds said that the injury to your forehead came from you hitting it on the steering wheel when you crashed."

Alice sat forward. "Well, of course he's going to say that," she yelled. "Do you really think he's going to admit to bashing it against the door of my car? I mean, my God, you're a detective, can't you tell when someone's lying to you?"

The weariness residing in the man's face receded, paving the way for a smoldering look that left his pockmarks crimson. "As a matter of fact, I can."

"If that's the case," she said, crossing her arms, "then why are you sitting here talking to me?"

"Let's just say for the moment," he replied, turning his pen end over end, "that you're telling the truth. Why did you hit his car with yours?"

Leaning across the table, she tapped the piece of paper with her finger. "It's — in — the — report."

"The *report*," he said through a clenched jaw, "is confusing. That's why you're here."

Finding his hostility towards her baffling, she sat back in the chair and interlaced her fingers. "When I was pulling out of the alley, I was afraid for my safety, and in my hurry to leave, confused the brake with the accelerator."

The detective gave her a blank stare. "You confused the brake with the accelerator."

"Yes."

"*Four* different times?"

Alice scraped her teeth along her bottom lip in order to keep a grin from forming as the image of Michael screaming at her to stop — as she repeatedly plowed into his Beamer — began to play in front of her. Although she'd had every intention of carrying out his rapidly planned execution, logic had intervened at the last possible second, sending her car careening into the next best thing.

"Ms. Malloy?"

Tucking the memory away to enjoy for later, she returned her attention to the detective. "I was scared and upset," she said, forcibly making her voice shake, "and got confused."

The door behind the detective swung open and a lanky man with a shaved head and ruddy cheeks

189

walked in. "Hayes, there's someone outside needing to talk to you."

"They're going to have to wait until I'm done with my interview," he replied, keeping his eyes locked on Alice as he spoke.

The man placed his hands on the table and twisted his giraffe-like neck towards the detective's ear. "It's regarding Ms. Malloy. There's—"

The vent lodged in the ceiling above Alice's head began to vibrate and then rattle as the heat cycled on. Straining to hear, she sat forward, but the forced air blowing down around her drowned out the rest of the man's words.

Detective Hayes pushed his chair across the floor and stood up. "Stay with her," he grumbled, grabbing his pad from off the table. "I'll be right back."

THE RAIN PINGED SOFTLY against the side of the window, turning the layer of dirt that was clinging to it into a watery red mess before sending it streaking down the tempered glass. Peering through the small area in the upper-right hand corner of the pane that the rain had yet to touch, Olivia stared at the peach tree Liam had planted after they'd first bought the house. In spite of the fact that he'd told her it would take at least three to four years for it to bear fruit, she couldn't help thinking that with its stunted growth — three years had already passed and it had yet to reach her eye level — and the white barnacle-like things sticking out of its slender trunk, that it was dead ... just like everything else in the yard.

Lowering her gaze, Olivia sighed for no other reason than to make noise. Although she couldn't remember the last time she'd been home in the middle of a weekday, the house seemed unusually quiet. It was so quiet, in fact, that she found herself wondering if Harlan had somehow fallen and knocked himself unconscious; it was a nagging feeling — yet one that she had no intention of acting upon.

Crossing her arms, she leaned forward and rested her forehead against the pane. The cold instantly penetrated the glass, burning the skin above her eyebrow, but no more concerned for her own comfort than she was for her father-in-law's, forced it to remain there as she ran her hand along the sill. The peeling layers of paint flecked off beneath her fingernails, stirring her memories ...

*Although spring had sprung a little over two months ago, a late frost had sent the temperature plunging, making Olivia bounce on her toes in an effort to keep warm as she waited for Liam to unlock the door. After several moments of jiggling the key, and a little help from his boot, it finally relented.*

*"Ladies first," he said, extending his arm.*

*Fashioning a small smile, she wiped her shoes on the rotting welcome mat and stepped inside the darkened house.*

*"So," said Liam, closing the door behind her, "here we are in the foyer."*

*Olivia looked down at her feet. By definition, a foyer was a large entrance hall near the front door of a home or apartment. Not eight squares of parquet flooring.*

*"Let me show you the kitchen," he said, brushing past her. Walking over to the sink, he reached up and pulled on a tangled cord.*

*Olivia bristled as the dilapidated blind slid upwards, filling the galley-sized kitchen with dusty daylight. Darkly painted cabinets hung above a butcher-block counter that had more pot burns than she could count, while an avocado-colored refrigerator and stove flanked the sides. Sensing that Liam was waiting for her to say something, she gave the rest of the room a quick once over with her eyes and nodded.*

*"You have to come in here," he insisted, motioning at her with his hand.*

*Pursing her lips, Olivia reluctantly made her way over to where he was standing.*

*"Look," he said, turning her around, "this is what's called an open-concept kitchen. You can see right into the living room."*

*Olivia's gaze shifted from the yellow-brick linoleum beneath her to the room on the other side of the counter. Although it was decidedly bigger than the kitchen was, the orange shag carpet and paneled walls made it seem gloomy and boxed in.*

"Look over there," he said, pointing to the open door just off the living room. "That's a huge den."

Tilting her head in order to see inside, Olivia noticed that the room had the same dark paneling and carpeting as what lay in front of her.

"And did you see the garage when we drove up?"

Before she could answer, he hurried back across the 'foyer' and into a small laundry room that had a large brown stain running down its striped wallpaper.

"Do you know what that means?" he asked excitedly, pointing to a battered door that stood next to a harvest-gold dryer.

"What?"

"It means," he said, pausing to open it, "no more having to scrape the ice off your windshield in the mornings. What do you say to that?"

As the smell of mildew mixed with gasoline fumes wafted in from the attached garage, Olivia lifted her eyebrows as high as they would go in the hopes that it would draw the corners of her mouth upwards.

"So, what do you think so far?"

"I think," she said, scratching the top of her head, which all of a sudden felt as if something were crawling on it, "that it needs a lot of work."

Dismissing her concerns with a dimpled grin, Liam started towards the living room. "Come on," he said, tugging on her hand, "I haven't shown you the best part yet."

"How did you find this house again?" she asked, eyeing the peeling plaster on the ceiling.

"I told you," he replied, glancing at her over his shoulder. "Eddie — "

"I know. Eddie, your real estate agent friend, told you about it and loaned you the key. But you seem to know an awful lot about this house considering this is the first time – " Her steps faltered. "Wait, this place wasn't the scene of a crime was it?" she asked, pulling out of his grasp.

Liam laughed. "Why would you even think that?" he asked, giving her an incredulous look.

Olivia's hands flew to her hips. "Why are you answering my question with a question?"

"I'm not. I was just – "

"Was someone murdered here?"

"No," he said, shaking his head emphatically.

"I can tell when you're lying."

"I'm not lying."

"Look me in the eye and tell me that no one died here."

Scratching the back of his neck, his gaze skittered across hers.

"Liam!"

He held out his hands. "The death was ruled an accident."

"Oh – my – God," Olivia muttered, starting towards the door.

"He was an elderly man," Liam called after her. "He fell and hit his head."

"Is that supposed to make me feel any better?" she yelled, making her way across the uneven floor.

Liam caught her by the belt of her coat. "Please don't go. You haven't seen the whole house yet."

"I've seen enough," she answered, trying to wrangle herself free.

"But you haven't seen the best part."

*Olivia looked into those big blue pleading eyes of his and stopped struggling. "Make it quick," she said with a sigh.*

*His grin returned, highlighting the handsome curve of his jaw. "Come on."*

*She let him lead her over to a faded set of curtains in the living room that spanned the length of the back wall.*

*"Close your eyes."*

*"Liam ..."*

*"Just humor me."*

*"Fine."*

*"Keep them closed."*

*"Hurry up," she snapped.*

*There was a loud swooshing noise followed by a bright light that pierced her lids.*

*"Okay, you can open them now."*

*A set of sliding glass doors that had a broken broom handle wedged in the bottom of its track appeared in front of her. On the other side of them, a rusty swing set, several creepy-looking gnomes, and other various lawn ornaments were scattered across a weed-infested yard.*

*"What do you think?"*

*Swiveling her head towards her husband, Olivia started to ask him if he'd lost his freaking mind but stopped when she noticed the serene look his face held. Following his gaze, she saw that just beyond the overgrown backyard lay a flat prairie, and just beyond the prairie were the Black Hills. She felt her breath catch in her throat as she stared in awe at the rugged, luscious sea of green ascending towards the heavens. "It's beautiful," she whispered.*

*Liam slipped his arm around her waist. "Not as beautiful as you."*

*Olivia inhaled deeply as his lips brushed against her cheek. The last few weeks had come and gone at a frantic pace, and she felt the desperate need to drink in every second of this perfect moment.*

*"I know this house isn't exactly what you had in mind," he said, resting his chin on the top of her head, "but it's within our price range. Things will be tight for a while, but over time, we'll get it fixed up. And when we're done, it'll be the home of our dreams."*

*"Promise?" she asked, wanting to believe him.*

*Liam drew back to look at her. "I promise," he answered, his locks falling across his forehead as he slid his hand along the small round bump protruding from her belly. "We could start by converting the den into the nursery. I can replace the paneling with drywall and paint it a pale blue."*

*"Or pink," she chided.*

*"Well, we could," he said, grinning down at her, "but I think it might confuse him."*

*Olivia giggled. "What makes you so sure it's going to be a boy?" she asked, wrapping her arms around his neck.*

*Liam's eyes twinkled brightly at her. "I just know."*

"Olivia!"

Olivia ground her teeth at the sound of her father-in-law banging on the door. Turning from the window, she stalked across the floor and jerked it open. "*What?*"

The startled look on Harlan's face was quickly absorbed by his gruff disposition. "Liam wanted me to check on you."

As Olivia stood there, debating on how to answer him, she found herself wondering how many days in a row he had worn that flannel shirt; besides being stained with ketchup, it was untucked, unkempt, and smelled heavily of all things Harlan. "Well, as you can see," she said, swinging the door around, "I'm fine—"

Harlan put the front leg of his walker in the path of the door.

"What?" she repeated, having neared the threshold of her tolerance for him.

"Liam wants you to give him a call."

"Fine," she lied.

The upbeat melody that Olivia had recently come to hate began to play. Swiping her cell phone off the dresser, she glanced at the screen and saw that it was the office of Dr. Feldspausch. During her forced trip to the ER last night, she'd learned that Dr. Ellis was the physician on call and had decided to kill two birds with one stone by telling him about her recurring pelvic pain in the hopes of getting a renewed prescription for Hydrocodone, as well as the note for the judge—but instead, had walked out with a handful of muscle relaxers and an appointment to see a specialist. Turning off her phone, she looked up to find Harlan still standing in the doorway.

"Is there something else?" she asked, sucking in her breath.

"Uh ..." He paused to scratch his head, sending a plethora of dandruff raining down upon his shoulder. "It's past noon. Don't you want some lunch or somethin'?"

Olivia's gaze involuntarily shifted from him to the living room. From where she was standing, she had a perfect line of sight into the den. Where there had once been a crib, adorned with blue sheets and hand-sewn gingham bumpers, now stood an unmade bed littered with newspapers, dirty underwear, and potato chip bags.

"Well? Do ya?"

Returning her attention to Harlan, Olivia pushed his walker out of the way and shut the door.

ALICE TENDERLY PRESSED her fingertips against the golf ball-sized lump sitting in the middle of her forehead and winced. Glancing at the spindly man Detective Hayes had put in charge of watching over her, she cleared her throat to get his attention. "I need to call my daughter."

"You'll have to wait until Hayes comes back," he replied, giving her a curt nod.

Alice looked away as her panic began to set in. Her daughter, not to mention Mrs. Chen, were probably wondering where the hell she was. The sound of footsteps brought her eyes back to the door. Unable to restrain her anxiety any longer, she stood up and pushed in her chair as Detective Hayes walked inside. "I've answered all your questions," she said, drawing strength from the countless episodes of *Law & Order* she'd watched over the years, "and legally, you have no right to keep me here."

The detective's mouth dropped open, allowing a deep-seated chuckle to come tumbling out of it as he closed the door. "What cop show have you been watching? Because that's not how this works."

Alice smoothed the hair from her face, trying to hold back her embarrassment. "I'm late in picking up my daughter—"

"Your boyfriend's refusing to press charges," Hayes said, tossing his pad of paper on the table.

Alice felt her body flood with relief. "So, I can go?"

The detective held up his hand. "That's the good news," he said, a cold smile spreading across his lips. "The bad news is that the Orand County Sheriff is here for you in regards to another police matter."

Alice blinked. "The Orand County—wait—I don't underst—"

Hayes reached behind him and opened the door. "Sheriff?"

Suddenly finding herself unable to breathe, Alice grabbed hold of the back of the chair. A moment later, Liam Matthews — all six-foot-two-inches of him — appeared, propelling her heart into her throat.

"Feel free to use the room," Hayes said to him as he leaned across the table to gather his things. "We're all done here."

"Thank you," replied Liam, letting him and the other man pass before closing the door.

The heat coming through the vent shut off without warning.

Certain that he could hear the beating of her heart as it painfully slid back down her esophagus, Alice pressed her arms against her chest.

Turning from the door, Liam's eyes seemed to hesitate and then slowly rose to meet hers. "Alice," he said, removing his hat.

With her heart tucked safely back inside its cavity, Alice felt it begin to flutter. Although it was barely noticeable at first, it grew more volatile with each breath she took. It was reminiscent of a butterfly with a broken wing; the harder it tried to fly, the more it flopped around.

Walking farther into the room, Liam gestured at her forehead. "Are you all right?"

"Why are you here?" she managed to ask, yet the words had no sooner jerked from her lips before she was struck by a single chord of terror. "Oh my God, did my mom get into an accident on the way up here?"

"No." Liam's hands shot up in front of him. "She's fine. I promise."

"Then why are you ..." She took her fingers away from her lips as another thought, more horrific than the one before, infiltrated her brain. "Oh—my—God. Did she call and tell you that I'd been arrested?"

He shook his head. "Not exactly."

Rolling her gaze towards the ceiling, Alice threw her arms up in disgust. "Un-freaking-believable. I can't believe she told you!"

"No, that's—" Liam stopped and let out an exasperated sounding sigh. "That's not why I'm *here*, Alice." Leaning around her, he pulled out her chair and motioned for her to sit. "I need to tell you something."

Refusing, Alice shoved the chair back underneath the table and grabbed her coat. "I have to pick up my daughter," she said, starting for the door.

Liam stepped in front of her, blocking her escape. "This is important."

His breath fell across her face as he spoke, causing her cheeks to feel as if they were made of molten lava. As the intense heat began to spread to her extremities, she dropped her gaze and shook her head. "If you'll give me a ride," she said, uncertain of the current whereabouts—or condition—of her car, "you can tell me whatever it is you need to tell me on the way." Then, deciding it would be in her best interest not to give him a choice, clumsily brushed past him and yanked on the handle of the door.

It opened to the sound of flushing toilets, ringing telephones—and a disheveled-looking Michael, who was standing in the middle of the corridor speaking with Detective Hayes.

Hunching her shoulders, Alice started towards the exit, hoping to slip past the both of them unnoticed, but as she drew near, Michael turned his gaze upon her. "I want you and that daughter of yours out of my house—*today*," he said in a low voice as his right hand curled into a fist.

Refusing to acknowledge him, Alice forced her feet to keep moving.

"Did you hear me, bitch?" he yelled, sliding in front of her as she tried to go around him. Sticking his reddened face in hers, his eyes began to fill with the same black rage that had consumed him in the parking lot. "I said that I want you and that fucking daugh—"

Liam's forearm jammed itself under Michael's throat. "Sir, you need to take a step back," he stated, then helped him do so by shoving him against the wall.

"Come on, Edmunds," said Hayes, sighing as he grabbed him by the collar of his shirt. "You've said your peace. Now you need to let it go."

"Do you hear me?" shouted Michael, clawing at the wall like a rabid animal as Hayes wearily pulled him along the corridor. "I want you to get the fuck out of my house!"

Feeling an odd sensation, Alice looked down and saw that Liam was in the process of wrapping his hand around her upper arm. It was strong and comforting and — giving it a rough jerk, he strode towards the exit, making her have to run to keep up with him.

Michael's voice grew faint, but the vulgar obscenities spewing from his mouth were still loud and clear, and suddenly, the magnitude of what she had done — what they had both done — began to set in.

As her stilettos wobbled beneath her, the tears that had pooled in the rims of her eyelids sloppily spilled down her cheeks.

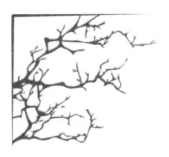

# Chapter 17

The cars and buildings flew past Alice in a blurry haze as she stared out the window. Her head was pounding and her neck ached from keeping it locked in the same position, yet she refused to turn from the glass, as Liam Matthews was the last person in the world she wanted to see right now, let alone be confined inside a vehicle with.

"Which way?"

"Right," she murmured, dragging the tip of her knuckle across her face. Although her tears had long dried, they had left the skin around her eyelids feeling crusty and tight. As Liam slowed to make the turn, she involuntarily stole a sideways glance at him and saw that the knot that had been protruding from his jaw in the corridor of the police station had disappeared. "Thank you for what you did back there."

"There's no need to thank me," he replied, keeping his eyes on the road.

Discerning that he seemed to be making as much of an effort to avoid looking at her as she was at him, Alice shifted in her seat and pointed her knees towards the dash. As she pressed the back of her neck into the contour of the headrest, Michael's hurtful words and deeds began to swirl in front of her, seeking to take refuge in the irrational part of her brain that still cared for him. Struggling not to let them in, she rolled her eyes towards Liam and latched onto the first thing that popped into her mind. "My mom told me about your mother's passing."

Liam's hands tightened around the steering wheel.

Realizing that probably wasn't the best statement to have led with, Alice shook her head while rushing to rectify it. "She was always so nice to me. I'm sorry."

"Thanks," he replied in a clipped tone.

Clasping her fingers together, she sought out another avenue of conversation. "How long have you been Sheriff?" she asked—yet thanks to her mother already knew the answer.

"A few months."

"Did your dad retire?" she asked innocently.

A ringing sound filled the cab.

Liam grabbed his phone from the console. "Yeah?"

Alice tried to respect his privacy, but the man speaking on the other end of the phone had a very deep and distinctive voice, making it difficult for her to keep from hearing what was being said.

"I got the cell phone dried out. It's charged and working."

"Did you find anything useful on it?"

There was a long pause.

"It's not the girl's phone. It's Hector's."

The tops of Liam's knuckles grew white. "Are you sure?"

"Positive. And there's something on it you need to see."

"I'll be there as soon as I can."

"Is everything all right?" asked Alice, feigning ignorance as he ended the call.

"Which way?" he demanded, wagging his finger at the upcoming intersection.

"Left and then straight."

Liam cut the wheel hard, causing Alice to have to grab onto the armrest in order to keep from sliding across the seat and landing in his lap. As the truck straightened, the sun came out from behind the clouds and shone through the windshield, drawing her eyes to the wedding band on his finger. "How long have you been married?"

There was a lengthy period of silence before he spoke. "Three years."

"What's her name?"

"You wouldn't know her. She's not from Weeping Rock."

"I didn't *ask* where she was from. I asked what her name was."

The knot found its way back onto Liam's jaw.

Beginning to think that his anger had less to do with the phone call and everything to do with her, Alice decided to stop trying to make small talk and sat back. "Take a left up here. It's the last house on the right."

He did as she instructed but in a slower and more even manner this time.

As the house came into view, Alice's stomach began to churn at the sight of Nancy Chen peering out its front window. As she sat there trying to collect her thoughts on what she was going to tell her, the sound of Liam's door opening made her turn her head. "What are you doing?" she asked in a high-pitched screech.

He gave her a puzzled look. "Getting out so I can open the door for you."

"I can open my own door," she snapped, having no wish for him to be seen by Nancy Chen or any other mother that happened to be lurking behind the curtains.

Liam's chest rose and fell sharply, sending a heavy sigh hurtling from his nostrils.

"What was it that you came here to tell me?" she asked, finding that she was no longer in a hurry to retrieve Claire.

"This isn't the right time — or place," he replied, glancing towards the house. "Let me take you home first."

Home. Alice's throat tightened at the word and the sudden realization that she no longer had one. "When my daughter gets inside this truck," she said, struggling to keep her voice steady, "she's going to ask a million questions that I'll have to answer because there'll be no peace until I do. So, trust me when I say that there is absolutely nothing you can tell me that's going to make my day any worse than it already is—or is going to be."

Liam's eyes took on a somber expression. "It's about your husband."

Alice sucked in her breath. "I'll tell you what I told your father when *he* was sheriff," she said, yanking on the handle of the door. "I don't know anything about the money Dom took—"

"Alice—"

"And I don't know where he went."

Reaching across her lap, Liam grabbed the door and held it closed.

With her cheeks burning, she forced herself to look at him. "Let me out—"

"Yesterday morning," he said, talking over her, "we pulled his car from Crow's Foot Lake."

The anger that had been quietly thriving inside Alice for the past eleven years began to fluctuate. Suddenly deprived of its oxygen, it slammed itself repeatedly against her chest in an effort to breathe, making her words come out in the form of a jagged sob as she clutched at the sleeve of Liam's coat. "Wh—what about Dom?"

Liam's face softened as he let go of the door. "His remains were found inside."

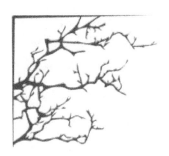

# Chapter 18

"Just aim it right there ... no — *there* ..." An unsteady arm clad in a black leather jacket came into view, and from it, a trembling finger extended into the darkness. "See where I'm pointing?"

"Uh-huh," replied a girl's voice.

The arm lowered and Hector Ramirez's grizzled face appeared. "Make sure you stay behind this tree and don't make a sound."

"How long will you be?"

Hector scratched at his neck, leaving a trail of bright red marks along his unshaven throat. "Not long," he said, turning away.

"When we're done, you're going to drive me to the bus station, right — "

"Stop worrying about the goddamn bus station!" yelled Hector, looking back. "I told you that I would and I meant it! But right now you need to concentrate on what's about to happen—because if you screw this up I'm gonna leave your ass here in the middle of fucking nowhere!"

The clouds behind him began to part, allowing the light from the moon to fall across the bluff, as well as the dark, still water below it.

Something reminiscent of a groan passed between Hector's lips. "No," he said, shaking his head, "don't you dare cry. Please—" He stopped and ran his hands through his hair. "Look, this is just ... I've got a lot riding on this, okay?"

There was a jerky breath followed by a loud sniff.

The corners of Hector's mouth relaxed. "I have to go. Just do what I said, and when I get back I'll drive you to the bus station, okay?"

"How far away is it?"

"How far away is *what*?"

"The bus station."

The frozen ground crunched beneath Hector's feet as he began walking away. "Not far."

"Mister, wait!"

"*What*?"

"The battery on your phone's flashing. It's down to twelve percent."

"Turn it off!" he shouted.

The camera zoomed in on Hector's shoes.

"I said, 'Turn it off'!"

"I'm trying—"

"*Shh*!"

Hector's face appeared again, the muscles in his neck straining as he twisted his head towards the bluff. In between his heavy breathing, the faint sounds of an engine could be heard in the distance. "Shit!" Shoving a branch out of his way, he began scrambling down the small incline.

"Mister, wait!"

"Just keep recording!" he shouted, running towards his Jeep that was parked along the edge of the road. Leaping in front of it, he leaned against its grill and gave a quick glance in the direction he'd just come from before folding his arms across his chest.

Seconds later, a car with one headlight came barreling around the curve and slowed to a stop.

The foliage of a scraggly pine suddenly came into view, blocking what was happening beyond it. As the sound of a door opening resonated in the imposing darkness, a slender hand with a familiar trio of tattoos appeared; with fingers outstretched, it grabbed the limb in front of it and pushed it down, once again providing a clear shot of Hector, who was still in front of his Jeep but no longer leaning against it. Metal slammed against metal, and boots could be heard clomping along the pavement. Taking a stiff stance, Hector uncrossed his arms and—

"That's all there is, Sheriff."

Liam sat back and rubbed his jaw.

"Do you want to see it again?"

Liam shifted his gaze from the frozen image of Hector to Aaron, who was perched on the corner of his desk. "Can you make it any brighter?" he asked, hoping to get a better look at the car.

Aaron shook his head. "It's as bright as it will go."

Letting him have his chair back, Liam stretched as he made his way over to the coffee machine. Although Enid's coffee was the last thing in the world he wanted, the day had been as long as it had miserable and he needed something to put inside his growling stomach. "When was the video taken?"

"According to the time stamp on his phone," Aaron replied, "February sixth at eleven forty-seven."

In spite of the fact that the video helped to fill in a piece of the puzzle regarding Hector's whereabouts, it appeared to hold more questions than it did answers, and Liam could feel the pressure mounting inside him as he poured the watery black liquid into his mug.

"There's something else you need to see, Sheriff," said Aaron, handing him a piece of paper. "Hector made over twenty calls to the same number, including three to it the night he was killed."

Liam scanned the dates and times that Aaron had highlighted. The calls went as far back as December.

"I tried the number," Aaron continued. "No answer."

"Probably a burner phone," Stiles offered, clasping his fingers behind his head as he leaned back in his chair.

"Did you show the girl's picture to the schools?" asked Liam, directing his attention to Gordon as he pressed the mug to his lips.

"I did, but no one recognized her," he answered, propping his feet on the side of Aaron's desk. "And if I'd seen this footage first, I wouldn't have bothered going over there at all."

Liam forced the burnt-flavored coffee that was floating on his tongue down his throat. "And why's that?"

"Because she believed Ramirez about there being a bus station in Weeping Rock for *one* thing," he said, using the same belligerent tone on him that he had in the chapel, "and the other is that she kept calling him Mister. It's obvious she didn't know him."

"How did she come to be standing on the bluff with him, then?"

Gordon cut his eyes over to Aaron. "It's called hitchhiking. Ever hear of it?"

Aaron's nostrils flared. "Have you ever heard of *iníla yaŋka yo?*"

"What did you just say to me?" asked Gordon, placing his feet on the floor.

"He *said,* shut up," Liam snapped, setting his mug on the table.

The bell above the door clanged.

Glancing over his shoulder, Liam saw a short, heavy-set woman with brown wavy hair coming towards him. "Mrs. Boyd," he said, hiding his grimace behind a tight-lipped smile.

"Sheriff Matthews," she replied, then tilting her head, peered around his shoulder. "Boys."

Liam listened to Stiles and Red Elk clearing their throats.

"Ma'am," they mumbled in unison.

The woman shifted her large almond-shaped eyes back to Liam. "Is this a bad time?"

"No," he said, leaning across Aaron's desk to retrieve Hector's phone.

"Then might I have a word with you?"

"Of course," he replied, straightening.

Loretta Boyd arched a thin, misshapen eyebrow at him. "In private?"

Holding onto his sigh, Liam extended his hand towards his office and reluctantly followed her inside. "Is this about the infant we found the other night?" he asked, swinging the door closed.

The woman's eyebrow rose higher, increasing the wrinkles on the right side of her forehead. "Is there another one I don't know about?"

Liam's face flushed. "No."

"Then what do you *think*?" she replied, plopping herself down in the chair across from his desk.

Biting his tongue, Liam grabbed the back of his own chair and sat down.

"Now, what can you tell me about the mother?"

"Nothing," he said, placing Hector's phone on a stack of files. "We haven't been able to make a positive ID on her."

Loretta Boyd's condescending expression grew deeper, causing the extra layer of fat surrounding her neck to drop into the folds of her paisley scarf. "How old would you say she was?"

"Thirteen, maybe fourteen."

"She's probably a runaway. Have you checked with the surrounding counties?"

Liam dug his elbow into the arm of the chair and leaned back. "Her picture was sent out yester—"

"That's fine," she said, flicking her hand at him as if she were swatting away a fly. "I don't have much time, so I'm going to cut to the chase."

Resting his chin on the pad of his thumb, Liam pressed his knuckles against his lips ... waiting.

After crossing her legs, which reminded him of two ham hocks stuffed inside a pair of heels, she reached down and pulled a manila folder from her purse. "I spoke with the attending pediatrician at the hospital this afternoon. He told me that the baby's doing much better and should be released sometime next week."

Liam let go of his anger long enough to offer up a silent prayer of thanks. "That's good news."

"Which is why you need to locate the mother's family as soon as possible."

"We're working on it."

"Time isn't exactly on our side here, Sheriff," she stated, "so let me give you some unsolicited advice.

You need to spend less of it trying to track down who killed that baseball player and more of it attempting to find this girl's relatives, or at the very least, the baby's father."

Liam pressed his knuckles harder against his lips. There were lots of things he missed about being a deputy, and having the luxury of handing Loretta Boyd off to his father was one of them. "We're doing everything we can to identify her," he finally said.

"Well, until that happens, I need to place the baby with a foster family, and right now I don't have any with the means to currently care for an infant—which brings me to the reason I'm here."

Reaching across his desk, Liam took the folder she was offering and flipped it open. As the words on the paper came into focus, he felt his chest tighten. "This is—" He stopped to clear the emotions that had swarmed his throat. "This is from a year ago."

"Yes—well, organizational skills weren't one of my predecessor's strongest attributes. I found your approved application mixed in with another file a few weeks back." Settling into her chair, she gave Liam a bemused look. "I take it that you were never told you were approved?"

"No," he replied, the word coming out in a half-whisper.

"Well, surprise," she said dryly, "you are."

Liam sat forward. "Are you saying that my wife and I can adopt this baby?"

"No, I'm saying that you can *foster* this baby until the mother's family is found. And depending on what happens after that, adoption is certainly a possibility."

In disbelief of what he was hearing, Liam turned his hand over. "Just like that?"

The woman laughed. "Yes, just like that," she said, yet her never-before-seen smile had barely registered on her lips before it ran in the other direction. "Unless something has changed that I need to know about."

Liam forced his gaze to remain locked with hers. "No."

"Good," she said, slapping her hands against her knees, "I'll be in touch."

Jumping up from his chair, Liam hurried around his desk to get the door for her, bumping into two filing cabinets and a trashcan along the way. "Thank you."

The woman's eyes glimmered beneath the fluorescent lighting as she turned to look at him. "I'll talk to you tomorrow."

Sliding his hands in his pockets, Liam pressed his back against the doorjamb and took several unencumbered breaths as he watched her leave.

"Everything all right, Sheriff?"

He shifted his gaze to Aaron who was watching him from across the room. "Everything's fine," he answered, yanking his coat off the back of the chair. "I'll see you in the morning."

ALICE CUPPED HER HANDS around the stream of water coming out of the faucet and splashed it across her face. The warmth of it stung her cheeks, making her close her eyes. She would've liked nothing more than to indulge in a hot shower, but knowing her mother's cleaning habits — or rather the lack thereof — decided against it. Patting her face dry with a towel that smelled of mint toothpaste, she opened her eyes and stared into the small mirror mounted over the vanity. The swelling in her forehead had gone down some, but the skin circling the knot was in the process of turning a purplish black. Hitting the light switch with her elbow, she walked out and made her way towards the room at the end of the hall.

Claire was sitting cross-legged in the middle of the bed, her phone inches from her face.

"You know," said Alice, summoning a small smile as she nodded at the poster of the unicorn hanging above the headboard, "this used to be my room."

"I *know*."

Alice sat down on the bed beside her and reached out to stroke her hair. "Sweetheart, listen — "

"How long do we have to stay here?" Claire asked, looking up from her phone.

Alice tilted her head in a sympathetic manner. "For a while."

Returning her gaze to her phone, Claire's stoic expression began to fluctuate.

"I'm sorry," said Alice, putting her arms around her.

Claire promptly slid out of her clutches and flopped onto her side.

Having learned over the past year that this was her daughter's way of shutting down—it had started the week before the arrival of her first period and never left—Alice ignored the motherly instinct to caress her mottled cheek and slowly stood up. "Goodnight, sweetheart. I love you," she said, and although she didn't expect a reply along the same lines in return found herself listening hard for one anyway as she walked towards the door.

The sound of canned laughter trickled in from the hall, drowning out the silence.

Swallowing her sigh, Alice closed the door behind her and wearily made her way into the living room, where she discovered her mother bent over the sofa as she tucked the ends of a sheet between its cushions. She started to tell her not to bother, but upon realizing that it would help to mask the smell of twenty-plus years of cigarette smoke, crossed her arms instead and leaned against the wall. On top of everything else that had transpired today, her mother's appearance had come as a shock, and although she wouldn't say why she'd chosen to dye her beautiful red locks the color of a banana, Alice suspected it might have had something to do with her having turned sixty last month.

"*Aawwwwwk*! Who's a pretty boy?"

Alice cut her eyes to Petey, her mother's parakeet. Strutting across the wooden dowel that was serving as his perch, his blue-feathered head bobbed up and down like a cork on a string as he pecked at the mirror fastened to the bars of his cage while making kissing noises at it.

"Is Claire asleep?"

"Not yet," replied Alice, returning her attention to her mother, who was still fussing with the sheet.

"Well, maybe if she'd put that damn phone down for a minute, she would be."

"She's upset," Alice said, the muscles in the back of her neck growing taut as she pushed herself away from the wall, "and if she wants to stay up and talk to her friends, I'm not about to tell her that she can't."

"You know, in my day, talking to someone meant a verbal exchange of words—not typing LOL with a smiley face," her mother grumbled. "Just how much of a meaningful conversation can you have with someone spelling their feelings out in acronyms and sending you tiny cartoon pics?" Straightening, she turned from the sofa. "Besides, what in the world does she have to be upset about?"

Picking up the remote, Alice aimed it at the TV, which had become unbearably loud, and gave her mother a disbelieving look. "You can't be serious," she said, dropping her arms. "I just yanked her away from her friends, as well as the only real home she's ever known—and on top of all that, I had to tell her that her father was dead."

Her mother grabbed a red and gold afghan off the back of the chair and began spreading it across the sheet. "Well, I don't see how it's possible for her to be upset over losing someone that she has absolutely no memory of." Letting go of the afghan, she cast a set of piercing green eyes in Alice's direction. "Unless you've been filling that mind of hers up with *fairy tales* about him."

The stiffness in Alice's neck expanded to the left side of her jaw. "They weren't fairy tales," she replied in a defensive tone. "You didn't know Dom the way I did. He was—"

"No different than Michael!" her mother snapped, gesturing at the bruise on her forehead.

A sharp breath found its way inside Alice's lungs. "Well," she said, arching her brow, "like mother like daughter."

Her mother's pale cheeks ignited, consuming her entire face.

Silence and sunflower shells crunched beneath Alice's feet as she stalked past her and flopped onto the sofa. Knowing that tears were imminent, she hurriedly pulled the afghan around her shoulders and drew her knees to her chest.

"It is beyond me," her mother finally said, smoothing her hair as if it had been ruffled by

Alice's words, "how you can be sitting there mourning a man like that, *and* ..." She paused to shake her head. "Unless that two hundred and fifty thousand he stole was in a waterproof bag, you can bet that everyone else in this town's going to be wondering the same thing."

"Petey's a pretty boy ... *aawwwwwk!*"

Regretting the fact of ever having called her mother, Alice turned her face into the afghan, letting the scratchy yarn absorb her tears.

"*Was* the money in the car?"

A large truck rumbled down the street, rattling the front windows of the house.

Twisting around, Alice parted the curtains hanging behind the sofa and peered outside.

"Alice Mae?"

Refusing to meet the expectant look that had undoubtedly accompanied her mother's question, Alice continued to stare out the window, watching the taillights of the truck grow smaller and smaller until they were swallowed up by the darkness. "Liam didn't say."

CLOSING THE GARAGE door behind him, Liam hurried across the foyer and into the kitchen. "Olivia?" he called, setting the box on the table. "Olivia—"

"Pizza, huh?"

Liam hid his disappointment at the sound of his father's voice. "Where's Olivia?" he asked, retrieving two plates from the dish rack before conducting a search of the cluttered countertop for napkins.

"I already answered that question for you once today," his father grumbled.

Giving up on the napkins, Liam reached under the cabinet and tore off several sheets of paper towels instead.

"I don't like mushrooms."

"That's not for you," said Liam, snapping the lid on the box closed. "*This* is."

His father took the sack he was holding out to him and peered inside it. "What is—"

"A meatball sub. And I need for you to eat it in your room."

"Why?"

"I just do," said Liam, raising his voice.

Shoving the sack into his caddy with a scowl, his father started across the kitchen floor.

Liam pursed his lips. "You're going the wrong way."

"I need somethin' to drink."

"I'll bring you a beer in a minute," he said, turning his walker in the opposite direction.

"I can do it myself," his father snapped, jerking it out of his grasp. "What are you tryin' to do, anyway? Make up for them dead flowers?"

"Something like that," Liam replied, glancing towards the hallway. When he looked back, he saw that his father hadn't moved. "Dad — "

"I'm goin', but first give me an update on the Ramirez case."

Liam shook his head. "I'll show you later."

His father's eyebrows knitted together, making it look as if a fuzzy gray caterpillar — the kind that inflicted pain when touched — had taken up residence on his forehead. "Show me what?"

Out of the corner of his eye, Liam saw the unmistakable silhouette of his wife's slender figure standing in the entrance of the hall.

"Show me *what*?"

"*Later*," Liam hissed, waving him away.

Picking up his walker, his father gave him another scowl before shuffling out of the kitchen.

"You're home early."

Wiping his hands on his pants, Liam turned to Olivia. "Hi," he said, offering her a hopeful smile. She didn't reciprocate but didn't stomp back to the bedroom either. Encouraged, he nodded at the table. "I thought we could have — "

The door to the den slammed shut.

" — dinner together," he finished.

Olivia's gaze went from Liam to the den, and then back to Liam. Emerging from the hallway, she walked into the kitchen and sat down.

Choosing the seat closest to her, he flipped open the lid to the pizza box and handed her a plate.

"Thank you."

He flashed her another smile. "You're welcome." Despite the exchange of pleasantries, however, the tension between them remained, causing Liam to feel as if he were suffocating. As he reached up to unbutton his collar, his radio gave off a series of beeps. He listened intently to the chatter on it for a moment and then turned the volume down.

"Do you have to go?" asked Olivia.

"No," he answered, uncertain if he heard disappointment or relief in her words. Without thinking, he reached over and placed his hand on top of hers as it lay upon the table. "I'm sorry about last night … and I'm sorry about your job."

Her knuckles tensed beneath his palm, yet remained where they were. "It's all right," she finally said.

Finishing his bite of pizza, Liam wiped his mouth on the paper towel as he tried in vain to recall the imaginary conversation he'd had with her on his way home, but as he listened to the jumble of sentences trouncing around in his brain, he became acutely aware of how stupid they all sounded. Not helping matters was the *COPS* theme song, which had begun blasting through the walls of the den.

"Is there something wrong?"

He looked up to find Olivia staring at him. "No," he said, clenching the paper towel between his fingers, "but there *is* something I need to talk to you about."

Olivia returned her gaze to her plate. "What is it?"

Taking in a small breath, Liam leaned forward. "Loretta Boyd from Child Services came to see me earlier. Our application from so long ago got lost in the cracks, but it's been approved. And you know the baby that was found at the truck stop?" Unable to contain his excitement, he paused to grin at her. "Well, she wants us to foster him."

Several seconds passed — and then the curve of Olivia's jaw began to harden. "You are unbelievable," she said, jerking her hand out from underneath his.

Liam's grin faded.

"All of this," she shouted, making a sweeping gesture with her hand as she got up from the table, "was nothing more than a way for you to push your own agenda!"

Slumping against his seat, Liam rubbed his forehead. "I don't have an *agenda*, Olivia."

"And your father doesn't *disgust* me," she countered, turning away.

"You're missing the point," he called, doing a poor job of hiding his anger as he watched her march out of the kitchen.

"Am I?" she yelled.

Determined not to let this go sideways, he got to his feet and started after her. "Olivia, wait," he said, throwing his hand up to keep their bedroom door from slamming in his face. Pushing it out of his path, he stepped inside and caught her by the elbow, stopping her before she could escape into the bathroom.

"Let go!"

"Listen to me," he said in a soft voice, cupping her chin in his hand. "I know how much you want a baby, and I also know that adoption isn't your first choice. But after the last time ..." He paused to swallow and shook his head. "I thought we'd come to terms with the fact that one's not going to happen without the other. That's why we filled out the application."

Olivia's eyes flickered, causing their blueness to disintegrate. "I think *you're* the one who's missing the point," she said, shoving against his wrist. "Several of them, in fact."

Letting her go, the shag carpeting scraped along the bottom of Liam's socks as he walked over to the foot of the bed. "What am I missing?" he asked, forcing himself to sit down.

"First of all," she began, "fostering a baby isn't the same as adopting one."

"I know that," he replied, struggling not to snap at her, "but Loretta Boyd said that we could —"

"We would end up caring for him just long enough to get attached, and then have to give him back."

"I don't believe that's going to be the case with this baby," he said, knowing that his chances of identifying the girl diminished with each passing day.

"It's a baby that isn't *ours*, Liam!" she shouted. "He's the by-product of some fourteen-year-old runaway — who most likely chose crack over prenatals and is probably *brain-damaged* because of it!"

Giving a subtle glance towards the den, Liam wearily got to his feet. "There's been no indication from the doctor of either of those things."

"You know what — fine! Let's just say for the sake of argument that you're right. I'm going to go out on a limb here and guess that you haven't told Loretta Boyd about my arrest!"

His gaze faltered.

Olivia's hands flailed out from her sides. "My God, Liam! You know she's going to hear about it from someone in this town sooner or later! What do you think's going to happen then?"

The wind outside began to howl, rattling the windowpane beside them.

"An arrest doesn't matter," he answered, talking loud enough to be heard over the noise. "What matters is that you haven't been convicted. The hearing next week is only for the defense to present their evidence to the judge for him to determine if there's enough to warrant a trial."

Her mouth began to tremble. "You and I both know that's only a formality."

Belinda G. Buchanan

"If that's the case — and that's a *big* if," said Liam, holding up a finger for emphasis, "I'll go straight over to Loretta Boyd and talk to her."

"And tell her *what*?"

The tears that had started down Olivia's hollowed cheeks carved their way through Liam's heart like a jagged piece of glass. Reaching out, he wrapped his arms around her and pulled her close. "Sweetheart," he whispered, kissing her tenderly on the side of her face, "you're worrying about things that haven't happened."

"Just stop," she said, pushing against him.

"*What*?"

Bowing her head, Olivia ran the tip of her knuckle up and down the bridge of her nose. "Even if all these things you said come to pass," she finally said, "adopting this baby isn't going to magically fix our marriage."

The whole house shuddered, dimming the lights, as the wind screamed to get in.

Dropping her hand, Olivia slowly raised her eyes to meet his. "*You* know it, and *I* know it."

A burning sensation began to fill Liam's lungs. "Olivia," he said, reaching for her again.

Shaking her head, she took a step backward. "Tell me I'm wrong."

Liam's breath grew labored in the piercing silence that followed. Her statement had absolutely no merit, and yet as much as he wanted to refute it … could not find the words to do so.

230

Olivia's chin flattened, cutting a swath of dimples across the middle of it. "That's what I thought," she whispered.

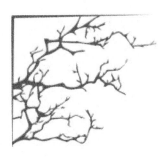

# Chapter 19

**A**lice inserted her card into the ATM reader and rolled her neck along her shoulders as she waited for the next prompt on the screen.

*This card is invalid*

She pulled it out and reinserted it, making sure to push it all the way in.

*This card is invalid*

Thinking she'd put it in the wrong way, she checked it and tried again.

*This card is invalid*

As a small sense of uneasiness began to circle her, she calmly removed the card and wiped it on the sleeve of her coat several times before returning it to the slot.

*This card is invalid*

"Goddamn you, Michael!" she swore, ripping the card from the reader.

A gruff laugh rang out. "I guess her shoppin' excursion's been canceled," said its owner in a loud voice.

A second laugh followed, yet was different from the first; obnoxious and high-pitched, it sounded more hyena than human.

Clenching the card between her fingers, Alice turned and saw two men, who between them didn't appear to have a whole set of teeth, grinning at her in a deprecating manner as they sat in their bibbed overalls and greasy ball caps drinking coffee. Dropping the bankcard into her pocket, Alice cut her gaze hard across their faces as she walked past them, hoping that the serrated blade she'd attached to it would draw blood. It didn't, but it did succeed in slicing the smile right off the lips of the smaller man.

Satisfied, she shifted her eyes to the front of the store and continued on. As she came to the end of the aisle, she paused to grab a bag of Claire's favorite chips—only to put it back when she saw the ridiculous price that had been stamped on it. Marching past the register, she threw all her weight against a door plastered with beer and energy drink posters and swiftly exited *Jolly's Stop-N-Save*.

The cold instantly seized her, stinging the small cut that sat nestled in the middle of the welt adorning her forehead. As she hurried across the dimly lit parking lot, it wasn't long before she felt something warm beginning to slide down her cheeks. Forcing herself to maintain her pace, she was uncertain if this sudden onslaught of waterworks was due to the fact that her stay in Weeping Rock had just been extended indefinitely ... or the painful realization that she'd wasted the better part of three years of her life on Michael.

Licking the salt from her chapped lips, Alice shoved her thoughts to the side as she turned the corner and started down the decaying sidewalk that stretched the length of Lummis Court. As she wiped at her face, the top of the sun began to peek over the houses, casting its pale light upon their frost-covered roofs.

While growing up, she'd always thought it odd that the houses in her neighborhood, as well as the ones lining the two streets that sat on either side of it, were identical. From their green asphalt shingles, to the white siding, to the small covered stoops serving as porches, there was nothing that differentiated one from the other. Walking home from school, she used to have to count the driveways. Hers was the thirteenth on the left. Most days she wouldn't count, but rather look for the one with the dark-blue truck in it. Traipsing up the drive, she would run her fingers along the top of its chipped hood, its engine still warm from where her father had ended his shift at the textile mill, and glance towards the porch where he would be waiting.

Leaning against the decorative iron column, he'd put out his cigarette on the bottom of his boot and squat down, scooping her up in his orangutan-like arms while calling her by some corny version of her name like Alice Malice has a Palace or Alice the Chalice. She would laugh, and he'd squeeze her tight, pinning her face against his shirt where the smell of nicotine, detergent, and whiskey always lingered.

Alice sighed and buried her chin deeper inside the collar of her coat. She'd spent her formative years demanding her father's attention, and her teenage ones ignoring him. She'd been good at both, yet had excelled at the latter, driving a wedge between them so tight that she couldn't even bring herself to say goodbye to him the day he'd packed up and left her and her mother for good.

A blaring horn rose out of the waking darkness, startling her.

Jerking her head in the direction it had come from, she saw that a man in a red Dodge truck was waiting for her to get out of the middle of his driveway so he could back up. Retreating to the sidewalk, she locked eyes with the man as he rolled past. Recognizing him as her mother's longtime neighbor, she gave a friendly wave. Narrowing his gaze, he answered her with a squall of tires. As Alice watched the pickup haul ass down the street, she slowly came to realize that although eleven years had come and gone, the people of Weeping Rock were not about to forgive her for her husband's transgressions ...

*"Where are we going, Mommy?"*

*Alice paused to tuck a frazzled lock of hair behind her ear before unbuckling Claire from her car seat. "To see Daddy for a minute."*

*Taking her fingers out of her mouth, Claire smiled and raised her arms.*

*Smiling back, Alice wiped the traces of grape juice from her chin as she lifted her out.*

*The heat coming off the pavement seeped through the bottoms of Alice's sandals, causing the heels of her feet to slip against their imitation leather as she hurried past the small, plastic-like flags that had been hung from the lampposts to commemorate the Fourth of July. Cutting across the street, she made her way towards the tan brick building that sat on the corner.*

*A blast of cold air greeted them as they stepped inside.*

*"Where's Daddy?"*

*"I'm sure he's in his office," Alice answered, glancing at the closed door on her right.*

*"Where's Diane?"*

*Shifting her gaze to the empty desk in front of her, Alice stared at the stacks of papers strewn across its top. "Diane might not be working today," she replied, although the faint sounds of a shredder could be heard running in the back room.*

*"Why?"*

*"Because today's a holiday."*

*"What's a howiday?"*

*Alice responded with an impatient sigh to what had to have been her two-and-a-half-year-old daughter's fiftieth question since having left the house all of twenty minutes ago. Fortunately, for both of them, the shredder cut off and high heels could be heard clicking across the wide-plank flooring.*

*A moment later, Diane Travis appeared carrying a black garbage bag. "Alice!" she exclaimed. "I'm sorry. I didn't hear you come in."*

*"It's okay," she replied, dismissing her apology with a wave of her hand.*

*Setting the bag on the floor, Diane turned her attention to Claire and grinned. "Hi, sweetie."*

*Claire's exasperating curiosity was suddenly consumed by a bout of shyness, causing her to do a sharp head dive into Alice's shoulder.*

*"Aww, what's the matter?" The ends of Diane's long raven hair fell across her silk blouse as she tugged at Claire's toes. "Cat got your tongue?"*

*Clutching the chain of Alice's necklace with her sticky fingers, Claire giggled and kicked her feet.*

*"So," said Diane, her eyes towering above Alice's as she straightened, "what are the two of you doing out on such a miserable day?"*

*"I'd rather be at home right now, believe me," Alice said, hoisting Claire farther up her hip, "but I need to see Dom for a second. Is he here?"*

*"He's in his office. You can go on in."*

*"Thanks," Alice replied, starting towards the door.*

*"Do you want me to take your jacket?"*

*Alice glanced down at the faded denim covering her arms and shook her head. "No, I'm fine. It's always a little too cold in here for my taste."*

*Diane laughed. "Well, I'm burning up just looking at you," she said, fanning herself with her hand.*

*The telephone rang, its subdued tone reminding Alice of a chirping cricket.*

*Excusing herself, Diane hurried around the desk. "Thank you for calling Black Hills Term Life Insurance," she said, the diamond on her ring finger sparkling brightly in the light as she held the receiver to her ear. "How may I help you? I'm sorry, but Mr. Malloy is with someone at the moment." She turned and gave Alice a wink. "Can I take a message?"*

*Grasping the knob with her free hand, Alice pulled her thoughts together and walked inside.*

*Dom was standing in front of the window with his back to the door, his broad shoulders, housed in a crisp blue button-down, blocked most of the sun's light as it streamed through the slatted blinds. "Yeah," he said, speaking into the mouthpiece of the corded phone, "whatever you have available. It just needs to be today."*

*Switching Claire to her other hip, Alice closed the door behind her.*

*Dom turned sharply at the sound and clasped his fingers over the receiver. "What are you doing here?" he asked in a tone that told her his mood from last night hadn't improved.*

*"Hi, Daddy — "*

*"Yes?" he said, taking his hand away from the phone. "No, just email me the confirmation. ... Okay, thanks."*

*"Daddy?" Claire reached out for him as he placed the receiver back on its cradle.*

*"What are you doing here?" Dom repeated, moving away from the window.*

*"You left your PDA on the nightstand," Alice said, adjusting her grip on Claire to keep her from tumbling*

*out of her arms when he made no motion to take her. "I thought you might need it."*

*He took the instrument from her and placed it on the edge of his desk. "Thank you."*

*The sound of the shredder starting up again filtered through the transom above the door, filling the room with a nervous hum.*

*"Daddy?"*

*Alice leaned forward, thrusting Claire's tiny, outstretched arms into Dom's. "Give Daddy a kiss," she said, forcing him to interact with his daughter.*

*Small wisps of fine red hair fell across Dom's neatly trimmed mustache as Claire planted a slobbery kiss on his cheek.*

*Wiping his face, he kept his gaze locked on Alice. "I'll see you at home."*

*Determined to say what she'd come here to tell him, Alice took a deep breath and shook her head. "No, you won't."*

*Dom's hands moved to his hips. "What the hell does that mean?"*

*"I'm going to be staying at my mother's for a while," she said, using Claire as a buffer between them.*

*A thin white line formed across Dom's knuckles, yet after several seconds, it, along with the darkness in his face, began to recede. "Well, I guess that's probably for the best," he replied.*

*Alice blinked, bewildered by his answer. She had done nothing all morning except prepare herself for the argument that she knew this particular moment would bring. It was a moment that should not have come and gone this easily.*

*"If anyone should call and ask about me while you're there,"* he said, lowering his hands. *"I don't want you talking to them. Understand?"*

Alice gave him a wary look. *"Who's anyone?"*

He shrugged. *"Just — anyone."*

Apprehension flooded Alice's throat, sending her breath rushing out of it. *"What have you done, Dom?"*

*"It doesn't matter what I've done!"* he yelled, knocking his PDA to the floor. *"What matters is that you follow my fucking directions!"*

Claire recoiled against Alice with a whimper, burying her face in her chest. Clutching the back of her head, Alice turned and hurried towards the door.

*"Alice, wait."*

Unable to keep herself from glancing over her shoulder, she saw that Dom's chiseled features had taken on a pained expression.

*"I'm sorry for losing my temper just now, and I'm sorry about last night."*

*"Somehow, I doubt that,"* she replied, the words rolling off her tongue in short order.

With lightning speed, he caught her around the waist and pulled her towards him, making her wince as her upper arm fell against his collarbone.

*"Dom, please …"*

Straddling her feet with his own, he placed his other hand on her neck. *"I never meant to hurt you,"* he said in a voice that was suddenly as broken as it was tender. *"I swear it."*

The rims of Alice's eyelids began to burn.

"And I know it's no excuse," he continued, shaking his head, "but this audit with the IRS has really got me stressed out ..."

As he pleaded his case, his breath roamed intently along Alice's exposed skin, prickling her flesh.

"I'm going a little crazy right now."

"It's all right," she said, her frustration with herself growing by leaps and bounds as she felt her anger towards him slipping away. Fighting to hold onto it, she forced her mouth back open. "But I need some time."

A single tear, small and irregularly shaped, rolled down the left side of his face, yet evaporated before reaching the outer fringes of his mustache. "I want you to call me when you get to your mother's," he said, his coal-black eyes penetrating hers as he caressed the edge of her cheek with his thumb. "And remember what I told you."

With her surroundings fading from her sight, she moved her head up and down in obedient fashion.

"I promise you," he whispered, bringing his mouth closer to hers, "that we're going to get through this ..."

Although Alice had heard it all before, the hope inside her sprang eternal — and as the heat from his lips radiated towards her own, the lower part of her body began to thrum ...

"Where have you been?"

Alice looked up to find Claire leaning out the back door of the kitchen. "For a walk," she replied, shivering as the warmth of Dom's touch left her.

"You don't *walk*."

Stamping her feet on the welcome mat, Alice brushed past her and headed straight for the coffee machine. "You're up early," she remarked, hoping to change the subject.

"You can blame Grandma's bird for that."

Alice slid the can of coffee towards her. "Where *is* your grandma?"

"In the shower. She says that it's her early day and that she has to be at the beauty shop by seven."

Being grateful for small favors, Alice scooped the grounds into the filter and began filling the coffee pot with water.

"Mom?" Claire appeared beside her. "The sheriff that took us to Michael's house to pack before bringing us here," she said, running her fingers along the edge of the sink, "do you know him?"

"Why are you asking?"

"A simple yes or no will do," Claire said in a tone that was eerily reminiscent of her mother's.

Dumping the water into the top of the machine, Alice set the pot on the burner and turned around. Her daughter's eyes were almost level with her own, and bore an arrogance that was beyond her years. "What makes you think I know him?" she asked, refusing to placate her.

Claire sighed and folded her arms. "Because you kept calling each other by your first names."

Feeling her face flush, Alice grasped the knob on the cabinet in front of her and pulled it open. "We used to date," she said, hiding behind the painted door as she searched the shelves for a mug that wasn't chipped.

"You're kidding."

Alice's lips grew taut. "Is that really *so* hard for you to believe?" she asked, slamming the cabinet closed.

"*No,*" replied Claire, dragging the word out as she gave a sarcastic shrug.

"Then why are you acting so surprised?"

"Because during the entire ride here," Claire said, leaning against the counter, "he seemed really mad at you."

THE SUN YAWNED AND stretched its sleepy rays, flooding the ground beneath Liam's feet with daylight as he waded into the overgrown brush. Treading carefully, he headed towards a scruffy pine that wasn't much taller than the weeds surrounding it and crouched behind its slender trunk. Reaching out with his hand, he grabbed hold of the drooping branch in front of him and pushed it out of his way. His truck, which had been parked deliberately near the edge of the bluff, came into view.

Certain that this was where the girl had hidden while recording Hector, Liam knelt and began scouring the wet earth below him in the hopes of finding something she may have left behind. After ten minutes of searching through the muck and leaves, however, it became clear that there was nothing to be found. Pushing himself to his feet, he wiped his hands on his pants and sighed.

Up until yesterday, he had assumed the girl was a local, yet after reviewing the footage on Hector's phone was inclined to believe Gordon's theory that she'd been hitchhiking that night. Logistically, it made sense, as *Ike's Truck Stop* sat adjacent to Highway 81, which ran for thirty miles east to west across the county — before branching off into I-90 — and was less than a mile from Hector's house.

Retrieving his phone from his pocket, Liam pulled up the photo that Gordon had snapped of the girl just before she'd been placed inside the body bag. His jaw stiffened as he ran his thumb along the edge of the screen. The girl was in the wrong place at the wrong time. Hector had stumbled upon her by pure chance, and in her desperation to flee whatever it was she was running from, had agreed to help him — only to end up dead.

A series of beeps sounded.

"County to any available unit. Signal 2 at 339 Bethel Road."

Hoping that a passing state trooper would handle the call, Liam remained quiet, yet after several seconds of silence grabbed his radio. "This is Sheriff Matthews responding. ETA twenty minutes." Clipping the instrument back to his belt, he made his way down the small incline and started across the road.

As he drew closer to his truck, he could see the mist rising off the lake and stopped to peer over the edge of the bluff. Minus the jagged outcropping of rock, it was a seventy-five-foot drop straight down from where he was standing, and he found himself hoping that Weeping Rock's "golden boy" had been killed prior to being tossed over its side.

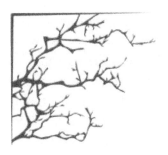

# Chapter 20

The phone lines at the front counter rang nonstop, their shrill bleats, combined with Enid's pinched voice, making Liam press his fingers harder against his temple as he sat at his desk scrolling through Hector's cell. A little while ago, Dr. Fuller had released a statement informing the public that Hector's death had been ruled a homicide, sending the press into a frenzy.

Setting the phone aside, Liam leaned back in his chair and rubbed his eyes. Although he had been at it for close to two hours, he'd yet to come across anything of value. Apart from the mystery number Hector had called, he hadn't been in touch with any of his four hundred plus contacts besides Kiki in months, and other than one sloppily misspelled text he'd sent in January pledging his undying love to her, the rest were short and to the point and had to do with their reality show. Kiki's replies were even shorter, usually answering him with a single word — except for the 'fuck you' in all caps she'd sent to him on Christmas Day.

The bulk of the phone's memory consisted primarily of shirtless selfies of Hector either standing in front of his bathroom mirror or lying in bed beneath a strategically placed sheet, all of which had been posted to his followers through his numerous social media accounts.

There were no emails in any of his folders, except for two unopened notifications from his bank informing him that he was overdrawn on his checking account. In regard to his voicemail messages, there were none, saved or otherwise, leading Liam to believe that despite his fame, Hector had led a very lonely existence.

"Here you go, Sheriff."

Looking up, Liam took the messages Enid was holding out to him and began sifting through them. They were all from various news outlets across the country wanting an update on Hector's case. "Don't give me any more of these," he said, tossing them on the pile with the others. "Or better yet, just don't even write them down."

"No more messages," said Enid, walking out of his office. "Got it."

"From *news stations*!" he yelled.

"Got it!" she yelled back.

Shoving the slips of paper out of his way, Liam picked up Hector's phone once more. Clicking on its browser history, he saw that Hector had looked up two restaurants in Atlanta, done fifteen searches of himself, and visited three porn sites. With the next page showing more of the same, he started to close out of it—but stopped when he noticed that buried in the middle of it all, was a single search on how to forge a prescription.

Reaching across his desk, he flipped open Hector's file and began sorting through the photos until he found the one he was looking for. Among the drug paraphernalia discovered in Ramirez's Jeep were several empty prescription bottles. A closer look revealed that all of them had been prescribed by a Dr. Randall Shaw in Rapid City and filled by *Elmar's Drug Mart*.

"Stiles?" called Liam, rising from his chair.

A moment later, his deputy came shuffling in. "Yeah?"

Liam handed him the photo. "I need you to pay a visit to this doctor. Find out if he actually saw Ramirez."

Stiles glanced at the picture and cocked his eyebrow. "Oxy, huh?"

"Yeah," replied Liam, "and I have my doubts that he came by it legally."

Gordon returned the picture to him. "I'm leaving now to transport an inmate from County over to Regional for a psych eval," he said, pulling a pack of Camels from his shirt pocket. "I'll stop by Shaw's office on the way back."

"Which inmate?"

"Bertram."

Liam frowned. Ever since Gilbert Bertram's mother had passed in November, the frequency of calls to his residence had increased, yet aside from one instance of public indecency in his front yard, most of the complaints had been for noise, and he was considered to be nothing more than a harmless nuisance. Things had unfortunately taken a turn for the worse last week, however, when he'd broken into his neighbor's house and assaulted him with a shovel. "What's the reason for the psych eval?"

"He tried to set the mattress in his cell on fire this morning," replied Gordon, digging a cigarette out of the pack. "Claims his neighbor was hiding inside it."

Liam gave a small sigh. "Let me know what you find out from Shaw," he said, sitting back down in his chair.

Twirling his keys around his index finger, Stiles turned and walked out of his office.

After hearing the front door to the station open, Liam's gaze promptly shifted to the window, where he watched his deputy pause in the middle of the parking lot to light his cigarette — and smoke it — before slipping inside his truck.

"Sheriff?"

Liam sucked in his breath. "What?"

"I've got Myrtle Jespersen on the phone. She's demanding to know when she's gonna get the three thousand dollars back that Dominick Malloy stole from her."

Tilting his head to the left, Liam cracked his neck. "Tell her I'm still sorting it out," he said. Aside from it being low on his list of priorities, he had absolutely no idea how to even go about handling such a task.

As the phones continued to ring, he returned his attention to Hector's cell. Pulling up the video, he fast-forwarded it to the last few seconds and silently watched as the car appeared in the frame. He'd spent most of the morning reviewing the footage and had noticed that there was a considerable distance between the headlight and taillights. As the video neared the three-minute mark, Liam hit the pause button and brought the phone closer to his face. The moon glinted off the car's rear quarter panel as it came around the curve, enabling him to see that it sat low to the ground and was light in color, maybe gray or —

"Sheriff?"

"*What!*"

"Loretta Boyd's on line one," Enid called, matching his snarky tone.

Liam's anger faded as quickly as it had come. "Tell her I'll talk to her later," he said, half-heartedly returning his attention to the video.

"Uh, Sheriff?"

He looked up to find Aaron standing in front of his desk.

"Fuller's office just faxed over the tox screen on Ramirez," he said, flicking his gaze towards the pink slips of paper that were scattered across the floor.

"*And?*"

Aaron looked back at him. "And his blood tested positive for heroin."

Shoving Hector's phone into the drawer, Liam got to his feet. "Feel like taking a ride?"

ALTHOUGH LIAM WAS GRATEFUL to be away from the ringing telephones at the station, he soon found the silence inside the cab of his truck to be just as irritating as his thoughts began to drift. Olivia's reaction to his news last night was the last thing in the world he'd been expecting, and her words that had followed had left him more than a little unsettled.

"Did you catch the game last night?" he said to Aaron, determined not to let himself dwell on Olivia — or the state of their marriage.

Aaron yawned and stretched his legs underneath the dash as far as they would go. "No, I missed it. Who won?"

"I don't know," Liam replied, pulling into the gravel parking lot on his right, "that's why I was asking."

Opening his door, Aaron let out a small sigh as he shook his head. "My evening consisted of watching three straight hours of Nickelodeon with Caleb."

"You sure it wasn't *Here Comes Kiki*?"

Aaron spread his fingers across his chest. "What kind of father do you think I am?"

"The kind that likes Kiki Grey," answered Liam, grabbing his hat off the dash.

As they began making their way towards the entrance of *Greer's Bar*, Liam took notice of the mildew growing along the building's cinderblock foundation, as well as the rotting plywood covering up most of its windows; outside the front door, beer cans and cigarette butts floated in the lower half of a whiskey barrel overflowing with stagnant rainwater and trash.

In spite of the establishment's run-down state, not to mention the fact that it had changed owners and lost its liquor license too many times to count, its clientele remained loyal … and judging by the number of vehicles already crammed in the tiny parking lot, Liam guessed that they were eager to get started on wasting their day.

Stepping over a puddle of urine, Liam squared his shoulders and went inside. Startled by the intrusion, men with wrinkled hands and hardened faces looked up from their drinks, while their eyes, glazed with a mixture of equal parts whiskey and sadness, began to flicker with apprehension as he walked past.

"What do you want, Sheriff?"

Liam shifted his focus to the other end of the bar, where he found Hank Crowell, the current owner, peering at him over the rims of his glasses as he sat sipping his coffee. "Information on Hector Ramirez," he said, heading in his direction. "When was the last time he was in here?"

Crowell flipped the page of the newspaper that lay spread out in front of him. "Damned if I know. It's not my job to keep track of people's comings and goings."

"What about the ones coming and going through there?" Liam asked, gesturing at the door behind the bar. "I bet you keep track of *them*."

"I don't know what you're talking about," said Crowell, hiding his face behind his coffee mug.

The distinct sound of poker chips being shuffled filtered underneath the door.

"I think you do," replied Liam, watching Crowell shift his weight on the stool, "and the last I heard, you didn't have a gaming license."

"Okay—look," said Crowell, setting his mug down. "Ramirez came in here a few times, but I honestly don't remember the last time I saw him."

Gripping the counter, Liam leaned in close. "I bet you could if you tried."

The deep crimson that had enveloped Crowell's face migrated to the top of his head. "It was around three weeks ago."

"And who did he talk to when he was in here?"

"Everybody," Crowell snapped, wiping the bead of sweat from his upper lip. "He was a goddamned celebrity."

"Sheriff?"

Liam cut his eyes to Aaron.

His deputy gave a subtle nod towards the back room and started walking.

As Liam turned to follow, he became aware of the looks being thrown in Aaron's direction and bit down on the inside of his cheek. Since joining the Orand County Sheriff's department three months ago, it seemed to him that his deputy only received two kinds of stares: one of curiosity, stemming from ignorance, or one of disgust, born out of inbred hate — neither of which saw him for the man he was.

"Guess who's here?" murmured Aaron, who was either oblivious to — or unfazed by — the interest being shown him.

Before Liam could offer a reply, a familiar laugh rang out in front of him, filling him with a vague sense of dread.

"I told ya you couldn't make that shot, asshole! You owe me twenty bucks."

"Let me try again. Double or nothin'!"

Frank Colter stood in the middle of the room with his elbow propped on a pool stick. "Go ahead," he said, waving his hand. "It's your money."

Grabbing the cube of chalk, Jesse Colter ground it back and forth on the tip of his cue. "No talkin' this time!" he yelled. Planting his grimy fingertips on the red felt, he stretched his lanky body across the table and pulled the stick backward along the webbing of his thumb, then closing his left eye, carefully lined up his shot. With a clean snap, he sent the five ball spinning towards the left corner pocket — where it promptly glanced off the rail and rolled to a stop.

Frank doubled over in laughter. "What'd I tell ya?"

"Fuck you!" shouted Jesse, limping around the table. "A hundred bucks says I make it!" Bending down, he hurriedly pulled the stick back and closed his eye.

"Last I heard," said Liam, stepping into his line of sight, "you were locked up in County over in Pennington."

The light hanging above the pool table cast a rectangular shadow across the side of Jesse's face. "They let me out for good behavior."

"When?"

Jesse returned his attention to the ball in front of him. "A couple of days ago."

"A couple of days ago," Liam repeated, exchanging glances with Aaron. "Just in time for you to do some early morning shopping at *Mobley's Hardware*."

Straightening, Jesse shot a nervous look towards his brother.

"What are you doing here this time of day, Sheriff?" asked Frank, dragging his pool stick across the floor as he made his way towards him. "Shouldn't you and Sitting Bull there be over at *Lonnie's* drinkin' coffee and eatin' donuts?"

Aaron glanced behind him in the pointed silence that followed. "Oh," he said, turning back, "you mean me." He paused to study his reflection in the cracked mirror that ran along the wall behind the pool table. "You really think I look like Sitting Bull?" Lifting his chin, he pensively stroked the side of his jaw. "I don't know … I think I'm more the Dwayne Johnson type." He turned from the mirror. "What do you think, Sheriff?"

Liam folded his arms across his chest, hating it when he did this.

"I mean, I may not have guns like The Rock," Aaron continued, flexing his arms beneath his coat, "but I've definitely got the same chiseled face." Striking a pose, he tilted his head and raised his eyebrow. "Am I right?"

"We're here," said Liam, drawing Frank's gaze back to his own, "because we want to talk to you about Hector Ramirez."

Frank took a deliberate step closer. "What *about* him?" he asked, setting the bottom of the pool stick on the floor in front of him.

Resting his hand against his holster, Liam kept a careful watch on Frank's movements as he stared at what was left of his nose, which had been bitten off during a fight with another inmate last year while serving time in Durfee. "A nickel bag of heroin was found among Hector's things. Would you happen to know anything about that?"

A gap-toothed grin unfolded across Frank's face. "Sorry, I don't use anymore," he replied, cupping his hands over the tip of his pool stick. "It would be a violation of my terms with the Drug Court."

Liam took in a small breath and held it, trying to suffocate the anger that had started to swirl inside him. In his opinion, the establishment of the Drug Court was the worst thing that could've ever happened to Orand County, because the one percent of people it helped was no comparison to the ninety-nine percent that used it as a way to avoid jail—and thanks to the sympathetic judges that oversaw it, that's exactly what Frank Colter had done. "I'm not talking about you *using*," Liam said in a low voice.

Frank's grin widened as he rested his chin on his knuckles. "What *are* you talking about, then?" he asked, batting his eyelashes.

"When was the last time you spoke to Hector?"

"Hmm ... let me think," replied Frank, scratching his head.

Out of the corner of his eye, Liam saw Jesse lean over and pick up the cue ball. Aaron saw him as well and walked around the pool table. Tossing the ball towards the ceiling, Jesse caught it on the way down, then, seeming to relish the attention being shown him, repeated his actions.

Frank turned his head to see what was going on, enabling Liam to discern that if it weren't for the two holes protruding from the jagged crater of skin perched above his lips, his profile would've been completely flat. "Oh, I remember now," he said, looking back at Liam. "That would be never."

"You *never* talked to him while he was in here."

"Can't say that I did."

"Did he ever call you?"

"Nope," replied Frank, making a popping sound with his lips as they parted.

"We recovered Hector's cell," Aaron interjected. Pulling his own phone from his coat, he swiped its screen and held it up for Frank to see. "Hector made several calls to this number, including the night he was killed. Do you know whose it is?"

"Nah, man," said Frank, doing a noticeably poor job of pretending to study the number. "I don't know who that belongs to."

"How about you, Jesse?" asked Aaron, turning it towards him.

Jesse began shaking his head before his eyes ever focused on the screen. "No."

Liam gestured at Aaron. "Why don't you try calling it again?"

"That's a great idea, Sheriff," he chirped, tapping the screen with his thumb. "Who knows? Maybe we'll get lucky this time."

Several seconds passed, and then Liam watched the veins in Frank's neck puff up like thick cords of rope as the rectangular shape bulging beneath the pocket of his jeans began to vibrate.

"I'm going to need you to come down to the station to answer a few questions," said Liam, reaching for his arm.

Clutching the ball in his fist, Jesse started across the floor.

"Stay right where you are," ordered Aaron, stepping in front of him. "Or I'll put a bullet in your other leg!"

As the scene on his left played out, Liam saw Frank's shoulder twitch—an advantage he hadn't had the last time—and instinctively ducked out of the way as his head came barreling towards his. Grabbing the back of Colter's thick neck as it hurtled past, Liam shoved it towards the pool table, slamming his face hard against its wooden edge. Knocking the stick out of his hand, Liam then threw all his weight on top of him in an attempt to force him to the floor. Legs kicked, elbows flailed, and profanities were uttered as they both fell to the concrete. Scrambling to keep the pool stick away from him, Liam rolled over onto his hip and jammed his knee between his shoulder blades, expelling whatever air Frank had left in his lungs through the gap in his teeth.

"Talk to me, Sheriff!" yelled Aaron.

"I'm good," said Liam, his words coming out between ragged breaths as he reached behind him for his cuffs. "You?"

"I'm fine."

Glancing up to make sure that he was, Liam's gaze went from the cue ball rolling around on the floor beside Aaron's boots to Aaron; his Glock was drawn and trained on Jesse, who was on his knees with his fists clenched and eyes ablaze.

When both brothers were secured, Liam grabbed his radio. "Enid, do you copy?"

"Go ahead, Sheriff."

"Show us as 10-15M … two males in custody." Taking his finger off the button, Liam paused as he waited for his adrenaline to subside. "I need you to get hold of Donovan," he said after a moment, "and have him meet me at the station."

"Copy that."

"Let's go," said Liam, hauling Frank to his feet.

"Donovan, huh?" Smiling, Frank leaned over and spat on the floor, covering the top of Liam's boot in a red spray. "Don't worry, little brother," he called over his shoulder. "We'll be back here before noon."

"Come on." Jerking Frank by the arm, Liam began leading him through the crowd of inebriated men that had gathered around the doorway, while at the same time, trying to dismiss the feeling of uneasiness that had accompanied his remark.

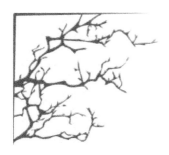

# Chapter 21

Staring at the small gap beneath the oak-paneled door on her left, Olivia impatiently tapped the heel of her shoe against her chair as she kept a vigilant watch for any signs of an approaching shadow. With each passing second, the sense of urgency that was churning inside her grew, causing the pads of her fingers to join in on the angry beat her foot was keeping. She hated doctors, but hated waiting for them more.

When she'd played back the message on her phone that Dr. Feldspauch's office had left for her yesterday, it was to inform her that due to a last-minute cancellation, they could see her this afternoon. Knowing that specialists were booked weeks—sometimes months—in advance, Olivia took the appointment for two very important reasons: The first being that regardless of what transpired today, she would most assuredly walk away with a prescription for Hydrocodone. The second was that it got her out of the house and away from her father-in-law. In her mind, both of those things were worth the drive to Rapid City.

Leaning back in her chair, she forced her gaze away from the door and set it wandering about the spacious office in search of a distraction. It eventually settled upon a row of pictures hanging on the wall opposite her. The wooden frames—six in all—each held an intimate portrait of a pregnant woman. Shot in exquisite black and white, the women were standing sideways with one arm over their bare breasts and the other under their round bellies, and even though their ages, race, and trimesters all varied, there was one constant: the jubilant smiles etched across their glowing faces as they looked into the camera.

A renewed sense of hope began to flutter in the back of Olivia's throat, making her breath quiver—and yet, before she could fully immerse herself in the feeling, her argument with Liam from last night came rushing to the forefront, grounding her in reality. Sinking her nails into the leather arm of the chair, she suddenly found herself wondering why she'd bothered to come here at all.

"Mrs. Matthews?"

She turned her head at the sound of her name to see a tall, slender woman standing in the doorway.

"I'm Dr. Feldspausch," she said, extending her hand. "I'm sorry to have kept you waiting."

"That's all right," Olivia lied, noting the warmth of the woman's fingertips in comparison to her own.

"It's been one of those days," she continued, taking a seat behind a sleek mahogany desk that was overflowing with charts and paperwork, "and my assistant being out with the flu isn't helping matters."

Although Olivia knew it would have been polite to respond to her statement in some manner, she remained quiet, finding that she couldn't care less about the woman's staffing problems.

"Okay, then ..." Dr. Feldspausch opened up the chart she'd brought in with her and slipped on a pair of purple-rimmed glasses. "Let's see what we have." Plucking a pen from the pocket of her lab coat, she began moving it back and forth across the paper, skillfully winding her way through the medical jargon adorning it. Occasionally, her tired brown eyes would stop and narrow in on a section of bold print, where they would hover there for the briefest of moments—sheltered behind an unreadable expression—before continuing on. "How much do you know about your condition?"

"What do you mean?" asked Olivia, finding her question to be as vague as it was odd—especially considering the fact that they lived in a world where everything could be looked up on the internet.

Dr. Feldspauch frowned, causing a flurry of deep lines to form around her mouth. "I mean, did

Dr. Ellis *explain* to you what a unicornuate uterus is?"

"Yes," Olivia replied, supplementing her answer with a nod. "I essentially have half a uterus."

"Well, there's a little bit more to it than that," said Dr. Feldspausch, her silvery bob coming to a sharp point on either side of her chin as she peered at her over the rims of her glasses, "but I suppose it's a start."

Olivia's tongue forced itself between her front teeth and upper lip. "I also know that one of my ovaries is in the non-communicating rudimentary horn attached to it," she stated, rigidly crossing her arms, "and that endometriosis is present in my other ovary."

Dr. Feldspausch's eyes widened, momentarily erasing the crow's feet surrounding them. "That's a fairly accurate assessment," she said, flipping to the next page of the chart.

Taking no satisfaction in being able to explain the internal failings of her female organs to her, Olivia slumped against the back of the chair.

"I see that you've had three miscarriages."

"Two," Olivia corrected.

The doctor frowned again. "The information I have from Dr. Ellis shows three."

Olivia took in the smallest of breaths. "My last two pregnancies ended in miscarriages, but my first child was stillborn," she said evenly. "He was thirty-seven weeks."

Dr. Feldspausch silently mouthed Olivia's

answers as she scribbled them down in the margin of the page. After she'd finished, she turned in her chair and retrieved a bright red folder off the credenza behind her. Pulling a flimsy piece of paper from it, she held it up for Olivia to see. "This is a sonogram of a unicornuate uterus in a thirty-one-year-old woman. You'll note the banana-like shape of it, as well as its decreased cavity size," she said, running her finger along the curve of it, "and just like you, her left ovary and fallopian tube are inside a non-communicating rudimentary horn. Your miscarriages were most likely due to the restricted blood flow to your uterus because of its abnormal shape ..."

Over the years, Olivia had managed to create a thick shell around the lining of her heart; hard and virtually impenetrable, it had its downsides, but there was no denying its usefulness when it came to deflecting the thoughtless comments made by well-meaning friends, extended family members — and insensitive doctors.

"... this compromises the placenta, which can lead to your body performing a spontaneous abortion of the fetus."

And yet, as she sat there staring at the sonogram, she began to feel the sobering sting of tears starting to form. Perhaps after years of defending herself from the numerous assaults, her heavily constructed shell had developed a crack in it.

"Additionally, your uterus is so limited in volume that it generally cannot accommodate a developing fetus …"

Or maybe it was because Dr. Feldspauch kept referring to her babies as fetuses.

"… are in a very rare percentage, in that only about one in four thousand women have this."

"That's why Dr. Ellis referred me to you," Olivia said, doing her best to rid herself of the abject misery that had gathered behind her eyes. "He said you specialized in this sort of thing."

Laying the photo aside, Dr. Feldspausch removed her glasses. "I wouldn't exactly use that term to describe it," she replied, clasping her hands together. "I've been doing this for twenty years, but have only seen a handful of women with this problem."

"But you *have* had success treating them," Olivia said, nodding her head in an attempt to make the doctor follow suit.

The lines around the woman's mouth softened. "Yes."

Olivia felt the tightness that had been residing in her chest begin to fall away.

Dr. Feldspauch was quick to hold up a single ruby-ringed finger. "Some — *not all* — were able to get pregnant by IVF and carry to full term. This type of condition can make it extremely difficult to conceive, especially after suffering two or more miscarriages. There's no guarantee."

Unable to contain the excitement that was now coursing through her, Olivia uncrossed her legs and leaned forward. "I understand," she said, nodding again.

Seeming to visibly recoil from the enthusiasm being thrown her way, Dr. Feldspausch lowered her hand and returned her attention to the file in front of her. "It's been a year since your last miscarriage. Have you been actively trying to conceive the old-fashioned way?"

Olivia hesitated, as several answers ran through her mind. "Yes," she finally said, deciding it would be best to err on the side of gross exaggeration in order to keep things simple.

"And when was your last period?"

"December."

Dr. Feldspausch looked up from her writing. "Had they been regular up until then?"

"They had—until this past miscarriage," Olivia replied, avoiding the woman's pointed stare. "Since then, I've only had a few."

"How many is a few?"

"Four."

Shifting in her chair, Dr. Feldspausch tapped her pen on the paper. "Dr. Ellis noted in your file that you have a long history of pelvic pain, as well as pain with your periods."

Olivia felt her exuberance beginning to fade.

"Are both of these still happening?"

"Yes."

"That's not uncommon," said Dr. Feldspauch, scribbling in the chart. "As pelvic discomfort almost always exists in those who have a non-communicating horn, not to mention the number of endometriomas—or chocolate cysts—your last ultrasound revealed to be present deep within your good ovary." Laying her pen aside, the woman leaned back in her chair and steepled her fingers. "And *that's* the part I'm most concerned about."

The outline of the doctor's face began to grow blurry as Olivia listened to her go on.

"At first glance, it would be ill-advised of me to even attempt IVF ..."

Fighting back her tears, Olivia focused all her efforts on the silver picture frame sitting on the credenza.

"Mrs. Matthews?"

She shifted her gaze from the young mother holding a healthy, chubby baby in her arms to Dr. Feldspauch, whose haggard appearance had been replaced with a look of impatience.

"Do you have any questions for me?"

She had several, but suddenly saw no point in asking any of them. "No."

Dr. Feldspausch closed the file. "Well," she said, rising from her chair, "let's get you into an examining room so we can see exactly what we're dealing with."

Olivia blinked and then stumbled to her feet. "Thank you," she replied, her words coming out in a sputtered whisper.

The doctor's impatient expression diminished, paving the way for a small smile to form on her lips. "You're welcome."

Utter elation began to fill every crevice in

Olivia's body as she blindly followed Dr. Feldspausch out the door.

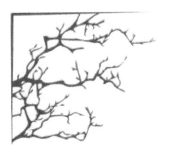

# Chapter 22

Harlan dropped his toothbrush in the glass and spit the turquoise foam, laced with bits of bacon, into the sink, then wiping his mouth on his sleeve, grudgingly locked eyes with the old man standing in front of him. Noting that he looked older than usual this morning, Harlan brought his hand to the side of his face and began running the tips of his fingers along the crevices in his skin, but stopped when he came upon the small scar embedded in his cheek. Lowering his arm, he sucked in his gut and straightened, yet his once tall and strapping frame refused to comply, having been replaced by a bent and shriveled form with thin, rounded shoulders.

Turning from the mirror with a sigh, he hobbled out into the hall and began his long trek towards the den, all the while being thankful for the fact that he didn't have to worry about bumping into Olivia, who'd left the house two hours ago without saying a word.

As he passed by the sliding glass doors in the living room, the desire for a cigarette made his hand twitch, but knowing that giving in to the temptation also meant having to put his coat and shoes on, he persuaded his feet to go the rest of the way across the floor and into the den.

Once inside, he pulled a small cardboard box from the lower shelf of his closet and eased himself down onto the bed with it. Having been forced into retirement at fifty-nine, but not ready to be put out to pasture, Harlan had brought home all of Orand County's unsolved cases that had occurred during his tenure as sheriff, with the intention of solving each and every one.

A sense of frustration surrounded him as he stared at the box. Unfortunately, he'd had neither the enthusiasm nor the energy these past few months to even try.

Peeling back the dusty flaps, he grabbed hold of the first file, knowing exactly which case it was by the single piece of paper it held and slipped on his reading glasses.

As the report detailing the hit and run that had left him with a shattered hip and a fractured jaw came into focus, his mind began to fill with a vague recollection of the events from that night. It had been another twelve-hour day, and he was on his way home to the house he shared with Enid when he'd had to pull off the side of Dixon Road to move the splintered remains of a pallet out of the middle of it. Bright lights, the squall of tires, and the sound his head had made as it hit the pavement were the only things he remembered … and with no witnesses or evidence to speak of, he knew his chances of finding the person who did it were slim to none.

Tossing the file back in the box, Harlan rummaged through the rest of the folders until he found the one labeled 'Malloy'. A thick, musty odor rose up to greet him as he flipped it open.

Other than the fact that Dominick Malloy had married the Johnston girl, Harlan didn't know a whole lot about the man, but all that changed on the morning of July fifth when he received a frantic call from Bernice Hickman, a retired schoolteacher whose husband had recently died, asking him to meet her at *Black Hills Term Life Insurance*. When Harlan had arrived at the building, he'd found Mrs. Hickman, Malloy's ashen-faced secretary Diane Travis, and an IRS agent all waiting for him. A quick check around the office revealed that the safe in the back room had been emptied and the hard drive on Malloy's computer was missing—as was Malloy.

After speaking at length with the IRS agent, Harlan learned that Malloy was using a bank in Rapid City to cash the checks made out to *Black Hills Term Life Insurance,* yet none of the money was being credited to any of the policyholders' accounts.

Slipping his knuckles underneath his glasses, Harlan rubbed his eyes. News about what Malloy had done had spread through Weeping Rock like wildfire, engulfing the struggling town in a raging panic that was only going to be quenched by either the return of their hard-earned money or Malloy's head on a spike — yet with there being no opportunity for recourse, due to the fact that Malloy was an independent insurance agent, Harlan gathered it would be the latter.

Amidst the uproar, he had quietly gone to question Malloy's wife. Tracking her down at her mother's house, she'd seemed completely shocked by what he'd had to tell her, and yet he knew from past experience what a manipulative liar she could be. Unable to link any of Malloy's illegal dealings back to her, however, he'd had no choice but to rule her out as an accomplice.

Days went by without so much as a word on Malloy's whereabouts … followed by weeks. And then as the leaves on the trees, shriveled and brown from the dry summer, began to flutter towards the hardened ground, Harlan watched the people in the town miserably come to accept their fate.

Leaning back against the headboard, he brought the file closer to his face. Staring at his handwriting from over a decade ago, he read the last interview he'd done with Alice Malloy, who — in between shouting obscenities at him — had repeatedly denied having any knowledge of her husband's wrongdoings.

Dropping the file in his lap, he grabbed his phone off the nightstand and pulled up the pictures of the briefcase that had been retrieved from the floorboard of Malloy's car. It contained close to two hundred and fifty thousand in large bills, which in spite of having been submerged in lake water for the past eleven years, were in relatively good condition, Malloy's muddied passport, and the fragmented remains of an email confirmation … for two plane tickets to Mexico.

"DO YOU UNDERSTAND THESE rights as I've read them to you?"

With his arms bound behind his back, Frank Colter's chest heaved as he stared at Liam through a narrowed set of eyes that were as dark as the circles lining the skin beneath them.

"Having these rights in mind," Liam went on, "do you wish to talk to me?"

Colter ran his tongue over the split in his bottom lip. "Why the fuck would I want to do that?"

"Because it would be in your best interest to do so," replied Liam, tucking the card he had been reading from into his shirt pocket. "Otherwise, I'm going to pick up the phone and inform Judge Lewis that you were in a bar, which is a flagrant violation of your terms with the Drug Court, not to mention the gram of heroin that was found on your person."

The network of throbbing veins crawling along the side of Colter's throat began to subside. "Go ahead," he said, as a misshapen grin unfurled across his swollen mouth. "I'll just cry in front of him and ask for mercy. He likes me, you know. Says I remind him of his dead grandson."

Liam picked up the chair in front of him and turned it around. "Well, I could always arrest you for attempted assault on a police officer," he said, straddling the seat. "And if memory serves, you have a pair of assault convictions already. A third would be a felony — and that's an automatic two in the state pen."

The smug look on Colter's face began to harden.

"Of course, that would *also* get you kicked out of the Drug Court program," continued Liam, "so I'm thinking — I don't know … another year on top of that?"

The smell of dried blood and stale beer drifted across the table as Colter let out a stilted breath. "What do you want to know?" he asked, curling his upper lip.

Opening the file, Liam slid a piece of paper towards him. "Why did Hector Ramirez call you twenty-one times between the thirtieth of December and February sixth?"

"I don't know," said Colter, shrugging. "I guess he was just lonely — "

"No," said Liam, shaking his head, "that's not how we're going to do this. You either answer my questions in a truthful manner or I'm taking you down to booking right now."

"You asked me why he called. I told you."

Getting to his feet, Liam motioned for Colter to stand up. "Let's go," he said, reaching for his arm.

"All right," said Colter, shrinking from his grasp, "I figured he was lonely because of what he asked me to do for him every time he called."

"Which was what?"

"Hook him up with girls."

"Girls," Liam said dryly.

"Yeah." Colter paused to suck the gap between his teeth. "But now that I think about it, I guess it was probably less about him being lonely and more about him wanting to get his rocks off."

Liam's toes curled inside his boots as his frustration with Colter grew. "I need their names."

"Let's see, there was Amber ... Destiny ... Violet—"

"How much of a cut did you get?"

"For what?"

"*You* know for what," Liam countered.

"Look, it ain't my problem if those bitches charged Ramirez for showing him a good time. I just gave them his number." Relaxing his shoulders, Colter sat back and flicked his gaze across Liam's face. "You know, you're lookin' pretty lonely there yourself, Sheriff. Maybe I should hook you—"

Shoving the chair out of his way, Liam leaned across the table. "Here's the problem I have with what you're telling me," he said, tapping the paper with his index finger as he struggled to rein in his temper. "This is a list of all incoming and outgoing calls on Hector's phone, and no number belonging to a Violet or Amber is on there—plus Destiny's been in County lockup for the past sixty days."

The smile returned to Colter's face. "Well, I've never been good with names," he said, cocking his head to the side, "but now, tits … tits are a different story …"

As the conversation ran away from him, Liam slid a picture out from between the folder, trying to wrangle it back.

"If you were to show me their—"

"This is what I want to show you," said Liam, slamming it down in front of him.

"Goddamn," exclaimed Colter, letting out a soft whistle as he stared at the photo of Hector's corpse, "someone's got some real anger issues."

Liam's phone rang out. Seeing that it was his father, he silenced the ringer and shoved it back into his pocket. "Hector called you three times the night of February sixth," he said, returning his attention to Colter. "The last one—at eleven—went on for more than five minutes. What'd you talk about?"

"The weather mostly. We may have talked about tits, too, but I think it was mainly the weather."

"Where were you that night?"

"Um … what was the date again?"

Liam placed his hands on his hips. "February sixth."

"Oh, I remember now," said Colter. "I was at home reading my Bible."

A heavy knock sounded against the door.

Turning, Liam saw Gordon motioning at him through its window. Picking up the file, he walked around the table, being careful not to bump against the stack of banker's boxes that—thanks to a burst water pipe last week in the evidence locker—had been stacked floor to ceiling around the perimeter of the tiny room.

Once outside, Liam rubbed his hand back and forth across his jaw, trying to get rid of the anger that had settled in it before talking to Gordon. "What'd you find out?"

"I spoke with Dr. Shaw, and he told me—"

"Whassup, Stiles?"

Liam watched Gordon's neck stiffen as his gaze found its way over to Jesse Colter, who was sitting beside Aaron's desk with his left wrist handcuffed to the radiator. "When'd you get out?" he called.

Jesse stretched his legs in front of him and laughed. "Why does everyone keep asking me that?"

Returning his attention to Liam, Gordon took a step closer. "What's going on?" he asked, nodding at the interview room.

"Frank Colter's cell was the one Hector had placed all the calls to."

Gordon let go of a small sigh. "Why am I not surprised?" he murmured.

Liam felt the upper part of his thigh begin to vibrate. "What did Shaw have to say?" he asked, jamming his hand inside his pocket to turn off his phone.

"That he never saw Hector—for anything. So I stopped by the pharmacy at *Elmar's* and got this from Walter Rafferty."

Liam looked down at the piece of paper Gordon had given him and saw that it was a prescription from Dr. Shaw's office made out to Hector for Oxy. Aside from the ridiculously large amount prescribed, it was obvious that it had been printed off a computer before being poorly cut down to the size of a prescription pad.

"Hector apparently never had any problems getting them filled through Jerry McCormick," Gordon explained, "but Rafferty saw them for what they were and refused."

As Gordon spoke, Liam began to understand the role Frank Colter had played in all this. With Hector's unwitting—or perhaps uncaring—source having retired to Florida, it stood to reason that he'd go in search of another supplier, and with his dwindling bank account, nickel bags of heroin did the same job as prescription pain killers but were much more affordable.

"Gordon?" said Enid, balancing the telephone receiver on her shoulder as she leaned across the counter. "We've got an overturned livestock truck

279

at Ash Creek Road and Saddlebrook. Cows are runnin' loose everywhere."

Gordon's lips flattened against his face. "Red Elk," he called, jerking his gloves from his coat. "Let's go. You're better than I am at herding these things."

"Yeah," chimed Jesse, "get along there, Geronimo."

Grabbing his hat off the corner of his desk, Aaron stood up and started across the floor. "I spoke with Jesse's parole officer," he said, stopping in front of Liam, "and he confirmed that he was released from Pennington on the fourteenth."

Jesse held out his free arm. "Isn't that what I've been tellin' you all along?" he snapped.

As Aaron followed Stiles out of the station, Liam stole a sideways glance at Jesse. Tall and rail-thin, he had a boyish-looking face that held a set of dimples, dark ruby lips, and a pair of eyes the color of the ocean. He would've been any mother's pride and joy if it weren't for the derogatory tattoos covering his neck; running along the edge of both jaws, they curved behind the lobes of his ears before slithering up the back of his shaved head. At twenty-four years of age, he'd already spent nearly a third of his life behind bars.

"Sheriff? Donovan's on his way."

Acknowledging Enid with a nod, Liam tucked the paper inside Hector's file and started for the interview room.

"Hey," called Jesse, rattling his cuffs against the radiator. "You heard what Crazy Horse said. Aren't you gonna let me go?"

Liam shook his head. "You're in the same boat as your brother. Being in a bar is a violation of your parole."

Jesse sat up and yanked on his cuffs, trying to free himself from the radiator. When that failed to work, he thrust his middle finger high in the air. "Yeah — well *fuck you!*"

Jesse's admiration for Liam carried into the interview room, causing Frank to look up.

"Why is my brother yellin'?"

"Because he's going back to jail," said Liam, closing the door behind him.

Frank's shoulders slumped forward. "Come on, man," he said in a voice that was almost close to pleading. "He just got out."

"I might be convinced to look the other way," replied Liam, sitting down across from him, "if you answer the rest of my questions."

Colter sat back, slamming his shoulder blades against the chair with such force it dislodged the greasy strands of hair that had been clinging to his face for the past half hour.

Taking his silence to mean that he had his attention, Liam pointed at the phone log that was still lying on the table. "This was the first day Hector called you. After that, he phoned you like clockwork every two days, with each call lasting less than twenty seconds. I want to know why—and I want the truth this time."

"You know why," he answered.

Liam folded his arms across his chest, waiting to hear him say it.

Colter's face darkened. "He was buyin' heroin off me."

"How much?"

"A bundle every time."

"So, ten nickel bags—at fifty dollars a pop—every couple of days." Liam arched his eyebrows. "You were making some pretty good money off him."

"Yeah," said Colter, looking about as proud as any drug dealer could, "I was."

"Until you jacked up your price."

Colter's high regard for himself plummeted to his lap.

"The call Hector made to you on February second," Liam said, circling the date on the page with his pen, "lasted over three minutes, then there was nothing for four days."

"Yeah, I raised my price on him," said Colter, the lines around his mouth growing taut. "So what?"

"Oh, don't get me wrong," said Liam, holding up his hand. "It was a wise business decision on your part, plus it was really, *really* smart of you to do it over the phone." He paused to shrug. "I mean, that way, if Hector got mad and lost his temper, at least you wouldn't end up with a bullet in your leg—like your brother did last year when the two of you tried pulling the same thing on that guy from Keystone."

An oozing oil slick of black began to seep from Colter's pupils, devouring everything in its path.

"Anyway," Liam continued, "here's what I think happened next. Out of options and desperate, Hector broke down and called you on the sixth, and after negotiating back and forth, the two of you finally came to an agreement on a price. You then drove out to the bluff at Crow's Foot to meet him — only to have him tell you that if you didn't give him the goods for free, he was going to report your illegal activities to the authorities." Pushing his chair back, Liam slowly got to his feet. "I'm guessing that's when you lost your temper and killed him."

Colter's gaze slowly rose to meet his. "You can't prove *any* of that," he said in a low voice.

Walking around the table, Liam placed his hand on the back of Colter's chair and leaned down. "We have a witness who saw you do it."

"Man, that girl didn't see *nothin'*!"

Liam's fingers tightened around his chair. "I didn't say it was a girl."

Colter's knee began to bounce uncontrollably as he pulled against his restraints.

"You either saw or heard her that night," Liam stated, "and when you found out where she was hiding, you drove your car out to the truck stop and killed her — just like you did Ramirez."

Colter's knee suddenly grew still. "You've got a big hole there in your theory, Sheriff," he said, as something along the lines of a sneer started to take shape on his face.

"And what's that?" asked Liam, watching Colter's eyes return to their turd-brown color.

"I don't own a car."

The door to the interview room swung open.

"Sheriff Matthews?"

Stumbling over Colter's words, Liam absently looked over to find Brooks Donovan standing in the threshold.

"About damn time," said Colter.

Donovan's gaze went from Liam to Colter and then back to Liam. "Let's talk."

Not nearly as excited to see the deputy state's attorney as he had been five minutes ago, Liam forced his feet to follow Donovan out the door. Catching up to him, he cleared his throat and gestured towards his office. "Go on in," he said, before veering in the opposite direction. "I'll be right there."

Donovan tapped his watch. "I've got court in half an hour."

"I just need a minute," said Liam.

"Hey, Brooks!" Jesse called from across the room. "How's it goin'?"

Donovan stopped in his tracks and turned.

"I know. I'm out. Big surprise, right?" Jesse leaned the back of his head against the wall and grinned. "So tell me somethin' … how's that fat wife of yours?" he asked, grabbing his crotch.

Pivoting around in his shiny loafers, Donovan and his reddened cheeks quickly disappeared inside Liam's office.

Walking up to the counter, Liam snapped his fingers to get Enid's attention. "Listen to me," he said in a hushed tone. "I need you to *quietly* check with the DMV and find out what cars are registered in the Colter brothers' names. I don't care if you call or do it through the interface, but I need the information yesterday. Understand?"

She nodded. "Got it."

Doubting that she did, he remained in front of her until she set her coffee mug down and placed her pygmy-like fingers on the keyboard. Satisfied, he pushed himself away from the counter and started for his office.

Donovan was sitting in the chair across from Liam's desk, scrolling through his emails on his fancy smartwatch. "All right, Matthews," he said, lowering his arm when he saw him walk in, "give me the rundown."

"We found Ramirez's cell," Liam began, noting that Donovan's face was still inflamed as he closed the door behind him. "He made several calls to Frank Colter, including the night — "

"Did Colter confess to murdering him?"

Liam's jaw shifted. "Not yet."

Crossing his legs, Donovan returned his attention to his emails. "What do you have in terms of evidence?"

"He's admitted to selling Ramirez heroin on several occasions—"

"That's not evidence, Liam," said Donovan, looking up from his watch. "It just proves that there's a shared link to Ramirez, and it's circumstantial at best." He uncrossed his legs and got to his feet. "I wouldn't even be able to get an indictment."

"I've seen you prosecute with less," Liam argued.

"Only because I knew the accused would plead guilty to a lesser charge offered. And if that's all you've got on Colter, there's no way he'll take a plea deal."

Wanting to tell him about the car in the video, Liam glanced anxiously at the door, hoping to see Enid coming through it.

Donovan frowned, drawing the bags under his eyes farther down his face. "Look, this trial—if and when—it ever takes place, is destined to be a media circus. It's going to be televised, scrutinized, and cost the taxpayers of Orand County tens of thousands of dollars. The case has to be airtight, and there *has* to be a guarantee of conviction."

"I know in my gut that Colter killed Ramirez," said Liam, pointing towards the interview room. "You just can't walk away from this."

Smoothing the rumples from his coat, Donovan shook his head. "I'm not about to jeopardize my career based on your gut feeling, Liam," he said, opening the door. "Have a good day."

Liam's fingertips sank into his palms as he watched Donovan slink towards the exit.

"Why the long face, Sheriff?"

Jerking his head over his shoulder, Liam took one look at the amused grin plastered on Jesse's lips and tore out of the station after Donovan. "Brooks!" he yelled, scrambling down the steps. "When are you going to stop playing it safe and do your goddamned job?"

Donovan stopped and turned—as did several passersby. Flipping up the collar of his coat, he walked back to where Liam was standing and drew a sharp breath. "Get me a confession," he said in a low voice, "or a concrete piece of evidence placing Colter at the murder scene, and we'll talk."

The wind bit through Liam's shirt, making his body grow rigid, as Donovan stalked off towards the black Escalade that was straddling the line in the parking lot.

Taking notice of the deliberately slowed pace and curious murmurings of passing pedestrians, Liam turned and started back up the steps. A pair of suede boots attached to a tight pair of pants suddenly appeared in front of his lowered gaze, and—finding that he was unable to stop himself from following the shapely curves belonging to the figure underneath them, soon found his eyes resting upon a familiar face.

"Liam."

"Alice," he said, forcing a nod.

A nervous smile spread between her lips, highlighting the patches of matching freckles on her cheeks. "Can we go inside and talk for a minute?" she asked, gesturing at the door behind her.

Glancing at the station, he shook his head. "This really isn't a good time."

"I gathered that," Alice said flatly, "along with everyone *else* within a two-block radius."

"Why are you here?" asked Liam, his words riding on the wave of a heavy sigh as he rubbed the back of his neck.

"I need to talk to you about Dom."

"It'll have to wait," he said, brushing past her.

"I need a signed death certificate for him."

Liam paused by the door and turned around. "Don't you think you should at least let his bones dry out first?"

Alice's long red locks began to lick at the edges of her face like fiery flames as she stomped up the last two steps. "Look, I get it that you hate me. God knows you have every right to. But don't you *dare* stand there and judge me!" she yelled, tapping her fingers against his chest. "I've got *no* money, *no* job and — until I can collect on Dom's life insurance and social security, I'm stuck living in this godforsaken town with my mother and her narcissistic *parakeet*!"

"I wasn't—"

"I'm only here because I just got off the phone with that lazy-ass coroner of yours," she said, pointing in the air at nothing in particular, "and he told me that it would be at least a week before he could get around to signing the certificate. I need you to call him and tell him to do it now, so I can get things moving."

Liam waited for several seconds to pass in order to make sure she was finished, as well as to allow time for the chest hairs that were now standing at attention under his shirt to relax. "First of all," he said, staring down at her, "Abrams works for the county, *not* me. And second, I wasn't judging you."

"*No?*" Tilting her head, Alice crossed her arms. "What would you call it then?"

Irritated that she couldn't see his cutting remark for what it was—as a means to hurt her—he reached for the door and yanked it open.

"Oh," she yelled, "are we done talking?"

Slamming the door behind him, Liam made his way into his office, where he promptly kicked the trashcan beside his desk. The small plastic bin went sailing across the room, striking the far wall before crashing to the floor.

"Uh ... Sheriff?"

He turned to find Enid standing behind him, her usual look of indifference having morphed into something along the lines of fear. Lowering his foot, he placed his hands on his hips. "What is it?"

Pushing the door to, she slipped on her cheaters and raised her notepad. "Frank Colter has a tan 2010 Ram 1500, as well as a blue 1996 Ford Bronco registered in his name. Jesse has a green 1999 Toyota 4runner."

Bowing his head, Liam ran his fingers through his hair. "What about a car?" he asked in a despondent voice.

"There's no car registered to either one of them."

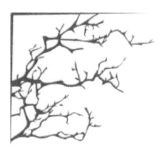

# Chapter 23

Darkness began to fall, awakening the streetlamps one by one as Liam turned onto Glenn Avenue. Duplexes with brown wooden-siding and overgrown bushes lined both sides of the street, their small porches sagging beneath the weight of discarded appliances, mattresses, and other pieces of junk.

Several dogs barked and gave chase as he drove past, dragging their chains through well-worn paths of mud and dirt that snaked their way around cars sitting on concrete blocks.

Liam couldn't help but scowl. The Glenn Housing Project came under fire every few months or so when a disgruntled citizen would take their ignored complaints to the city about it being an eyesore directly to the local newspaper. The city, in rebuttal, would promise to get it cleaned up, which translated to dozens of citations being issued by the sheriff's office. A few occupants would heed the warnings and make an honest effort, but after a couple of weeks, the paper would lose interest in the story and the matter would quietly die — until someone's house the next street over got broken into, and then it would start up again.

Pulling alongside the curb of the duplex that he knew all too well, Liam saw a woman dressed in only a tank top and shorts come running out of the front door on the left and yell for the two boys playing in the yard to get inside. They obeyed without question and the woman gave Liam a wary glance before shutting the door.

Shifting his gaze to the right half of the duplex, his grip inadvertently tightened around the steering wheel as he saw the flickering light of a TV through the tattered blinds in the window. Thanks to Donovan, Frank Colter had walked out of the station this afternoon a free man. In retaliation — and certainly what hadn't been one of his finer moments — Liam had reneged on his offer to Frank to look the other way and had arrested Jesse for violation of his parole, waiting until the last possible second to book him to ensure that he wouldn't make bail until sometime tomorrow.

Dismissing his guilt, he turned his attention to the driveway where a green 4runner, blue Ford Bronco, and a Ram 1500 that had been badly painted to resemble camouflage sat parked ... yet there was no car of any kind visible. Lowering his window, Liam pressed his aching shoulders into the back of the seat. As the cold air rushed inside, he forced his eyes and ears to remain focused in the hopes that they would pick up on something that would give him just cause to search the duplex and surrounding property.

As the minutes ticked by, it wasn't long before Liam found his fingers wrapped around the handle of his door, knowing how easy it would be for him to say that he heard someone outside the residence screaming for help, yet before he could act on his impulses, a bright yellow Neon came barreling down the street. It slowed as it drew near Colter's duplex, but upon seeing Liam's truck turned into the driveway opposite it and started to back out.

Hitting the lights on his dash, Liam pulled forward, blocking it. Stepping out of his truck, he approached the car from the rear and motioned at the driver to lower his window. As the tinted glass disappeared into the doorframe, the pungent aroma of weed rolled out.

Liam shined his flashlight inside the car. Two teenage boys with pupils as big as dimes stared back at him. Letting out a disgruntled sigh, he grabbed his radio. "Sheriff Matthews to County."

"County. Go ahead, Sheriff."

"10-53," he said, giving Colter's duplex a longing glance as he reached for his cuffs. "Requesting backup at 130 Glenn Avenue ..."

STANDING ON THE STEPS in the garage, Liam rested his shoulder against the door as he struggled to shove the events of the day to the back of his mind before allowing the ones that had been plaguing him for the past few weeks to the forefront.

The knob suddenly twisted out of his fingers, knocking him off balance.

"Did you get my messages?"

"All twenty of them," Liam snapped, brushing past his father.

"Why didn't you call me back, then? I've been waitin' around on ya all day."

"I've been busy."

"Well, so have I," his father retorted, thrusting a piece of paper at him.

"What's this?"

"A list of everything found in Malloy's car when it was brought up out of the water. Besides the money, do you see what else was in there?"

Liam glanced at the scrawled words his father had scratched onto the paper and shook his head. "Just tell me."

His father's nostrils flared as a noisy breath rushed out of them. "An email from a travel agency in Rapid City, confirming two plane tickets to Guadalajara."

Handing the paper back to him, Liam took off his coat and tossed it over the hook.

"So, did you talk to Malloy's wife like I told you to?"

"As a matter of fact, I did."

"And?"

"And what?" asked Liam, walking out of the laundry room.

"Did she say where she was the night her husband disappeared?"

"No, because I didn't ask."

"Why the hell not?"

Liam stopped in the foyer and turned. "Because she had nothing to do with his death. I read Abram's report. It was an accident, plain and simple. Case closed."

His father's eyes flickered. "I didn't say that she killed the son-of-a-bitch. I just wanted you to ask her where she was because I think she knew damn well what he was doin' and had plans to meet up with him later that night at the airport."

"She didn't—and she *wasn't*," answered Liam, clenching his jaw.

"How do you know?"

"I just do."

"Oh, I'm sorry," said his father, tilting his head. "I forgot that you were psychic."

Liam's upper lip disappeared inside his mouth. "She's an innocent victim in all this, just like half the people in this town."

"Well, if that's the case, what harm would it have done to question her?"

"Because you already *did* eleven years ago — several times if I'm not mistaken. And if you didn't find anything out then," Liam said, holding his arms out from his sides, "I'm sure as hell not going to find out anything different now."

His father shifted his weight to his good leg. "Sounds to me like you were afraid of hearin' her answer."

Turning on his heel, Liam made his way into the kitchen and emptied his thermos in the sink. Out of the corner of his eye, he saw his father pick up his walker — with surprising strength — and shuffle over to where he was standing.

"Or maybe you already know … and just don't wanna tell me."

Liam's throat began to thicken, suffocating his reply. Placing his thermos in the dishrack, he strode out of the kitchen and disappeared into the hallway. By the time he reached the bedroom, his entire body was shaking. Grasping the handle on the door, he pushed it open — only to stumble into darkness.

Seeing a slit of light coming from the bathroom, he felt his way over to the nightstand and sat down on the edge of the bed, being somewhat grateful that he didn't have to talk to Olivia at the moment, but as he went to remove his holster, the unmistakable sound of her crying brought him to his feet. Moving past the bed, Liam's own reflection greeted him as he flung open the door. His gaze traveled from the mirror to the floor, where he found her sobbing by the tub. "What's wrong?" he asked, dropping to his knees in front of her.

She answered him with another sob.

Cupping her face between his hands, Liam tilted it back until her eyes met his. "What is it?"

Black tears ran down her cheeks as she drew a fractured breath. "I went and saw a specialist today in Rapid City for the pain that I've been having … and she told me that the cysts covering my good ovary have damaged all of its healthy tissue."

Using his thumbs to wipe her face, Liam shook his head apologetically. "What does that mean?" he whispered.

Olivia's chin began to quiver as she clutched at his shirt. "It means that it's become non-functioning … just like the other one."

Wrapping his arms around her, Liam pulled her close. "I'm sorry," he murmured, holding the back of her head.

"It's not fair," she said, the words jerking out of her mouth in between sobs as she buried her face in his chest.

"No," he answered, pressing his lips to her cheek, "it's not."

Olivia's fingers uncurled from their tightly wound fists and slid around to the back of Liam's neck, grabbing the hair at his nape as she clung to him. Her breath, warm and uneven, fell across his throat, causing his blood to rush towards his extremities. Ashamed of his masculine instinct — but powerless to stop it — his lips, drenched from her tears, remained against her cheek.

Without warning, she drew back and looked at him. Her eyes were flooded with unmitigated anger, grief … and something he hadn't seen in months. Before he could say anything, she sank her fingernails into his skin and pulled his mouth towards hers.

Liam sucked in his breath as if he'd been awakened from a deep sleep.

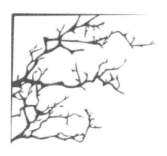

# Chapter 24

The sun began to stream through the curtains, bathing Liam's face in a bronze light as Olivia lay on her side watching him sleep. Her bleary eyes followed the patch of light-brown stubble running along the curve in his jaw, which for the first time she could remember was devoid of tension.

As his breath fell softly across her fingertips, she turned her cheek into her pillow in order to catch a wayward tear. The throbbing ache in her right side had woken her before dawn, but not wanting to disturb Liam by getting up to take one of the pretty white pills Dr. Feldspausch had prescribed for her, tried to lessen the pain instead by concentrating on other things. Unfortunately, her efforts had only succeeded in bringing back the anguish from yesterday, as well as summon an unrelenting fear for next week's court appearance.

The sound of the toilet flushing in the hall caused Liam to jerk awake, his disoriented gaze stumbling around the room before coming to rest upon Olivia. "Morning," he said, reaching out to touch her cheek.

Shoving her thoughts to the side, she forced a smile.

He stretched and lifted his arm, inviting her to lay her head upon his shoulder. "How long have you been awake?"

"Not long," she lied, snuggling against him.

"What have you been thinking about?"

She twirled his chest hairs around her fingers, searching for an answer. "The day we met," she heard herself say.

"Really?"

"Mmm-hmm," she said, running with it. "I was sitting at my desk, trying to get through my paperwork, when one of my tellers poked her head in my office and told me that a man was waiting outside with a power of attorney for his mother." Olivia grinned as the memory came rushing back to her. "I looked up, expecting to see some short, frumpy guy with a receding hairline and spare tire around his middle, but instead, this tall, blue-eyed, broad-shouldered sheriff's deputy, wearing a serious face and gentle smile, comes walking through my door."

"I remember that day, too," said Liam, pointing to a small pink spot on the upper-left side of his chest. "See this?"

Olivia raised her head and squinted. "What? You mean your birthmark?"

"It's not a *birthmark*," he said, scrunching up his face, "that's a scar from where I was struck by Cupid's arrow. I don't know if I ever told you this, but I was smitten the moment I saw you."

She laughed as his feet tangled themselves around hers. "I know."

His right brow slanted upwards. "How could you tell?"

Propping herself up on her elbow, she ran her fingers through his hair, which was a sexy mess, and giggled. "Because you came back the very next day to open an IRA, and paid the minimum amount required with three crumpled twenties, two tens, nineteen ones, and four quarters."

"It wasn't my fault, you know," he said, tapping his chest. "It was the arrow."

Olivia patted the side of his cheek. "Well, whatever the reason, I thought it was sweet."

He leaned over and kissed her. "*You're* sweet."

Letting him pull her on top of him, she closed her eyes and took in a contented breath as his lips began to roam across her breasts — yet the slamming of cabinets, followed by the clanging of a pan, stifled her mood. "I guess your dad's up to stay," she declared with a sigh.

Resting his head against the pillow, Liam's voice broke the silence that had drifted between them. "I'm sorry about what the doctor told you," he said in a tender voice.

Finding herself unable to answer, she nodded as she struggled to let it go.

Echoes of thunder rumbled in the distance, causing the light in the room to fade to a dismal gray.

"I know I haven't said it lately, but I do love you," he said, staring into her eyes as he slid his hands around her waist. "You are my *life* ... and that's never going to change."

His face faded from her sight as her eyes flooded with tears. "What about when I'm in an orange jumpsuit, picking up trash along the highway?"

Liam's grip around her waist tightened. "That's not going to happen, because — I swear to God — I'll move heaven and earth to make sure it doesn't."

Hearing the conviction in his words, Olivia swallowed the ache in her throat and pressed her lips to his. The thunder outside grew louder, rattling the windowpane as he parted her legs with his own. Filled with desire, she clutched at the sheet beneath his shoulders as the warmth of his skin set her insides on fire. Tossing her head back, she let out a soft moan and rode the feeling until her body collapsed in a quivering heap against him.

As she lay there, curled up in his arms, the smell of burnt toast began to waft under the door, and she could feel the pain in her side returning, yet the grief that always accompanied it was nowhere to be found, leaving the hole it had made in her heart full of an unfamiliar — and unwavering — sense of peace.

"Liam," she said, running her fingers along his torso as she listened to the rain hitting the window. "I want you to call Loretta Boyd ... and tell her yes."

HARLAN PAUSED TO PICK the skin off of his scrambled eggs before shoveling them into his mouth. They were a bit on the rubbery side, and as he forced the remainder of them down with his blackened toast, he found his taste buds longing for a pan of Enid's homemade biscuits and gravy, which aside from his wife's were the best he'd ever had.

Sighing, he licked the grease from his lips and reached for his coffee, but the sound of the bedroom door opening caused him to shift his gaze to the newspaper instead, where he pretended to read the sports section.

A moment later, Liam walked into the kitchen.

"Mornin'," he said, looking up from the paper.

Liam answered him with a curt nod.

"Want some coffee?" prompted Harlan, his uneven tone disrupting the caustic silence surrounding them as he extended the small olive branch. As *sorry* wasn't a word in his vocabulary — an unfortunate trait that had been passed down to him by his own father — it was the only way he knew how to apologize, and yet, over the past few months, had noticed that the branch had started to become brittle.

Liam's gaze flicked across Harlan's face in the same unassuming manner it always did. "Yeah," he finally said, making his way over to the counter.

Harlan's elation was short-lived when he saw him pick up his thermos from the dish strainer. "I thought you might wanna sit down and have a cup with me."

"I can't today," he replied, keeping his eyes on his thermos as he filled it. "I'm meeting Dr. Neumann in half an hour for the girl's autopsy." He set the pot back on the burner and turned around. "Would you like to come? It'd give us a chance to talk on the way over."

Taken aback by his offer, Harlan hid his surprise by rubbing his hand along his jaw. "Seein' the insides of a person's body isn't somethin' I care to do," he said in a gruff tone.

Liam screwed the cap onto his thermos and leaned against the counter. "When I get home, I'll fill you in on the Ramirez case ... as well as a few other things, and you can tell me what you know about Malloy."

Fairly certain that the *other things* he was speaking of had to do with him and Olivia fostering the girl's baby — but not wanting him to know that he'd heard the two of them arguing about it the other night, gave him an innocent nod instead. "Sounds good," he answered, setting his mug down.

"I'll see you later, then." Pushing himself away from the counter, Liam walked out of the kitchen.

Glancing at the microwave, Harlan watched the back of his son's reflection disappear into the garage behind him. Upon hearing the overhead door bang against the concrete, he grabbed the edges of the table and hauled himself to his feet, then leaning over his walker, pulled the note he'd written for Olivia from the pocket of his caddy and placed it under the saltshaker. He knew she wouldn't give a rat's ass if he was gone or not, but didn't want to take a chance on her calling Liam when she realized he was missing.

After putting on his coat, he felt along the top of the refrigerator for the keys to his pickup—that Liam thought he'd hidden from him—and headed for the front door.

LIAM STOOD ON THE OTHER side of the metal gurney, watching Dr. Neumann as she fussed with the bright circular light above it. "I appreciate you taking time out of your Saturday to do this."

Satisfied with the position of the light, the woman lowered her arms. "Not a problem," she chirped, leaning over the girl, whose naked corpse lay stretched out between them. "After being around patients all day that do nothing but complain, I find performing autopsies to be quite cathartic."

"Can you tell me how old she was?"

Inserting a gloved finger into the girl's mouth, Dr. Neumann pulled her lower jaw down and peered inside. "Well ... she doesn't have any baby teeth, but it looks like her upper primary molar was just starting to come in. I'd say that, combined with the fact that she was old enough to get pregnant, puts her around twelve or thirteen."

Liam's gaze deviated to the plain white cabinets hanging on the wall as she began poking between the girl's legs.

"I take it you still haven't been able to identify her?"

"No," he said, focusing on the poster advocating for clean hands in the workplace that was taped to the far cabinet.

"There's bruising and tearing along the vagina that's consistent with having just given birth."

Liam shifted his feet and nodded, wishing she'd tell him something he didn't already know.

"So, how's Harlan doing these days?"

Upon hearing the biting sarcasm in her voice, Liam swerved his attention back to her. Still hunched over the table, the years embedded in the woman's face were a stark contrast to the electric-blonde ponytail that followed the curve of her spine. Along with being a part-time medical examiner, Gloria Neumann was also Orand County's only general physician; having been practicing medicine longer than he'd been alive, she stood a mere five feet tall, carried around a flip-style phone, a purse filled with butterscotch candies, and owned a razor-sharp tongue that could cut men twice her size in half—and had.

"Is he enjoying retirement?"

"Not really," replied Liam.

"Well, I can't say I blame him," she said, walking around the table. "If you ask me, he'd have been better off being hauled out of there in a pine box."

Arching his brow, Liam folded his arms.

"You know," she said, pausing to slip on a pair of glasses that had special lenses attached to the front of them, "I saw where you let Dr. Fuller up in Rapid City perform the autopsy on that Ramirez fellow."

Once more hearing the contempt in her tone, but knowing it would be pointless to try and explain his reasons for giving such a high-profile case to Fuller instead of her, Liam decided it would serve him best to remain silent.

Bending over the girl, Dr. Neumann cradled her face in her hands the way a mother would. "Come closer," she said to Liam.

He shook his head. "I'm good where I'm at."

The doctor peered up at him and let out a long, arduous sigh. "No, I mean—*come closer*. I need you to help me roll her over."

Liam felt a hitch in his breath. He didn't mind handling corpses, but he did mind handling the body of a teenage girl who had been stripped of all her dignity.

"Well, come on," she said, snapping her fingers. "I've got other things I want to do today, and it doesn't involve mollycoddling the new sheriff."

Pressing his tongue to the roof of his mouth, Liam forced himself to move in her direction.

"There," said Dr. Neumann, gesturing at a box of latex gloves on the counter. "Put on a pair. And the gowns are to your left."

After doing as she instructed, Liam slipped his hands under the girl's shoulders and rolled her onto her hip.

"That's good. Now, as you can see, the bullet entered here ... through the right occipital bone."

He looked to where she was pointing. The hole, about four millimeters in diameter, was centered in the lower right side of the back of her head.

"X-rays show the main fragments of the bullet are lodged in the frontal bone," she continued, removing a piece of scalp tissue near the wound with a set of tweezers, "but I won't know the extent of the damage until I open her up."

"Was she killed instantly?"

"If you want my preliminary answer—it's no. The bullet most likely caused immediate unconsciousness and brain death, but her heart probably continued beating for several minutes, which is why she had blood coming from her mouth and nose, and around the entrance wound."

Easing the girl back down onto the table, Liam turned away.

"I wasn't done —"

"Did you check her fingernails for DNA?" he asked, stripping off his gloves.

Dr. Neumann's shoes echoed sharply across the black-and-white speckled tiles. "Before you got here," she answered, stepping in front of him to retrieve a corded saw with a serrated blade off the counter.

"*And?*"

"The blood underneath them was her own."

Disappointment surrounded him. "Did you come across anything else of interest?"

Dr. Neumann waved the saw in front of him and smiled. "Not yet."

Having no desire to watch the girl's skull being cut open, Liam tossed his gloves in the biohazard bin beside him and tore off his paper gown.

"Don't you want to stay?" she asked in a manner that came across sounding more like an order than a question.

"I have other things to attend to," he answered, averting her penetrating gaze as he edged past her.

"Once I retrieve the bullet and its fragments, I'll get them to you, along with my detailed report."

Giving her a nod, Liam started for the door.

"Oh, wait! I almost forgot."

He stopped and turned.

"The hoodie she was wearing is in that bag over there, and she had *that*," she said, pointing at a small envelope lying beside the bag, "stuffed inside its front pocket."

Walking over to the counter, Liam picked up the envelope and emptied its contents into his hand. A silver key for *The Way, The Truth, and The Life Chapel* fell into his palm.

HARLAN PUFFED CONTENTEDLY on his cigarette as he pulled up to the entrance of Orand County's impound lot and rolled down his window. Extending his arm, he entered the four-digit code that had only been changed once in the last twenty years into a weathered keypad and waited. The chain-link gate in front of him began to move, and he watched its rubber wheels bump along the uneven gravel as it slowly rolled past him.

After the gate had cleared the left front bumper of his truck, he drove through the narrow opening and started winding his way around a dozen or so vehicles — all of which were here no doubt because of his son's relentless enforcement of traffic violations. Parking along the back row, he stamped out his cigarette in the ashtray and shut off the engine.

Throwing open his door, he set his left foot down on the crushed rock and walked his butt cheeks across the ribbed seat until his right foot joined it. Using the steering wheel for leverage, he pushed himself to a standing position, then with movements lacking coordination or grace, reached into the bed of his pickup to retrieve his walker that he'd decided to call Roi. It was short for hemorrhoid, and the name fit because it was a pain in the ass and always attached to him.

As Harlan maneuvered Roi's legs around a puddle left behind from this morning's rain, his lungs began to shrink against the bitter cold, making him cough. Arriving at the entrance to the garage, he grabbed hold of the knob but it refused to turn. "Hey, Clark?" he yelled, banging on the door with his fist. "You in there?" Glancing around the deserted lot, Harlan dug the key out of his pocket that he was supposed to have turned in four months ago and jammed it into the lock.

The door gave way to a dark and damp space that reeked of gasoline, mineral spirits, and transmission fluid. Flipping on the lights, the garage, which was essentially nothing more than a pole barn, began to buzz with excitement as the fluorescent bulbs came to life.

With the shadows in front of him illuminated, Harlan started towards the black Monte Carlo parked at the opposite end. Other than the trio of salt trucks that the county kept stored here, the remaining space was utilized by the sheriff's office to hold and examine vehicles that had been used in a crime or involved in a fatality.

He ran his hand along the Monte Carlo's rusted roof and shook his head. It was as surreal as it was frustrating to find out after all these years that Dominick Malloy — and the money he'd stolen — had been resting at the bottom of the lake this entire time.

Pulling out his phone, he began scrolling through the pics of the car that Stiles had sent him. Having spent most of yesterday painstakingly going over each and every one of them in detail, he found that he was bothered by two things: The first was that the briefcase had been found on the floorboard behind the driver's seat. Harlan didn't know of many men who would risk letting a quarter of a million dollars out of their sight, much less their arms' reach. Second, the passenger-side window was down. Wincing as he forced his hip to flex, Harlan placed his hands on the car's doorframe and peered inside. It wouldn't have been unusual for the window to be down at all during a hot day in July — if it hadn't been for the fact that the air conditioner on the center console was turned up full blast.

Letting his gaze roam along the rest of the interior, Harlan's jaw began to ache as his thoughts turned to a certain pale-faced green-eyed girl with red tresses. Long before Alice Johnston became Alice Malloy, she had been Liam's significant other. Harlan had watched their relationship go from a slow-burn in high school, to fast and furious upon Liam's return from his deployment in Afghanistan, to ending abruptly six months later when she informed him that she was going to marry Dominick Malloy.

Harlan dug his fingers into the leather panel of the door. First loves were as hard to forget as they were to get over, and based on the evasive conversation he'd had with his son last night, he began to wonder to what lengths he would go to protect her.

"Hey," shouted a man with a raspy voice, "what are you doin' in here?"

Harlan looked over his shoulder to find Dennis Clark hurrying towards him. "It's just me, Denny," he called, ducking his head out of the car.

The man's frantic footsteps slowed. "Sorry, Harlan," he said, giving him an easy smile. "I didn't know it was you." As he drew closer, the relieved expression on his face quickly turned to confusion. "Uh, how'd you get in?"

Not wanting to relinquish his key just yet, Harlan searched for something to say. "The door was unlocked," he replied, knowing the bottle of whiskey that Denny kept in the drawer under his tool bench would lend credibility to his answer.

"Oh ..." Denny scratched his unshaven throat as he cast a worried glance around the shop.

Returning his attention to the car, Harlan opened the passenger-side door and after balancing all his weight on his good leg, leaned inside.

"What're you doin'?" asked Denny, kneeling next to him.

Scowling, Harlan turned up his elbow making him draw his head back. "Just havin' a look around."

"I figured you'd be goin' over Ramirez's Jeep," Denny said, straightening, "not this piece of shit."

"Well," replied Harlan, running his hand along the fold in the seat, "since I've been consigned to the scrap heap, I'll take what I can get." As he spoke, his index finger touched upon something small and hard. Grasping onto the object, he plucked it from its muddy tomb; a slender chain, broken at the clasp and covered in sediment, came with it. Rubbing it against his shirt, Harlan held it up to the light and saw that it was a gold initial that had been stamped in the form of a cursive A.

The driver's side door opened and Denny squatted across from him. "Need any help?" he asked, his bloodshot eyes appearing eager to be of assistance.

Harlan felt his lips tightening as he closed his fist around the necklace. "No, I've got what I need."

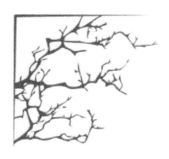

# Chapter 25

"**A**re *you* gonna tell me what I'm doing here?" demanded Caffrey, his boots clomping across the tile floor of the station as the door swung closed behind him. "Because your deputy here was too busy arguing with his girlfriend on the way over to fill me in."

Liam absently flicked his gaze to Stiles, who had his cell phone pressed to the side of his face.

"I've got to go," Stiles mumbled in a clipped tone.

Liam pointed to Aaron's chair. "Have a seat, Mr. Caffrey." Unable to deal with the confining space of the interview room, he felt it would be better on the both of them if he questioned him out in the open, as Saturday's were relatively quiet at the station.

"So, we're back to Mister now," mused Caffrey, the smirk he'd worn the other day returning to his lips as he plopped himself down in the chair. Removing his sunglasses, he placed them on the desk and snapped his fingers at Stiles. "Can I get some coffee?"

Gordon folded his arms. "Sorry, we're fresh out."

Leaning back in the chair, Caffrey narrowed his eyes at him.

Liam sat down at Aaron's desk and took in a shallow breath. "A key to your chapel was found on the girl that was murdered near the truck stop. Would you care to explain how she got it?"

Turning his attention to Liam, Caffrey shrugged. "She must've stolen it."

"From where?"

"I keep a spare under the welcome mat."

"There's no welcome mat outside your chapel."

"She must've stolen that too," said Caffrey, his smirk widening.

Liam's jaw flexed. "You have a pretty good sense of humor."

"Well, I find that it helps make the best of bad situations."

"Did you come up with that mantra while you were in prison?"

The grin nestled on Caffrey's face took a downward turn.

Leaning across the desk, Liam placed a piece of paper in front of him.

He shoved it away without looking at it. "That was a long time ago."

"Not for the girl you raped," said Liam in a low voice.

Caffrey's eyes flickered. "The person you see sitting across from you now is not the same man that committed that crime."

"How so?"

Slapping his left ankle across his right knee, Caffrey gripped the arms of the chair. "Because I found God in that prison cell and made a promise to myself that when I got out, I would devote my life to helpin' people." He paused to jab a wiry finger at Liam. "And it's a promise that I've kept for the better part of twenty years."

"Does that include lying to the law?" asked Liam, unmoved by his declaration.

"Look," Caffrey said, rubbing his hand over his face, "the girl showed up last week outside my chapel—cold, scared, and starved to death."

"Did she give you her name?"

Caffrey shook his head. "She wouldn't say, but when I asked her how she'd come to be here, she told me that her mother's boyfriend had gotten her pregnant and that when she'd finally confided in her mother what he'd done, she'd called her a liar and kicked her out. She then went on to tell me that she'd been trying to hitch a ride to the bus station when someone stole her backpack, which had all her money as well as her cell phone in it."

A heavy sigh sounded to his left, prompting Liam to steal a sideways glance at Stiles, who was leaning against the filing cabinet, texting. "Did she tell you where she was heading?" he asked, looking back at Caffrey.

"Lynnville, Tennessee. She said that she had an aunt that lived there. I offered her the use of my phone so she could get in touch with her, but she didn't know her number, address, or even her last name. I asked her how she was planning on gettin' to her house then, and she told me that she'd figure it out once she got there."

"What else did she say?"

"Nothin'. She begged me to drive her to the bus stop, but I told her that I couldn't."

"And why was that?"

Caffrey scowled. "Why do you think?"

"I don't know," said Liam flatly, "that's why I'm asking."

"How would it look—with my record—if I got pulled over with a fourteen-year-old runaway sittin' next to me?" Caffrey folded his arms against his chest. "I gave her a key, ten bucks to eat on, and a blanket from my truck. I told her I'd be back the next day and that I'd help her get to where she needed to go."

"When exactly was this?"

"The evening of the fourteenth, just after my prayer service."

Getting to his feet, Liam placed his hands on the desk. "Why should I believe any of what you've told me?"

"I'm tellin' you the truth."

"I'm not sure you know *what* the truth is," replied Liam, shaking his head, "because the other day you told me you'd never seen the girl, and — just less than five minutes ago — denied giving her a key."

"If I'd told you the truth the other day, you would've pulled my record and hauled me in here for questioning."

"And how is today any different?" asked Liam.

Caffrey's jaw hardened, forming a knot in the sunken part of his cheek.

The phone in Liam's pocket began to ring. "Sheriff Matthews," he said, turning away.

"Uh, yeah, this is Robert Jeffries. I'm the shipping supervisor at *Sanford's Farm Supply* in Sioux City returning your call."

"Thanks for getting back to me," said Liam, heading into his office. He paused to close his door before continuing. "Do you have any information for me regarding the message I left you?"

"Yeah, our records confirm that on the fourteenth, a W. Caffrey delivered a load at ten twenty-five that night …"

The siren starting up on the fire station's pumper truck sounded in the distance, drawing Liam's gaze to the window. "Can you describe what the driver looked like?" he asked, watching the truck and its lights as it went screaming past.

"I don't know him personally, but I pulled up the video footage from our dock and took a couple of pics for you. I just sent them to your phone."

"Thanks for your help." Ending the call, Liam went into his text messages and eagerly pulled up the pictures. A sense of despair began to course through him when he saw Caffrey and his silver-tipped boots talking to one of the workers on the loading dock.

Grabbing a pad of paper out of his top drawer, he jerked open the door and started across the room.

"Bad news?" asked Caffrey, lifting his brow.

"Write down everything you just told me," Liam said, tossing the pad in front of him. "Then I'll have Deputy Stiles drive you back to the truck stop."

"County to Sheriff Matthews. Do you copy?"

"Go ahead, county," he answered, feeling his anger rising as he watched a smug expression spread over Caffrey's face.

"We have a report of a signal 11. Eldridge Lane near the railroad tracks. There's a vehicle on fire."

BY THE TIME LIAM ARRIVED on the scene, the inside front of the car was fully engulfed in flames.

Thick black smoke poured from its windows, choking the air around him as he climbed out of his truck. "Is anybody hurt?" he called, running towards Mick Andersen, Captain of Orand County's only fire department.

"It appears to be abandoned," Andersen said, shouting to be heard over the noise as his men battled the blaze. "We'll know in a minute."

"Who called it in?"

"A woman walking her dog." Andersen paused to tilt his helmeted head to the left. "She's over there."

Peering through the cloud of smoke, Liam saw an older woman in a blue parka standing by the shoulder of the road with a large dog pacing anxiously by her side. "Ma'am," he said, making his way over to her, "I'm Sheriff Matthews. Can I get your name?"

The woman wrapped the handle of the leash tightly around her fingers. "Irene Standing Crow."

"Pretty dog," he said, gesturing at the white ball of fluff that was now sniffing his boots. "Is he a Pyrenees?"

A small smile formed at the corners of the woman's mouth, softening the lines in her face. "Yes."

Eyeing the progress the firemen were making, Liam bent down to pet the dog. "He's a big boy," he said, scratching the thick white fur on his back.

The dog hunkered at Liam's touch and ducked behind the woman's leg.

"More like a big baby," she countered.

"How old?"

"Almost a year."

"Well," said Liam as he straightened, "if that's the case, this time next year, I think he'll probably be walking you."

The woman blinked and then let out a deep-throated laugh. "He might just be," she said, sweeping a wisp of long gray hair off her forehead.

"Can you tell me what happened here?" he asked, hoping she wouldn't be offended by his impatience to get to the truth.

Irene Standing Crow's smile narrowed slightly. "We were walking down the road," she said, pausing to point towards the curve on her right, "when I heard a loud pop. It sounded like a gunshot, but I didn't think much of it because we're surrounded by woods. It wasn't long after, though that I smelled something burning. When I came over the hill, I saw the car on fire."

"Did you see anyone near the car? Some kids maybe?"

"Nope. No one."

"Sheriff?"

Glancing over his shoulder, Liam saw Mick Andersen motioning at him. He turned back to the woman. "Thank you for your time, ma'am," he said, pulling down on the brim of his Stetson. "Have a good afternoon."

"You too," she replied, tugging on the leash that was still wrapped around her knuckles. "Come on, Mató."

Obeying her command, the dog came out from behind her leg and happily began trotting ahead of her.

As Liam started across the road, the smoke surrounding the car began to clear, causing his impatience to turn into apprehension as the partially scorched body of a 1971 Impala materialized before him. Low to the ground and light silver in color, it bore the same gap in distance between its front and rear lights as the car in Hector's video.

Rigidly sweeping his gaze along the car's grill, Liam stopped and swore under his breath upon seeing that the outermost headlight on the driver's side was busted.

"Whoever did this used lighter fluid as an accelerant," stated Andersen.

Liam looked to where he was pointing and saw the charred remains of a small yellow-and-red can resting at the bottom of the metal frame that used to be the front seat.

"Captain?"

"Yeah?" answered Andersen, glancing at one of his men over the top of the car's smoldering roof.

The fireman, whom Liam had known most of his life and who went by the nickname of Curly, paused to wipe the sweat from his face. "There's something you might wanna see."

Stepping in front of Andersen, Liam made his way around to the other side of the car where the passenger-side door stood open. "What is it?"

"There," said Curly, pointing at the floorboard in the backseat as Andersen caught up to him.

Liam followed the tip of Curly's gloved finger to find a crowbar, about fifteen inches in length, lying in the midst of the rubble. The flat part of it was blackened and covered in soot, while the other end, which was resting on the hump of the floorboard, was relatively unscathed—allowing him to see the bloodstains along its curve.

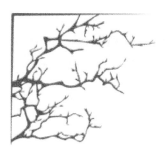

# Chapter 26

Spotting the address he'd been searching for on a dented mailbox, Harlan turned into the sloped driveway next to it, being careful to avoid its rain-filled potholes, and exited his truck by employing the same tactics he had at the impound lot. The tall steps leading up to the porch were a bit more cumbersome, however, and he had to grab hold of the iron column bolted to the concrete in order to pull himself up.

Leaning heavily against Roi, Harlan waited for his breath to return before ringing the doorbell. Unfortunately, the reaction to the chime was quicker than he'd expected and he found himself scrambling to scrape together his thoughts as the door swung open.

"Sheriff Matthews."

Harlan dipped his head in the direction of the woman standing in front of him. "Well, I used to be," he replied, his words getting lost in a white vapor as a strong wind began to stir.

Diane Travis pulled the ends of her gray cardigan tighter against her.

"I apologize for showin' up here unannounced like this," he continued, shifting his feet to ward off the cold, "but there are a few questions I need to ask you on the sheriff's behalf."

A taut smile unfolded across her lips. "I assume this is about Dominick?"

"Yes, ma'am. It is."

Taking a step backward, she motioned for him to come inside. "Would you like some coffee?" she asked, closing the door behind him. "It's still warm."

Although another cup of coffee was the last thing in the world he needed, Harlan felt his head move up and down the instant her velvety-brown eyes settled upon his.

Folding her arms against her, Diane Travis turned and, with movements as rigid as his, started across the living room floor.

As he followed along behind her, Harlan couldn't help but notice the eight-point buck that was mounted on the wall above the TV; its massive neck, covered in white fur and supporting a large head and rack that faced east, rose out of the wooden plaque it was attached to like a phoenix. As Roi's tennis-balled legs touched upon the linoleum, Harlan thought back to the meager four-point stag that hung above his own TV and sighed.

"How do you take it?" Diane asked, reaching into the cabinet.

"Black's fine," he answered, eyeing the stack of overdue bills that were lying on the desk next to the fridge. "So, where are you workin' these days?"

"For the past few years, I've been the assistant manager for a PR firm in Rapid City, but have been on medical leave since January."

"Oh, uh … what's wro—"

"Have a seat," she said, gesturing at the table beside him.

Relieved that he didn't have to finish his sentence, Harlan did as she asked. Sitting down in the chair, his gaze swept across the tiny kitchen, stopping briefly to take in the cluster of prescription bottles on the counter, as well as to note that there were no pictures of kids—framed or otherwise—in either of the rooms he'd been in, before coming to rest upon the side of her face. Although it was still every bit as beautiful as he remembered, there was something hauntingly familiar embedded in the small crevices that now lined it. "I was sorry to hear about Patrick," he mumbled, scratching his sideburn as he watched her fill the mugs.

Diane's posture stiffened, enabling him to see that the right part of her chest was caved in. When the coffee was dangerously close to spilling over the brims, she set the pot back on its burner and took an inordinate amount of time adding cream and sugar to the one on the left before turning around. "I'm sorry," she said, sitting across from him. "I know it's been thirteen months ... but it's still hard."

"Well, if there's one thing I've learned over the years," he replied, offering her a crusty smile, "it's that there's no set timetable for grief."

Keeping her gaze fastened on her mug, Diane gave a half-hearted shrug as she ran the tip of her finger along its chipped rim.

Fueled by an overwhelming desire to take her pain away, Harlan sought to expound upon his statement. "You know," he added, "some people have the ability to cry for a bit and move on, while others wallow in it for months as they thrive on all the sympathy bein' poured their way. And then there are those who are so consumed by it, it causes their insides to die a little each day—until there's nothin' left of them but a hollow, bitter shell ..." As his rambling, not-so-well-thought-out epiphany drifted across the table, the slender curve of Diane's jaw began to harden.

Shifting in her chair, she raised her eyes, now a coarse shade of black, to meet his. "So," she said pointedly, "which one of those are you?"

Feeling a twinge in his cheeks, Harlan brought his mug to his lips and took a long swallow, washing the remaining empathy he held for her into the pit of his stomach. When he was finished, he retrieved a battered notepad from his coat and curtly flipped it open. "I'm sure you know by now that we pulled Dominick Malloy's car out of Crow's Foot Lake this past Wednesday."

She tilted her head, seeming amused by his statement. "Everyone in Weeping Rock knows."

"How well did you know Malloy's wife?"

"I wouldn't exactly say that we were friends, but I knew Alice fairly well, I guess."

"Do you think she knew about her husband's illegal business affairs?"

"No." She paused to take a sip of her coffee. "She was so young at the time, that I doubt she even knew what the term *embezzlement* meant."

"And what about you?" asked Harlan, eyeing her closely. "Did you know?"

Diane met his gaze with an intense but guarded ferocity that was eerily reminiscent of his daughter-in-law's. "You've asked me these questions before, the *first* time you interviewed me."

Harlan leaned back in his chair. "I think they bear repeating."

Matching his gesture, Diane went a step further and crossed her arms against her uneven chest. "I had no clue what Dominick was doing. My job as his secretary was to answer the phone, print out contracts, and enter the clients' information into the computer."

"What about the garbage bags full of shredded files? Was that your doin'?"

"Dominick said there wasn't any reason to have dusty files taking up office space when the client's info could be called up with the push of a button."

Harlan stretched his leg under the table, trying to alleviate the pain in his hip. "Let's go back to July Fourth," he said, being careful to keep his boot away from her bare toes. "What was his mood like?"

"He was a little on edge because he'd just found out the day before that he was being audited by the IRS."

Checking his notes, Harlan saw that her answers were almost word for word the same as they were eleven years ago. "Did he make or receive any unusual calls, or did anyone come by to see him?"

"Alice stopped by with their daughter that afternoon."

"What did she have to say?"

"I don't know. They talked in his office."

"For how long?"

"Not very long. Less than five minutes, I guess."

Harlan turned the page on his notepad and saw that his questions had come to an end.

"Is that it?" she asked, taking another sip from her mug.

"We recovered a portion of an email sent to Dominick from a travel agency in Rapid City — that's now out of business — confirmin' two first-class seats with *Sprint Airlines* to Guadalajara on the night of the fourth."

Silence followed his words.

"If you're asking if I knew anything about it," Diane finally replied, setting her mug down, "the answer is no."

"You didn't make the bookin' for him?"

"When it came to traveling, Dominick always made his own arrangements."

Rain began to plink against the window, drawing her gaze.

Slipping his hand inside his coat, Harlan unbuttoned the pocket of his flannel shirt and grasped the chain of the necklace. "I found this in the front seat of Dominick's car this mornin'," he said, pushing it across the table.

The bottoms of Diane's long eyelashes fell upon her sunken cheekbones as she looked down at the initial. "Well, his wife's name *was* Alice," she replied with a laugh.

Harlan let several moments pass before he spoke again. "You know, my memory isn't what it used to be, but I seem to recall on the day I interviewed you that you had the beginnings of what was goin' to be a pretty bad bruise in the middle of your forehead."

Another laugh, more stilted than the one before, spilled from between her lips as she hugged her arms against her chest. "I guess your memory's better than mine because I don't have any recollection of that."

Reaching beside him, Harlan pulled Malloy's thick case file out of the caddy that was tied to Roi's front. "When Malloy disappeared, we went through his financials with a fine-tooth comb," he said, opening it up. "And on one of his credit card statements, we found a purchase made at *Burke Jewelers*. I didn't think much of it at the time, but I went down there this mornin' and spoke to Marvin." Harlan paused to shake his head. "You know, that old man has kept track of every transaction ever made since his store opened some fifty-odd years ago?"

Diane's gaze traveled to the crisp piece of paper he was holding. "I never did any of Dominick's personal shopping. As I explained to you earlier, I was his secretary — nothing more."

"Well now, you see," countered Harlan, "that's where our stories differ. According to Marvin's records, durin' the first week in June, Malloy came in and bought not one, but *two* necklaces, both of them with an initial A charm. One for his wife, and I assume the other ... for his mistress."

Diane dug her fingernails into the sleeves of her cardigan. "My name doesn't start with A."

Cutting his eyes to his right, Harlan stared at the window over the sink for a long time. "You know," he finally said, "when I was a boy I used to live down the street from a girl named Diane, but her momma and daddy always called her Ann." Turning his gaze back to her, he saw that her cheeks had been drained of their color. Leaning across the table, he tapped the initial with the tip of his finger. "Was that Dominick's nickname for you?"

Diane's chin flattened as tears the size of raindrops began to slide down her face.

"How long were the two of you havin' an affair?"

"A few months," she answered, keeping her eyes on the necklace.

"What happened that afternoon?"

Diane wiped at her face. "I walked into the back room to discover Dominick putting all the money from the safe into his briefcase. He explained that he was leaving for Mexico because he was in trouble, and then told me that he wanted me to go with him." She drew a ragged breath and shook her head. "I knew it was wrong, but I was in love with him and the idea of running away to Mexico with nothing but the clothes on my back was as exciting as it was romantic."

"How'd the car end up in the lake?"

The skin around her eyes bunched as they took on a distant look. "He was afraid we were going to miss our check-in at the airport and was driving too fast. It was beginning to get dark and he misjudged the curve." Propping her elbow upon her left wrist, she held her whitened knuckles against her cheek, but her tears continued to flow over them. "I woke up in a dazed panic to find the car filling with water. I started clawing at the window trying to get out and reached for Dominick. In the fading light, I could see him slumped over the dash with his mouth open ... the blood drifting from his head ..."

As Harlan watched the lines in her face darken, he swiftly came to realize just exactly who it was that she had been mourning. "How'd you get free from the car?"

She gathered the necklace between her fingers. "I managed to get the window down," she said, pressing the initial to her lips, "and once I made it to the bank, I half-walked, half-crawled the three miles to my house. Fortunately for me, Pat was still at work."

"*Fortunately*," Harlan repeated.

Her gaze shot towards him. "He was a different man back then," she said in a broken whisper. "He would never have forgiven me."

"Well, lookin' at how things stand now," stated Harlan, drawing his leg back underneath him, "it seems like that would've been the *least* of my worries."

Still clutching the necklace, Diane closed her eyes and dropped her head into her hands.

In the grim silence that followed, Harlan could feel his pity for her resurrecting as a silent sob wrenched itself from her throat … and for the first time in his life, he found himself wishing that he'd been wrong.

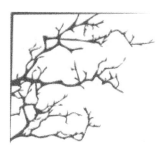

# Chapter 27

The strong smell of perfume and freshly cut flowers clogged what little air there was in the small space, while the sound of throats being cleared, impatient sighs, and silent stares that darted when met only served to enhance the awkwardness that came from riding in an elevator with eight strangers.

Chastising herself for not walking up the one flight of stairs, Olivia chewed on the inside of her lip as she waited for the stifling steel box to finish its ascent. It finally did—with a well-orchestrated jerk—and as the doors began to slide open, she turned sideways in order to squeeze past the large man standing in front of her. After unavoidably brushing her chest against his elbow and her backside against another woman's purse, she took in an anxious breath and started down the corridor.

As she drew closer to the set of double doors that led to the Neonatal Intensive Care Unit, she saw a sign posted that it was a restricted area and to call for admittance. Retrieving her phone, she clumsily entered the number, finding that her fingers were as nervous as the rest of her.

"NICU, how may I help you?"

"Uh — yes," Olivia stammered. "I'm here to visit one of the babies."

"What's the mother's last name?"

"I don't know. I'm here to see the infant that was found in Weeping Rock a few days ago."

There was a long pause.

"Are you a relative?" the woman on the other end asked in a wary voice.

"No, but I'm going to be fostering him and was hoping that I could hold him for a little while."

"What's your name, ma'am?"

Olivia politely answered the question and then listened as the earpiece filled with silence. "My husband, Sheriff Matthews, was in touch yesterday with Loretta Boyd regarding the matter," she added, hoping that the namedropping would help.

"Let me speak with my supervisor," said the woman. "I'll get right back to you."

Before Olivia could offer a reply of thanks, the call ended. Turning from the doors, she made her way over to a small waiting area that was currently unoccupied and sat down. As she leaned over to set her purse beside her feet, her phone, which was still in her hand, began to play. Thinking it was the

NICU, she held it up — only to have her heart skip a beat when she saw Dwayne Ballard's faceless avatar appear on the screen. Having no desire to discuss strategy, worst-case scenarios, or anything else regarding her upcoming hearing with him, she declined the call and forced herself to sit back. As the seconds ticked away, she was unable to keep her thoughts from straying to the reason that she'd had to cash in her 401-K to pay his retainer in the first place.

*It was Houdek Savings and Loan's annual Christmas party, and for the past half hour, she'd had to endure listening to Steve Montgomery, the vice-president of sales, brag about her work skills while simultaneously eyeing her cleavage. After checking her phone for any missed texts from Liam, who'd had to respond to an accident on the way here, she politely excused herself and ducked into the ladies' room.*

*Happy to have a moment's peace, she smiled at the secret she'd been carrying around inside her as she pushed opened the stall door. It was what made the party bearable and Liam's failure to attend it forgivable. She was five days late, and come morning would use the pregnancy test she'd bought earlier to confirm that fact. As she sat down, however, her smile faded against a backdrop of tears as her gaze fell upon the small red spot in the middle of her underwear.*

*Wanting nothing more at that moment than to be numb, she walked out of the bathroom and straight over to the open bar — where the rest of the evening quickly became a blur, except for the memory of the flashing blue lights in her rearview mirror … and her argument with*

*Liam as he drove her home from the Crawford County jail.*

A chiming noise caused Olivia to shift her attention to the corridor. Crossing her legs, she watched as the elevator doors slid open and dumped out four passengers before continuing on. An older couple, carrying a stuffed panda and pink polka-dotted gift bag, took a moment to study the directory mounted on the wall before turning excitedly in her direction.

Next, came a man dressed in khakis, his steps deliberate but slow as he held onto the hand of a little boy with golden curls; clutching the ribbon of a foil balloon that matched the color of his eyes, the boy grinned as he tottered across the floor.

Seeing the joy and anticipation in each of their faces as they passed by, Olivia wiped at her eyes as feelings that she had long buried began to stir. Twenty-nine months ago, she'd lain in a hospital bed on this very floor, her arms empty and her heart grieving, yet no one came to see her, except for Harlan, whom she suspected had done so out of obligation to his son. The notable absence of sympathetic words and gentle hugs from friends and co-workers that day had lingered among her tears, turning them bitter. And in the weeks that followed, she couldn't help wondering if they'd been too busy to come, hadn't known what to say — or just plain didn't care.

"Mrs. Matthews?"

Olivia saw a nurse in scrubs coming towards her. "Yes?" she answered, binding her emotions inside her as she got to her feet.

"I'm sorry you had to wait, but if you'll come with me, I'll take you to see Sweetpea." The nurse flipped her braid over her shoulder and smiled. "That's what we've been calling him."

Stooping to pick up her purse, Olivia smiled back as she walked with her through the set of doors and down the hall.

"So, you're Sheriff Matthews' wife?"

Olivia nodded. "I am."

"He's such a nice guy."

"Yes, he is," she replied.

The nurse's smile widened to a grin, pushing her cheeks closer to her enormous brown eyes. "He's quiet, though."

Olivia felt the corners of her mouth turn downward as feelings of jealousy began circling within her for no real reason. The nurse, who according to her ID badge went by the name of Melissa, led her into a large room, where nestled amongst the monitors and floor-to-ceiling equipment were several clear bassinets and incubators, each containing their own tiny human.

"Okay," said the nurse, handing her a gown. "Put this on and have a seat."

Taking off her coat, Olivia pulled the garment on over her sweater and jeans and sat down in a large blue glider as she watched the nurse reach into a bassinet with a card taped to the side that had '*Baby Doe*' printed on it.

"Here we are ..." Still smiling, the nurse bent over and placed the infant in Olivia's waiting arms.

The insides of Olivia's nose and throat started to sting as she cradled him against her chest. Taking a moment to warm her fingers in the palm of her hand, she reached up and smoothed his light-brown hair, being careful to avoid the I.V. needle in his scalp, before caressing his face and chin.

He jerked awake at her touch and began to cry.

"Shh," Olivia cooed, gently patting his bottom as she rocked him back and forth, "it's all right."

Upon hearing her voice, the baby's cries diminished. Pressing his little fists against his cheeks, he let go of a small yawn as he stared up at her with his bluish-gray eyes.

Smiling through her tears, Olivia's breath shook from her lips as her tethered emotions began to come undone, and before she could stop herself, the three words that she'd been unable to say to her own son came rushing out of her.

HAVING GOTTEN USED to the low hum buzzing in his ears as he walked the perimeter of the substation, Liam couldn't help thinking that its towering metal boxes would have blended in perfectly with the ever-graying sky if it hadn't been for the graffiti spray-painted across their panels. Because the station was situated off of a secluded road, in recent years it had become a favorite hangout spot for teens and adults alike, as the gravel lot surrounding it provided them with ample parking to engage in sex, drugs, and whatever the hell else they wanted to do.

As he paused to step over a cracked glass pipe, Liam's attention traveled from the barbed-wire fence circling the substation to the open field behind it where Hector's Jeep Wrangler had been found. Although the vehicle had been thoroughly searched, the area around it—with the exception of the immediate vicinity—had not, and if Caffrey was telling the truth about what the girl had told him in regards to her backpack, Liam felt there was an off chance it could be somewhere close by. As he headed towards the clearing, however, he struggled to dismiss the selfish hope that had been lurking inside him since yesterday that he wouldn't find it at all.

Sweeping his gaze across the blades of dead grass in front of him, Liam's thoughts unevenly bounced from the girl to Hector. Desperate to push forward after discovering the crowbar in the fire-ridden Impala, but knowing it would take a minimum of seventy-five days for the forensics lab in Pierre to process the blood found on it, he had called in a huge favor to Dr. Fuller, who'd agreed to test a sample. Although the results revealed it to be an exact match to Hector's, Reed Maxwell from the Rapid City PD forensics department had determined the crowbar, as well as the car, to be devoid of fingerprints.

Liam let go of a heavy sigh as he walked on. Without prints, there was no way to tie Frank Colter to Hector's murder *or* the car—which had come back as stolen—putting him right back to square one.

Emerging from the field, cold and empty-handed, the roar of an engine caused him to absently glance towards the road. A moment later, he saw Aaron's truck come around the bend.

"I figured you'd still be here," his deputy said, pulling off to the side.

"What are you doing out this way?" asked Liam as he drew closer.

"Hiram Murphy was walking down the middle of Canyon Lane drunk again."

"Was he wearing clothes this time?"

"Only his boots," said Aaron with a shudder. Lowering his window the rest of the way, he thrust his chin towards the substation. "Did you have any luck?"

"No," he replied, trying to hide his guilt that he wasn't disappointed by the fact.

Aaron reached across his seat. "Well, listen, I need to be getting on home, but I wanted to be sure and give you this before I left."

"What is it?" asked Liam, perplexed by the small gift bag he was holding out to him.

His deputy laughed. "Open it and see."

Reaching inside, Liam pulled out a pair of tiny moccasin boots; crocheted from soft blue yarn, they had delicate white stripes running along their tops. "How did you know?" he asked, feeling his face flush.

Aaron laughed again. "Because nobody comes out of a meeting with Loretta Boyd smiling, and judging by the size of the grin that was plastered on your lips the other night, I figured it could only mean one thing."

Putting the moccasins back in the bag, Liam nodded as he turned his gaze towards his deputy. "Thank you, and thank Naomi for me as well."

"I will," said Aaron, glancing at his watch, "but if I'm not home in the next twenty minutes, she's going to kill me."

"Why's that?"

"Her father's coming over for dinner."

Although Liam had met Aaron's father-in-law, who was a member of the He' Sapa Tribal Council, on a few occasions, he didn't know him well enough to form an opinion. To hear Aaron describe him, however, Jay Whitefeather was a man steeped in tradition, who disliked the fact that his son-in-law had given up his job with the tribal police and moved off the res—taking his only daughter and grandchild with him—in order to become a sheriff's deputy.

Aaron leaned his head out the window as he started his truck. "If you get any calls between six and nine," he said, talking over the engine, "be sure and send them my way."

Liam's phone began to vibrate. "So, I'm guessing that he still hates you?" he mused, offering his deputy a sympathetic shrug as he took a step back.

The good-natured expression behind Aaron's eyes wavered. "I think we're beyond hate. We've moved on to loathing now." Cutting the steering wheel to the right, he began easing the truck forward. "I'll see you tomorrow."

"Good luck," said Liam, giving him a wave. As Aaron pulled onto the road, he dug his phone out of his coat and saw a text from Olivia.

*'Someone wanted to say hi'*

Liam's heart swelled as he stared at the accompanying photo. His wife's smile, perfect, beautiful, and infrequent as of late lit up her entire face as she held the baby in her arms. *'Wish I was there'* he texted back and then added a heart emoji before hitting send.

Returning his phone to his pocket, he started towards his truck — only to have his gaze snag upon the ditch running alongside his tires. A fast-moving stream of water carrying trash and twigs rushed past him before disappearing into a large drainage pipe that ran underneath the entrance of the substation.

With his euphoria giving way to apprehension, Liam set the gift bag on the hood of his truck and retrieved his flashlight from his belt. Forcing his feet to move, he stepped down into the ditch and knelt in the freezing water. About a foot inside the culvert, he could see a pink backpack laying on its side. Shoving the top of his shoulder, which had grown rigid, against the edge of the pipe, Liam grabbed hold of its strap and dragged it out.

Carrying the backpack over to his truck, he set it in the passenger's seat and yanked on the first zipper. It opened up to reveal a compartment full of girl's clothes, food in plastic baggies, an assortment of makeup, and a tattered teddy bear missing an eye. In the second pouch, he pulled out two infant sleepers, a package of diapers, and a book on giving birth. Checking the rest of the pockets, he came across a cell phone with a cracked screen, a billfold containing close to two hundred in cash, and a library card for a town three counties west of here.

Liam stared solemnly at the name that was printed on the card. A lump began to form in the back of his throat as he ran his thumb along the photo of the familiar face sitting above it. In just a few short hours, the lives of Amelia Paige Adamson's family were about to be shattered forever … as was Olivia's.

As Liam climbed into his truck, the sun began to sink behind the trees, ushering his emotions to the forefront—along with a single, repeating, and horrific thought: one garbage bag and a dumpster were all it would take to make his problems go away.

"I TOLD YOU HE BITES."

Tears trickled down the sides of Claire's reddened cheeks as she sat forlornly on the edge of the bathtub.

After soaking a cotton ball in hydrogen peroxide, Alice dabbed it along the small puncture wound on the tip of her daughter's left forefinger.

Claire sniffed.

Knowing that her daughter's tears weren't stemming from the pain, but rather from the fact that Petey had hurt her feelings, Alice wet a washcloth and held it to the side of her face. Claire's relationship with animals had started almost before she could talk. Growing up, there had been an endless array of hamsters—all named Fluffy—because Alice had to keep switching them out upon their deaths. Next came Buddy the guinea pig, and then there was Sprinkles, their ten-year-old one-eyed cat who had to be given away because Michael was allergic. Suddenly consumed by guilt, Alice sighed and tossed the washcloth in the sink. "I think that bird was spawned from the depths of hell," she said, trying to coax a smile from Claire's lips.

It didn't.

Eyeing the sullen teenager in front of her, Alice began to suspect that the only thing her daughter loved more than God's creatures was her phone, which was currently clutched in the non-mangled fingers of her other hand. Tearing open the bandage, she wrapped it around the cut and sat back. "There," she said, admiring her nursing skills, "all done."

Claire's head snapped up from her phone.

"What?" asked Alice, confused by the hateful glare being thrown in her direction.

"Why did you lie to me about my dad?"

The tiny room fell silent.

Struggling to regain her composure, Alice straightened her shoulders as she shifted her weight on the toilet seat. "What do you mean?"

Claire's mouth twisted into an unnatural shape. "Everything you ever told me about him was a lie!"

"That's not true, sweetheart—"

"He stole a bunch of money and took off! It wasn't an *'amicable parting of the ways'* between the two of you like you said. He didn't *care* about us!"

Having always thought this day would never come, Alice leaned forward and placed her hands on Claire's knees as she searched for the words. "Your father was human, just like everyone else, and he made a mistake." She paused to shake her head. "I didn't tell you because I didn't want that to be the only thing you remembered when you thought about him."

The floor behind her creaked.

Glancing over her shoulder, Alice could see her mother's shadow moving underneath the door.

Pursing her lips, she turned back to Claire. "Everyone has done things in their life that they're not proud of," she said, raising her voice, "and regardless of what your father did … I do know that he loved you."

Claire's breath came tumbling out of her, paving the way for an angry-sounding sob. "Why should I believe you?"

"Because it's the truth," she replied, tightening her grip on her knees as she spoke. "Do you know what he said the day you were born?"

"No."

"That it was the happiest day of his life."

"Really?" asked Claire, her tone resembling that of a hopeful four-year-old as she wiped at her eyes with the backs of her hands.

Clenching the yellow bathmat between her bare toes, Alice forced a smile and nodded. "Yes."

OLIVIA TOOK LIAM'S collection of ties that he hadn't worn—since ever and stuffed them, along with the twenty-five ball caps that had never so much as graced the top of his head, inside the box she had marked for donations and got to her feet. Wiping her hands on her jeans, she glanced around the tiny room that sat at the end of the hall opposite the master and gave an inward shrug. There was still a lot to do before it would resemble a nursery, but she was making progress and hoped Loretta Boyd would see that as well when she came tomorrow for what was sure to be the first of many visits.

The room had been used by the previous owner as a library of sorts, and upon moving in, Liam had taken out the crumbling wall-to-wall built-in bookshelves and painstakingly spackled all seven hundred holes left behind in the plaster before painting it a soft yellow. It had been Olivia's original intent to turn the ten-by-ten space into an office complete with a pull out sofa in the event that her mother should ever decide to come for a visit, but unfortunately, the couch they'd picked up at a garage sale had been too wide to fit through the room's narrow doorway.

Fast-forward three years.

The couch was in the living room, her mother was still in Denver, and the office had become a catchall for everything they didn't have a use for.

Picking up the box, Olivia carried it out into the hall and set it on the floor next to the others. As she turned to go, she casually peered into the darkened living room and saw Harlan slumped in his recliner watching TV.

After several moments of deliberation, Olivia walked over to the sliding glass doors and pulled the heavy curtain shut before clicking on the lamp beside the couch. It was then that she realized her father-in-law wasn't so much as watching TV as he was staring at it. "Harlan," she said, bending over to pick up the newspaper off the floor, "it's after six. Would you like me to fix you something to eat?"

"I'm not hungry," he said, keeping his eyes fastened on the screen.

Olivia took her time putting the paper back together. He had been quiet ever since his return home yesterday from wherever it was that he had gone, and although she knew she should've called Liam and told him the moment she'd read the note, she had made the decision not to for a couple of very important reasons: one, it got Harlan out of her hair, and two, she didn't want the day that had started off so well to be ruined by listening to them argue about it.

Placing the newspaper on the coffee table beside him, she made her way into the kitchen and began rummaging through the cabinets in search of food. Upon spying a box of spaghetti, she dragged a pot out from underneath the sink and filled it with water; it was a quick and easy meal—especially when the sauce came from a jar—and was one of Harlan's favorites.

As she bent down to adjust the gas flame on the stove, her gaze caught upon the bottle of merlot sitting beside the microwave. Surmising that a glass of wine would be nice right about now, she gleefully reached for it only to stop. Dropping her hand, she rested it against the counter instead and sighed. The past few months had been tumultuous, at best, and even though she may have overindulged a few times, she didn't have a drinking problem — and resented the fact that Harlan thought she did. Still, with him sprawled in the recliner a few feet away, she didn't want to give him any more ammunition to rip her apart with in front of Liam.

The door to the garage opened and closed.

Turning from the stove, Olivia hurried across the kitchen floor.

A moment later, Liam appeared in the foyer where his eyes immediately gravitated to his father. "Dad," he said, giving him a nod.

Harlan lifted his chin in response to the greeting but remained silent.

"Hi!" said Olivia, throwing her arms around Liam's neck. "Guess what?"

"What?"

"Dwayne Ballard left a message this afternoon saying that the charges against me have been dropped."

He pulled back to look at her. "Why?"

"I don't know," she answered with a laugh, "and neither did he when I called him back. He just said that the Crawford County Sheriff's Office had decided not to pursue the case."

Liam's chest rose and fell at her explanation, but the relief she had expected to see on his face did not appear. "What's wrong?"

Setting his thermos on the counter, he took her gently by the arms. "I found the girl's belongings," he said in a low voice. "She was positively identified a little while ago by her mother."

Olivia's heart began to pound in her ears, causing her entire body to shake. As she stood there, trying to form the words, she saw Harlan rise from his chair and start making his way towards the den.

Lowering his gaze, Liam drew a small breath. "The girl's aunt is going to take the baby."

Tears flooded Olivia's face, setting her cheeks on fire. "No, Liam," she pleaded, clutching at his shirt. "You can't let them take him from me!"

"I'm sorry," he whispered, "but there's nothing that I can—"

A sickening thud sounded on the other side of the living room, making Liam turn his head.

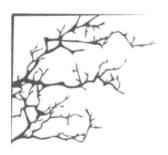

# Chapter 28

"He's had a heart attack. ... No, I'm waiting for them to come out and talk to me. ... Is Ronny with you? ... Where is he? ... *Where?*"

Leaning back in her chair, Olivia crossed her legs and rubbed her temple, wishing that the dark-haired woman sitting across from her would shut the hell up. She'd been talking on her phone nonstop since arriving in the small waiting area outside the ICU, and Olivia knew more about the woman's life — not to mention her dysfunctional family's — than she cared to.

"Can't his brother Jimmy lend you the money? ... No. ... Because I ain't *got* it! ... Well, he should've thought of that before he went and skipped bail."

Sighing, Olivia anxiously scanned the corridor for any sign of Dr. Graham before feeling her gaze being drawn to Liam. Sitting beside her with his head down and his elbows resting on his knees, he absently picked at the scab on his palm as he stared at the floor. Reaching out, she tenderly placed her hand on his forearm.

He stopped and gave her a bewildered look.

Gazing solemnly into his eyes, she squeezed his wrist.

After several moments, his lips did a slight upturn. Taking her hand in his, he slowly sat back.

Olivia matched his fragile smile as the world around them began to fall away. She knew it was strange, but they were never closer to each other than when they were reeling in the wake of tragedy. They were absolute masters at handling the initial stages of it together ... it was the aftermath that followed, however, that they needed to work on.

"Sheriff?"

Olivia glanced over to find Aaron Red Elk standing on the other side of the waiting area. As Liam got up from the chair, Aaron's piercing brown eyes shifted to her. "Ma'am," he said, removing his hat.

Dipping her head in acknowledgment, she found his gesture to be just as awkward as it had been a few months ago when Liam had invited him and his wife over for dinner. Aaron had said very little to her, his wife Naomi—even less. After dinner, Liam and Aaron had retreated into the living room, leaving her to clear the table with a woman who nodded and smiled a lot.

"I heard the call come over the radio," Aaron said in a hushed tone as Liam drew closer. "What's going on?"

"We don't know," answered Liam. "He just collapsed. We're waiting to hear something."

"Is there anything I can do?"

A pinkish hue slithered along Liam's jaw. "No, but thank you," he replied.

"You know," said Aaron, cracking a grin, "I was only joking about you sending calls my way."

A small laugh came from the back of Liam's throat. "How did things go?"

Aaron shrugged. "As expected. I'll fill you in on the dramatics of it another time."

"That bad, huh?" said Liam, arching his eyebrow.

"Hold on, I can't hear you." The woman who was talking on her phone shot Aaron a scowl. "Let me call you right back." Grabbing her coat and cigarettes from off the chair beside her, she stood up and walked over to the nurses' station. "I'm going outside to smoke. If the doctor comes lookin' for me, be sure and call me on my cell."

The nurse nodded at her without bothering to look up.

As the woman stepped onto the elevator, Olivia found her thoughts turning inward. Less than seven hours ago, she'd been back in the NICU rocking a little boy that she had come to call her own. Still conscious of Liam's voice as he talked with Aaron, she felt herself beginning to drown in her bitterness. She'd been struggling to keep her head above it for so long now that her legs had grown tired. Closing her eyes, she stopped fighting and let her body sink into its cold black depths.

"How is he?"

Taking in a deep but noxious breath, Olivia returned her gaze to Liam. From her new vantage point, she saw that Aaron had gone and Dr. Graham was now standing in front of him.

The doctor removed his glasses and gestured for Liam to have a seat. "Your father has suffered a massive stroke," he said, speaking in a slow and deliberate manner. "Initial tests show that there's significant impairment on his right side."

"How significant?" asked Liam, digging his fingers into the arm of the chair that the annoying woman had been sitting in.

"It's severely affected his breathing, among other things."

Liam shook his head. "Can't you put him on a ventilator to help him?"

The doctor scratched his graying temples and leaned forward. "Liam," he said, slipping his glasses back onto the bridge of his nose, "after your father shattered his hip last year, he signed a living will."

Olivia watched a shadow fall across Liam's face as it went from confusion to anger … and then to grief.

"We're giving him something for the pain to keep him comfortable," Dr. Graham continued, "but it was his wish that no extreme measures be taken to save his life."

THE SUN ROSE ABOVE Liam's shoulders, casting a pale light over the room as he sat in the corner of the ICU listening to his father's heartbeat. During the past few hours, he had become accustomed to its chaotic rhythm and found himself beginning to anticipate the beeps before they flashed across the monitor in jagged bursts of neon-green.

A nurse with short dark hair and an empathic smile moved quietly about, checking the equipment that his father was hooked up to, including the catheter that ran between his legs, and yet — despite this startling invasion of privacy — his eyes remained closed.

Locking his fingers together, Liam shifted abruptly in his seat, blaming his burning throat on the strong odor of disinfectant that hung thick in the air.

Olivia, who'd been asleep in the chair beside him, stirred at the sound. Placing her feet on the floor, she sat up and rubbed her eyes before glancing in his father's direction.

Liam waited for the nurse to leave the room before speaking. "There hasn't been any change."

Tucking her hair behind her ear, she met Liam's gaze with a reserved intensity. "I'm going to find a restroom and then some coffee," she said, handing him back his coat that she'd been using as a blanket. "Would you like some?"

"No, thanks."

"I'll be right back."

"Listen," he said, following her across the floor, "why don't you go on home? There's no need for you to stay."

Pausing in the doorway, Olivia eyed him for several seconds, her face unreadable. "Are you sure?" she asked, reaching up to caress his cheek.

Liam's pulse quickened at her touch. "I'll be fine," he replied, laying his hand over hers. Her knuckles slid stiffly down his palm and recoiled against her side. Fairly certain that the trembling in her lips wasn't because of his father, yet wanting to stop the tears that were pooling in her eyes, he leaned in to kiss her.

She turned her head, stopping him cold. "I'll be back in a few minutes," she said, edging past him.

Sticking his hands in his pockets, Liam slumped against the doorjamb. Even though he knew he wouldn't have been able to live with himself if he hadn't turned over the girl's backpack, he also knew as he watched Olivia walking away … that she was never going to forgive him for having done it.

A low moan sounded behind Liam, sending him scrambling back into the room. "Dad?"

After a moment, his father's eyelids, which were bruised and swollen from where he'd fallen, fluttered open.

"Dad? Can you hear me?"

His father's chest crackled as he drew a labored breath. "Where … am I?"

"The hospital," said Liam, hoping his slurred speech was due to the powerful drugs that were flowing through his veins.

Confusion swirled behind his father's left eye, turning it a cloudy gray. "What … happened?"

"The doctors aren't sure," Liam replied, clutching the railing of the bed. "They're going to run some tests later."

His father clicked his tongue. "You're a terrible l-l-liar," he said, the right side of his face remaining immobile as he spoke.

Letting go of the railing, Liam slipped his fingers inside his father's hand. "Well, I learned from the best," he said, giving him a wavering smile.

"What's g-going on with … Ramirez?"

"We found a crowbar inside a burning vehicle. The blood on it matches Hector's, but there were no fingerprints."

A frantic series of beeps echoed on the monitor.

"Your turn," said Liam, keeping his gaze on his father.

"My t-turn for what?"

"What's happening with the Malloy case?"

A vacant stare followed his question. "There's nothin' to talk about," his father finally replied.

"It's just like Ab-Abrams said. It was an accident … p-plain and simple."

An alarm sounded.

Jerking his head up, Liam saw that the jagged lines moving across the monitor were now inverted. "I'll be right back, Dad," he said, the adrenaline rushing through him causing his words to fluctuate as they tumbled from his lips. "I'm going to get the nurse." As he straightened to go, his father's hand clamped down onto his, stopping him.

"Don't bother," he said in a tired voice.

Liam's throat began to ache.

"So, t-tell me," said his father, a bluish tinge spreading across his mouth as his eyes slowly closed and opened, "do I get to be a grandpa?"

"No …" Liam's chin began to tremble as he paused to swallow. "His aunt is going to take him."

"That ain't right. Y-you need to talk to Loretta Boyd … and make her see your side of things."

"I already have. There's nothing else I can say that's going to make her change her mind."

"Then use somethin' besides w-words."

Liam laughed and shook his head, unleashing his tears. "I don't think Loretta Boyd can be bought."

"*Anyone* can be bought, Liam. You just have to know their pr-price."

The beeps on the monitor reached a frenzied pace.

"Dad?"

Lifting his hand, he placed it against the side of Liam's face. "Take care of that wife of yours."

Unable to answer, Liam managed a hurried nod.

"And tell Enid," he said, closing his eyes, "I'm sorry …"

"*Dad*?" Liam grasped his father's hand as it slid from his cheek. Pressing it to his lips, his shoulders began to convulse as a guttural sob tore itself loose from his throat.

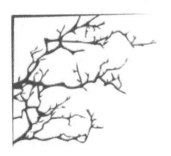

# Chapter 29

"To everything there is a season and a time to every purpose under the heaven ..."

The grass in the cemetery, still stiff from last night's frost, shimmered brightly in the sunlight, while the tips of its thawed blades nipped at Alice's bare ankles, making her wish that she'd worn pants instead of a dress as she slowly weaved her way through the crowd of mourners.

"... time to be born, and a time to die ..."

After stepping to the right of an older man in a gray wool coat, she saw the preacher standing in front of the casket with Bible in hand.

"... to plant, and a time to pluck up that which is planted ..."

Although she'd heard the words being spoken many times before, Reverend Harwick's tone added a certain glibness to them, as if he were overjoyed to be performing for such a large congregation.

"… time to heal; a time to break down, and a time to build …"

Partially cloaked behind the elderly man's fedora, Alice's gaze inconspicuously traveled from Reverend Harwick's pretentious face to Liam. Standing arrow-straight, his eyes were trained on the ground, his right hand was clasped tightly over his left wrist, and his jaw was set. He looked as if he'd been carved out of wood, and if it weren't for the steel-white puffs of air sporadically exiting his nostrils, he would have blended in perfectly with the trunk of the Sycamore that stood a few feet away.

"… to weep and a time to laugh; a time to mourn …"

Alice's attention shifted to the slender blonde that was clinging to his elbow. As her golden locks cascaded down around her shoulders, her utter beauty transcended the sadness reflected on her face. Staring at the gold band adorning her finger as it clutched the sleeve of Liam's coat, a sense of misery began to surround Alice, making her eyes sting.

*A faint boom echoed in the distance, followed by a succession of crackles and pops that exploded into a vibrant shower of orange twinkling lights.*

*"I hope my mom is letting Claire watch," said Alice as the colorful sparks fell from the sky. Lips, warm and tender, touched upon the side of her neck, giving rise to*

an army of goosebumps that marched in tight formation across the affected area of flesh before slipping into her bloodstream, where they began to flow throughout her body.

Turning from the window, Alice met Liam's lips with her own; locking them in a fiery embrace, her fingers clumsily groped his deputy's badge before finding their way to the buttons on his shirt. Liam's breath came out in an uneven rush across the top of her head as her teeth grazed his chest.

Parting her denim jacket with his hands, he slid it from her shoulders and took her by the arms, causing an unintentional whimper to spill from her mouth as he fell backward with her onto the bed.

"What's wrong?"

"Nothing," she replied.

In one swift motion, Liam sat up and turned on the lamp, flooding the tiny bedroom of his apartment with a soft light. Alice's cheeks began to burn as she watched the concerned expression on his face darken. "That son-of-a-bitch," he said, getting to his feet.

"Liam, wait!" she pleaded, grabbing at his wrist as he picked up his holster from the nightstand. "If you go over there – he'll know that we've been sleeping together!"

"That's going to be the least of his problems," he said, starting towards the door.

Leaping off the bed, Alice scrambled to get in front of him. "You can't do this!" she begged, pushing against his chest.

"I'm not going to just stand by and do nothing, Alice!"

"He'll take Claire away from me!"

"I won't let that happen," he said, brushing past her, "I promise."

Alice wrung her hands as he jerked open the bedroom door. "I left him today!"

Liam stopped. Wrapping his fingers around the doorjamb, he looked back at her. "For good?" he asked, his face hidden by the shadows.

Pausing to draw a hurried breath, she walked up to him and slid her arms around his torso, then forcing herself to look into his eyes, nodded. "For good."

The rigidness in his jaw fell away.

"Now ..." Alice smiled as she reached up and swept his locks from his forehead. "I told my mom I was going on a diaper run, and if I'm not back in the next half hour," she murmured, pressing her mouth against his, "she's going to grow suspicious."

Liam responded in kind, only to pull back after a few seconds.

"What's wrong?" she asked, tilting her head.

His gaze went from her face to the cluster of bruises lining her arm. Caressing them with his thumb, his breathing began to grow shallow. "Marry me," he whispered.

Alice felt her heart constrict. "Liam — "

"I'll be a good husband to you, and a good father to Claire," he said, rushing the words. "I'll love her as if she were my own."

"I haven't even filed for divorce yet," she countered with a nervous laugh.

"It doesn't matter. I'll wait."

"Liam," she said, letting go of a sigh, "it's not that simple."

*He shook his head. "I love you. I've always loved you, and I can't imagine ever loving anyone else as much as I do you right now." Cupping her face in his hands, his blue eyes sparkled brightly against the pale light as he smiled down at her. "Marry me," he repeated.*

*The fireworks sounded like cannons going off as they ascended into the sky one after the other, filling Alice's mind with a chaotic roar. Digging her fingernails into her thighs, she felt her lips begin to part. "Yes."*

*Liam scooped her up into his arms and carried her over to the bed. "We're going to have a nice life," he said in a hushed voice, spreading himself on top of her. "I promise."*

*Clutching at the back of his shirt, Alice closed her eyes and breathed in, yet as his body intertwined with hers … she found her disjointed thoughts turning to Dom.*

"In Christ's name, we pray. Amen."

As the crowd began to disperse, Alice took in an unsteady breath and made her way around to the front of the tent, drawing Liam's gaze as he bent down to accept a hug from an elderly woman. Murmuring something inaudible, the woman reached up and gently patted him on his cheek before turning to go.

Swallowing the knot that had formed in her throat, Alice instinctively followed the older woman's lead and stepped forward to give him a hug — yet the subtle movement in his jaw made her stop. "I'm sorry about your dad," she said, sticking her hands in the pockets of her coat instead. "He was a good man."

Liam nodded, allowing her to see the dark circles underneath his eyes. "Thank you."

Tension, awkward and obvious, rapidly filled the space between them, causing Alice to glance at the blonde who was still clutching his elbow.

"Alice, this is my wife, Olivia," Liam offered in a rigid tone. "Olivia, this is Alice."

The blonde gave her a smile that looked more like a mechanical grimace. "It's nice to meet you."

"You too," Alice replied, wondering why Liam hadn't bothered to mention her last name during the introduction.

"Where's your daughter?" he asked, shifting his feet.

"She's with my mom. They're having a sort of spa day."

"How old's your daughter?"

Alice turned towards Liam's wife to find her staring pointedly in her direction. "Thirteen going on thirty," she replied with a laugh, yet was uncertain if her chattering teeth were a result of the cool breeze that had begun circling her—or her own nervousness.

"I know you're cold," said Liam, placing his hand on the small of Olivia's back. "Why don't you wait in the car? I'll be right there."

Offering him what appeared to be a grateful nod, she returned her steel-blue gaze to Alice. "Nice meeting you."

Before Alice could respond, Olivia slipped past her, giving her a sidelong glance in the process, and disappeared into the thinning crowd. As the awkwardness resumed, Alice reluctantly forced her attention back to Liam. "I want to apologize for my behavior the other day outside the station."

"It's fine," he replied, watching Olivia make her way towards the car.

"The coroner did sign the death certificate, though," Alice continued, twisting the belt of her coat around her fingers as she stared at the scar running through his left eyebrow. "I should be receiving a check from Dom's life insurance policy in a few days, which—fortunately for *me*—wasn't done through *Black Hills*."

Liam gave her a hurried nod. "That's good."

Alice let the belt slip through her fingertips. "Well," she said, taking the hint, "I should probably get going."

"Thanks for comi—"

"I'm sorry for running out on you the way I did," she suddenly blurted, her conscience refusing to let her leave before she said what she'd come here to say.

Liam's mouth closed, forming a tight line across his lips as he looked at her.

"With Dom running off the way he did—or so I thought—and the town holding me accountable for his crimes by default, it was just easier for me to go than stay here."

Something flickered in Liam's face, making his gaze falter.

Realizing she'd just downplayed their entire relationship in one rambling sentence, Alice reached for his hand. "You know I've never been good with words," she exclaimed, shaking her head. "But I never meant to hurt you, Liam. I swear to God I didn't."

His chest slowly rose and fell, causing the black and white polka-dotted tie laying against it to quiver. "It's all in the past," he finally said, then lifting his eyes to meet hers, abruptly pulled his hand away. "I think it's probably best that it stays there."

"Liam," she whispered, blinking back her tears as he brushed past her, "I wouldn't have made you a very good wife."

He stopped and turned around, his expression unreadable. "Take care of yourself, Alice."

She wiped at her face as she watched him walk away, yet her tears continued to fall. Although he wasn't the only man she'd ever loved … she knew he was the only man who'd ever loved her.

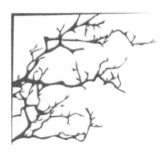

# Chapter 30

The house seemed unbearably quiet to Liam as he sat on the edge of his father's bed, clutching the bag of personal effects that the hospital had given him. His gaze, uneven and damp, drifted aimlessly around the room before coming to rest upon the nightstand beside him; its wooden top, faded from years of exposure to the sun and covered in old cigarette burns, held his father's cheaters, a pile of junk mail, and a small but tarnished picture frame.

Picking up the frame, he lightly ran his thumb across its dusty glass. His mother's sapphire-blue eyes beamed up at him as her long brown hair fell down in curls around the lace shoulders of her wedding dress. Liam smiled back, having forgotten how beautiful she was. It was a far cry from the last eighteen months of her life … in which she couldn't even recognize her own face.

He returned the picture to the nightstand and let out a heavy sigh. Licking the salt that had gathered on his lips, he got to his feet and stiffly made his way over to the dresser that stood on the other side of the room.

After pausing to steady his emotions, he reached inside the hospital bag and retrieved his father's shirt, where the scent of stale smoke and aftershave surrounded him. As his fingers closed around the soft flannel, he felt something crinkle beneath his thumb. Unbuttoning the shirt's frayed pocket, Liam found a folded receipt from *Zip Gram*. Opening it up, he saw that six days ago his father had wired the sum of two thousand dollars to a Melvin Davis. Lowering his arm, he gripped the edge of the dresser and closed his eyes, trying to unsee what his father had done.

"What are you doing?"

Jerking his head up, Liam stared at his wife's reflection as she stood in the doorway behind him. It had been thirty-six hours since the funeral ... and thirty-five hours since Olivia had spoken to him. And yet, now that she had, her tone crackled with animosity. "Attempting to come to terms with how much my father loved you," he replied, crumpling the receipt between his fingers.

She crossed her arms. "What's that supposed to mean?"

"It means," he said, turning from the mirror, "that he paid the Crawford County Sheriff to get rid of the evidence Kyle Robinson had against you in order to ensure that nothing stood in the way of you fostering the baby!"

The indignant expression Olivia wore wavered. "Well," she said in a half-whisper, "thanks to you, none of that matters now, does it?"

Liam's hands settled on his hips. "I took an oath, Olivia. It was my duty as sheriff to — "

"To do the right thing — I know." A sarcastic smile erupted onto her lips. "You're a regular saint, aren't you?" Pushing herself away from the doorjamb, she stumbled towards him. "You *always* have to do the right thing, whether it's allowing your father to come and live with us, missing birthdays and anniversaries because you just had to respond to a call, or ... let's see — oh yeah, turning in a dead girl's belongings."

"I'm sorry."

"*Are* you?"

Drawing a shallow breath, he rubbed the back of his neck. "If there had been any other way, I would have done it."

"You had a *choice*, Liam!" she yelled. "You could've looked the other way but you didn't!" The glassy film covering her eyes grew moist as she shook her head. "Why is it that you can do right by everyone but me?"

"That's not true."

"It's not? Oh, wait," she said, holding up a finger. "You *married* me, didn't you? I guess that counts."

Her words stung the side of his cheek.

"Oh, come on," she said, arching her brow, "are you honestly going to stand there and tell me that you didn't marry me because I was pregnant?"

"No," he said flatly, "because telling you anything at this point would be lost on you."

A burst of static sounded in the kitchen.

"County to Sheriff Matthews."

"Go on," said Olivia, making an exaggerated gesture towards the door, "don't let me get in the way of you doing the right thing."

Dropping his gaze, he walked past her and headed towards the kitchen.

"But don't expect me to be here when you get back!"

Liam's footsteps slowed, but he didn't turn around.

Three beeps echoed sharply in front of him, fracturing the deafening silence that had descended.

"County to Sheriff Matthews. Do you copy?"

Forcing his hand around the radio, Liam picked it up off the counter. "This is Matthews —"

A loud boom ricocheted throughout the house, rattling the dishes in the sink as the door to the bedroom slammed shut.

Closing his eyes, Liam's shoulders slumped forward as he brought the radio closer to his lips. "Go ahead, County."

THE STEADY BAND OF snow falling out of the darkness swirled haphazardly around Liam before dropping onto the pavement by his feet. Leaning against the bed of his truck, a shiver rolled down his spine as he watched the digital numbers on the gas pump tick by. The temperature had already dipped below freezing and he knew it wouldn't be long before the massive flakes began to accumulate.

The fingers on his left hand started to sting from the cold, yet he found the needle-like pain pricking his skin to be a welcome change, as Olivia's declaration had left him numb.

After responding to the call that had come over his radio, he'd desperately wanted to return home, but was too afraid of what he would find when he got there. So instead, he'd been driving around for the past three hours, trying to lose his thoughts on the winding back roads, yet they had stubbornly hung on, increasing in both number and decibel.

The trigger on the nozzle kicked back, cutting off the flow of gas. Twisting the fuel cap on the tank, Liam felt as if he were moving in slow motion as he walked across the deserted parking lot and through the front door of *Bucky's Mini-Mart*.

The man behind the counter looked up from his phone. "How's it goin'?"

"All right," said Liam, making his way to the coffee machine in the back. Choosing the largest cup available, he filled it to the brim and snapped the matching lid on top of it.

"Will this be all for you?"

Liam set the cup on the counter. "Plus the gas," he said, reaching for his wallet.

"Would you like some donuts with your coffee?" asked the clerk in a voice that was far too loud for this time of night. "They're on special: two for a dollar."

"No, I'm good," replied Liam, inserting his credit card into the reader beside him.

The clerk drummed his fingers on the counter as he waited for the transaction to process. "You havin' a slow night?"

"Yeah."

"Same here." Raising his left arm, the clerk scratched at the dry patch of skin on his elbow, causing the bottom of his shirt, which he seemed to have outgrown a bag of chips — or three — ago, to ride up. "Only four customers since midnight."

"Is that a fact?" asked Liam, glancing at the open energy drink beside the register as he hurriedly scrawled his name on the electronic pad.

"Yeah, it's usually really, really busy right about now," he said, tugging his shirt back down over his stomach. "I heard that the flu's goin' around, though. Could be everyone's got it. If that's the case ..." He gave a nervous laugh and held up his hands. "They can just stay at home—because I don't want it."

Stuffing his wallet back into his pocket, Liam picked up his coffee and started towards the exit. "Take it easy."

"Hey, Sheriff?"

Grimacing, Liam stopped and looked back.

The clerk pointed at the computer monitor behind the counter. "There goes somebody needin' a ticket."

Liam returned to the counter. A live feed, divided into six squares, was displayed on a large computer screen.

"See?" The clerk tapped the square at the top right corner. "There he goes."

Liam's gaze shifted from the speeding truck to the square on the bottom left. Set up to capture the activity behind the convenience store, the angle of the camera offered a straight shot down the alley where the back of Cal Mobley's hardware store sat. "Do these record?"

"Twenty four-seven. But after a month, it gets deleted."

"Can you pull up the footage for that one," asked Liam, gesturing at the bottom square, "for the morning of the fifteenth?"

The clerk's eyes lit up. "Sure thing, Sheriff." Pausing to take a quick gulp from his can, he cracked his knuckles and started sliding his index finger around the built-in mousepad on the keyboard. "What time?"

"Around seven."

The individual squares disappeared as the picture of an empty alleyway with a timestamp of 7:00 filled the screen.

"Can you fast forward it?"

Rotating the monitor so Liam could see it better, the clerk nodded and tapped the mousepad again. After a moment, two figures turned up on the screen, and even from this distance, Liam could make out Frank Colter's hulking frame. For the next two minutes, he and the clerk watched Frank and his brother, Jesse, empty Mobley's store and shove the items through a hole in the fence. Several trips were made until 7:09:04 when they tore out the back door. At 7:09:12, Cal Mobley emerged from it waving his shotgun at them. Frank took off down the alley, with Jesse limping along behind, and scaled the fence.

"That — was — *fucking awesome!*" shouted the clerk.

Keeping his eyes on the monitor, Liam saw brake lights come on at 7:09:18 and then vanish behind the rear of the building on the right. At the 7:09:28 mark, he felt his breath catch in his throat when a light silver Impala with one headlight came barreling around the side of it.

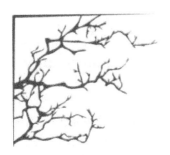

# Chapter 31

Morning broke across the horizon, shattering the surrounding darkness into fractured prisms of orange light that glistened brightly upon the new-fallen snow. As Liam watched them dance their way along the crumbling sidewalks that led to nowhere, a sense of loss, greater than he'd ever felt before, washed over him like a tidal wave, making him gasp for air as its powerful current dragged him under.

"You all right?"

Liam glanced at Stiles who was standing beside him and cleared his throat. "Yeah," he said, both embarrassed and startled by his deputy's empathy.

Shifting his weight to his other leg, Stiles sighed and took a long pull on his cigarette, drawing his cheeks inward. "You sure he's alone?" he asked, scratching his left shoulder blade against the side mirror of Liam's truck.

"As of eight hours ago, Jesse still hadn't posted bail," replied Liam, forcibly shoving his grief aside as he swept his gaze along the darkened windows of Frank Colter's duplex, "but there's always the possibility that he's got a girl shacked up in there with him."

Stiles snorted, sending a stream of smoke rolling out of his nostrils. "There ain't enough money in the world," he said, checking his watch. Pushing himself away from the mirror, he scowled as he looked towards the street's entrance. "Where the hell is Red Elk?"

Before Liam could answer, the distinct rumble of a diesel engine brought forth feelings of relief as well as apprehension.

"What took you so long?" asked Stiles, tossing his cigarette in the snow as Aaron stepped out of his truck. "Did you stop for breakfast?"

"Yeah," Aaron replied, walking towards him, "your girlfriend made it for me."

A deep crimson consumed Stiles' face, bringing the edge of his jaw to a hardened point.

"Did you get it?" asked Liam, holding in his sigh.

Swerving his gaze, Aaron patted his coat and nodded.

"Sheriff Matthews to County," said Liam into his radio. "Show us as 10-24 at 131 Glenn Avenue."

"County to Matthews. Copy."

As the three of them started towards the duplex, the thin layer of ice that had formed on top of the snow cracked beneath the weight of their boots, drawing the attention of the pit bull across the street. Pulling its heavy chain through the drifts, the dog ran back and forth in its yard—barking, growling, and doing its overall best to alert its owners of their presence.

"Shit," muttered Gordon, increasing his pace.

As they neared the driveway, Liam motioned for his deputies to stop. Crouching behind the front tire of Colter's Bronco, Liam peered around its rusted bumper and was grateful to find that the right half of the duplex was still dark.

"See anything?" asked Gordon.

"No—"

A shrill screech suddenly pierced the air above them.

Jerking his head up as his hand instinctively moved to his holster, Liam saw a Great Horned Owl soar past him and land on top of the light post across the street. Tucking its giant wings, which spanned at least four feet in length, against its sides, it aimed its big yellow eyes in his direction and let out another haunting screech.

Aaron clutched the medicine bag hanging around his neck and mumbled something under his breath that Liam didn't understand.

"Christ," said Gordon, shaking his head, "*this* is why you don't bring a Lakota to a gunfight. If a piss-ant crosses the street in front of them, they take it as a goddamned omen!" Rocking backward on his heels as he squatted by the tire, he gestured at Aaron. "I mean, look at him, Sheriff! He's about to shit himself because he thinks that owl is the harbinger of death and it's come for him. Ain't that right, Red El—"

Liam grabbed Gordon by the collar of his coat and slammed him against the fender of the Bronco. "That's enough, Stiles!" he said in a fierce whisper. "Do you hear me? Now stop running your fucking mouth and go cover the back!"

The surprised expression riding Gordon's face quickly succumbed to anger. Shoving Liam's arm out of his way, he got to his feet and started around the duplex.

"Hey, Stiles?" called Aaron.

He stopped and looked over his shoulder.

Aaron stood and gestured at the owl. "How do you know he hasn't come for *you*?"

Clenching his jaw, Liam placed his hands on his knees and straightened, catching Aaron's gaze. "Are we done?"

"Sorry, Sheriff," he murmured.

Liam shifted his attention to Stiles. "Radio when you're in position."

Stiles turned away without acknowledging him and resumed walking towards the back of the duplex.

With the dog still barking, the anxiousness inside Liam increased, making his heart pound in his throat as he and Aaron hurried up the steps that led to the front porch and took a low stance on either side of the door.

A moment later, Gordon's voice crackled over the radio. "Ready."

"Copy that," replied Liam, then jamming his right shoulder up against the wooden cladding, pounded on the door with the side of his fist. "Sheriff's Office!"

There was a loud thump followed by the sound of heavy footsteps.

"Frank Colter," Liam yelled, "we have a warrant for your arrest!"

"What the hell for?" shouted Frank through the door.

"The murder of Hector Ramirez!"

"I didn't have nothin' to do with that!"

"That's for the courts to decide," countered Liam. "Open up!"

Silence followed his command.

Exchanging glances with Aaron, Liam drew his Glock and held it against his thigh with his finger next to the trigger.

Releasing his grip on his medicine bag, Aaron gave him a stiff nod. Drawing his own gun, he swung his body towards the door and raised his leg.

A succession of deafening blasts ripped through the air, splintering the wood above the knob.

Staggering backward, Aaron's gun fell through his fingers as he crumpled against the steps.

Firing three rounds into the door, Liam jumped off the porch and grabbed Aaron by the flap of his coat, where he dragged him down the steps and behind a cluster of overgrown bushes. "Matthews to County!" he yelled into his radio. "10-99! Shots fired—officer down!" With his gun still pointed at the door, he knelt over Aaron and opened his coat. Dark-red blood oozed from a dime-sized hole just above his deputy's right hip, staining the snow beneath him.

As his radio began to fill with chatter, Liam placed his free hand over the wound, trying to stop the bleeding. "Listen to me, Aaron. You're going to be okay—"

The sound of breaking glass came from the right side of the duplex.

"He's gone out the window!" shouted Stiles. "Officer in pursuit. Suspect is heading south behind Glenn Avenue!"

Holstering his gun, Liam grabbed his radio. "Let him go, Stiles!" he said, feeling Aaron's blood seep through his fingers. "Backup is on the way!"

"I have him in my sights!" replied Stiles, his words coming out in sporadic jerks between breaths.

"Stiles, you need to stop and wait for backup."

The radio buzzed beneath Liam's lips.

"Goddamn it, Gordon! Answer m—" A cold set of fingers closed around Liam's, rendering him silent. Releasing the button on his radio, his gaze went from straining to see beyond the side of the duplex to Aaron, whose dark eyes were open and alert, but flickered with each jagged breath he took.

"Go on, Sheriff," he said in a rigid voice. "Help Stiles before he gets himself killed."

Taking Aaron's hand, Liam placed it firmly over the wound. "Keep pressure on it," he said, his tone coming out clipped as he struggled to keep his emotions from surfacing. "I'll be right back." Forcing himself to his feet, he paused to give his deputy a reassuring look before scrambling around the side of the duplex.

The frozen ground jarred Liam's teeth as he raced through Colter's backyard and into a tract of woods that ran parallel with the property. Following the snarl of footprints sprawled out in front of him, he jumped across a narrow creek bed only to find that the tracks in the snow had given way to scores of fallen twigs, pine needles, and leaves that were brown, wet, and ankle-deep. Cupping his hand around his mouth, he took a deep breath. "Stiles—"

The sharp crack of a single gunshot ricocheted through the trees.

"Stiles!" repeated Liam, frantically sweeping his gaze back and forth along the dense terrain for any sign of his deputy.

"Over here, Sheriff!" Gordon's voice, distressed and winded, drifted out of a thicket of pines on his left.

Reaching for his Glock, Liam ducked under a low-hanging branch and saw his deputy standing a few yards away; with his feet spread apart and arms extended, the barrel of his gun was pointed directly at Colter, who was on his knees — barefoot, shirtless, and bleeding. "You all right, Stiles?"

"Never better," Gordon panted, keeping his eyes locked on Colter. "Can you cuff him?"

"Gladly," said Liam. Holstering his Glock, he strode up to Frank and roughly grabbed his left wrist as it lay on top of his head.

"Ow, man," he groaned. "I need to go to the fuckin' hospital!"

"You'll live," said Liam, twisting his arm behind his back.

"I'm serious, Sheriff! I'm bleedin' out!"

"It's a flesh wound, you big baby," said Stiles. "I've cut myself worse shavin'."

As Liam slapped the cuff around Frank's other wrist, he saw him look over at Stiles. "Why the hell did you shoot me?"

Gordon shook his head. "Because you had a *gun* and wouldn't stop runnin', asshole."

"That was no reason to shoot me!"

Wanting to get back to Aaron, Liam jerked Colter to his feet. "Let's go."

The muscles in Colter's arm flexed as Liam forced him to start walking. "You told me everything was going to be fine, Stiles!" he yelled over his shoulder. "And then you show up bangin' on my door with an arrest warrant! I wanna know what the fuck's goin' on!"

Liam stopped in his tracks and glanced back at Gordon. "What's he talking about, Stiles?"

"How the hell should I know, Sheriff?" he answered, leaning over to pick up Colter's 9mm from off the ground. "He's a fucking idiot!"

The misshapen holes above Colter's upper lip opened and closed like gills on a dying fish as he struggled to break free of Liam's grasp. "Answer me, Stiles!"

Tightening his grip, Liam's gaze warily darted back and forth between Colter and his deputy.

Straining against his cuffs, Colter took a step towards Stiles. "You told me you were handling things!"

Gordon sighed and turned around. "I am."

A flock of starlings scattered from the treetops as the bullet tore through Liam's chest. Sinking to his knees, he managed to pull his Glock from his holster, yet it slipped out of his hand as a second bullet pierced his lung. The coppery taste of blood swarmed his mouth as the ground hurtled towards him.

"What the hell are you doing?" shrieked Colter.

"Cleaning up your mess!" answered Gordon. "Just like I had to do with that girl!"

"I *told* you I didn't know the girl was there!"

Frantic to keep Stiles in his sights, Liam dragged his hand underneath him and pushed himself onto his side, causing the blood that had pooled in his mouth to spill from between his lips.

"Whether she was or wasn't wouldn't have mattered if you hadn't gone and lost your temper!" shouted Stiles. "Caffrey told me she confided in him about everything that had gone on that night — which included seeing you beat Ramirez to death with a fucking crowbar!"

"He was trying to blackmail me," replied Colter, gritting his teeth.

"You should've let him go and come to me," said Stiles. "I would've taken care of him in a less conspicuous manner."

"All right, I screwed up!" Colter replied, and then shifting his gaze to Liam, shook his head. "But why did you shoot the sheriff — with *my* gun!"

Stiles gave a gruff laugh. "You just shot Red Elk!" he yelled, pointing in the direction of the duplex. "You're going to jail, *regardless* of the arrest warrant — and I *know* you! You'd roll on your own grandmother to cut a deal!" His expression turned bitter. "I'm not about to let you take me down with you."

Colter's eyes widened as Stiles raised his Glock. "Stiles — man — wait — "

A deafening roar filled Liam's ears as Colter's head snapped back; striking the tree behind it, his body slumped to the ground.

As the sirens screamed in the distance, Stiles angrily wiped away the flecks of blood dotting his face and started towards Liam. "I'm sorry it has to be this way, Sheriff."

Struggling to breathe, Liam's hand trembled as it felt along the ground for his Glock.

Stiles placed the tip of his boot against his shoulder. "I'm just glad Harlan isn't here to see this," he said, shoving him onto his back. Raising Colter's 9mm, which was still clutched in his other hand, he slid his finger around the trigger.

Refusing to let Gordon be the last thing he saw in this life, Liam turned his thoughts to Olivia. As he waited for the darkness to sweep over him, he concentrated on the delicate curves of her beautiful face, the sound of her child-like giggle, which could be contagious at times, and the warmth of her skin against his as they—the air exploded around him making his body jerk.

Gordon's arm dropped to his side. A silent panic filled his eyes as a thick gurgle came from the hole in the center of his throat. Turning away, he fell face-first against the ground.

"Sheriff ..."

Rolling his head to the right, Liam saw Aaron stumbling towards him. "Caffrey," he said, the pistons in his brain still firing.

Aaron nodded. "I heard," he answered, his voice barely audible as he sank to his knees beside him.

The cold seeped into Liam's veins making him shiver. "Tell Olivia ... I love her," he said, yet the words came out sounding garbled as they slid off his tongue in a wave of blood.

Spreading his fingers across his chest, Aaron leaned over him. "Stay with me, Sheriff!" he pleaded.

As a gray mist closed around Aaron's face, Liam felt something brush against his waist. Managing to look down, he blinked to clear his vision, and as the fog faded from his eyes, he saw that he was surrounded by tall blades of green grass, their pointed tips, soft and covered in dew, swayed back and forth in the warm, gentle breeze.

Lifting his head, Liam slowly came to realize that he was standing in the prairie that bordered his and Olivia's backyard. As the sun's heat began to soak into his skin, his gaze went from the white clouds drifting across the brilliant-blue sky above him to the flowers of every shape and color imaginable that were lining the back of his house.

The unmistakable smell of peach cobbler hung thick in the air, drawing his attention to the tree he'd planted outside his and Olivia's bedroom window; standing taller than their roof with a stout, healthy trunk, dozens upon dozens of peaches clung to its long and slender branches, making them droop towards the ground.

"Daddy!"

Liam's gaze rapidly slid down the trunk of the tree and stopped. A boy, about two or three, with iridescent blue eyes and hair the color of wheat, was sitting in front of it pushing a toy bulldozer around in the dirt.

Jumping to his feet, the boy toddled over to him and held out his arms.

Liam instinctively picked him up, where the scent of baby shampoo, powder, and Olivia's perfume washed over him.

Placing his tiny hands against Liam's face, the boy looked into his eyes and smiled, revealing a set of dimpled cheeks. "I've been waiting for you."

The corners of Liam's mouth trembled as he smiled back at him. "I've been waiting for you, too," he whispered.

"Can you swing me?"

Glancing to his left, Liam saw through his tears that the rusted swing set had been painted a bright red. Swallowing the lump in his throat, he nodded. "I'd love to," he said, giving him a kiss. As they started across the yard, Liam felt his heart flood with a sense of peace as the sunlight spilling from the heavens engulfed them.

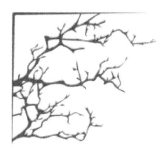

# Chapter 32

"For the latest on the shooting that took place in Orand County," said the news anchor, lifting a plucked brow as he stared into the camera, "let's go to Weeping Rock where Lynn Ainsworth is standing by."

The picture coming through the television switched from inside the WKZR news studio to a short brunette, whose perfectly styled hair was in the process of coming undone as the wind whipped it across her reddened cheeks.

Acknowledging the introduction with a small nod, she brought the microphone to her lips. "This past Saturday, Sheriff Liam Matthews and his two deputies arrived at this duplex behind me," she said, pausing to let the camera pan to the police tape surrounding it, "to serve an arrest warrant on Frank Colter, who—according to Delmar Lewis, the judge that signed the warrant—was wanted for the murder of Hector Ramirez. But something went horribly wrong, as just minutes later, Sheriff Matthews frantically radioed for help. When state police arrived, they found a grisly scene. Sheriff Matthews, along with deputies Aaron Red Elk and Gordon Stiles, were found shot in a wooded area behind the property—as well as Colter. Deputy Red Elk and Sheriff Matthews were airlifted to Regional Hospital in Rapid City, while Colter and Deputy Stiles were pronounced dead at the scene."

A mug shot of Frank Colter flashed on the television, followed by photos of Liam and his deputies.

"Deputy Red Elk is said to be in good condition, while Sheriff Matthews—"

"Lynn, I'm sorry to interrupt." The picture on the screen split as the news anchor from before materialized on the right side of it. "But we're getting word that Lieutenant Darryl Munson with the South Dakota Highway Patrol in Rapid City, who is the lead investigator in this case, is about to give a statement. Let's go there now."

The split picture on the screen transitioned to a tall, burly man, who—with his shaved head and broad shoulders—looked more like a marine than a trooper as he stood outside the steps of Weeping Rock's tiny courthouse. "Good afternoon," he said in a voice that was as crisp as his uniform as he spoke into the plethora of microphones taped to the wooden podium in front of him.

"First, I'd like to thank the citizens of Orand County for their patience, and on behalf of the Highway Patrol, I want to take a moment to extend our sympathies and prayers to the victims' families during this difficult time." Clearing his throat, Munson paused to smooth the piece of paper lying on the podium beneath his fingers.

"After speaking at length with Deputy Aaron Red Elk, who was shot by Frank Colter as the warrant was being served, and examining the evidence found at the crime scene, we have determined that Deputy Gordon Stiles shot Frank Colter … as well as Sheriff Matthews."

Cameras began to click as low murmurs filled the audio feed.

"Although I'm not at liberty to give the reason for Deputy Stiles' actions," said Munson, talking over them, "I can tell you that an arrest warrant was issued last night for Reverend Wayne Caffrey, who is wanted in connection with this case. He was picked up two hours ago by troopers outside Pierre, where they confiscated over five kilos of heroin from his tractor-trailer."

The questions erupted.

"How does Caffrey's arrest tie to the shootings —"

"Lieutenant Munson, it's been rumored that heroin was found at Deputy Stiles' residence. Was the motive for the killings drug-related —"

"Was Sheriff Matthews shot by friendly fire —"

"That's all I can say at this time," answered Munson, holding up his hands. "Thank you." Gathering his paper between his thick fingers, he turned abruptly from the cameras.

"I thought we were leaving."

Alice wiped at the tears that had formed in the corners of her eyes before glancing at Claire, who was standing beside the coffee table with her hands on her hips. "We are," she replied, turning off the television. "I was waiting on you."

"I've been ready for the past five minutes," said Claire, then lifting her backpack off the floor, swung it back and forth in front of her as if to prove it.

Pushing herself up from the sofa, Alice drew a stilted breath. "Tell your grandma goodbye and then go put your things in the car."

"The *car*?" Claire gave her a puzzled look. "Oh … you mean that small thing in the driveway?"

"You can drop the attitude."

Claire rolled her eyes as she walked into the kitchen. "Bye, Grandma."

Alice's mother turned from the sink. "Bye, sweetheart. I love you," she said, wrapping her arms around her.

"Love you, too."

As Alice watched Claire traipse towards the door, she found herself wondering why she was so quick to dispense her affections to everyone—but her.

"You can stay you know."

Swallowing her misery, Alice shifted her attention to her mother and sighed. "You and I both know that wouldn't work," she answered in a soft voice.

Her mother's eyes glistened as she tilted her head and shrugged. "You're probably right."

Grabbing a wayward strand of bright yellow hair, Alice gently tucked it behind her mother's ear. "Goodbye, Mom."

"Promise me that you won't let another eleven years go by before you see me again."

"I promise," she said, walking into her embrace.

"I love you."

Alice pulled back before the sob in her throat could manifest itself. "I'll call you tonight."

Hurrying out the door, she trotted down the steps and slid behind the wheel of the used Fiesta that she'd bought for fifty dollars down and a sensible payment plan at *Crazy Larry's AutoMart*.

"Are you okay, Mom?"

"I'm fine," she answered, surprised that her daughter had even bothered to acknowledge her presence, let alone pick up on the fact that there might be something wrong.

Claire eyed her closely as they backed down the drive — and then resumed her texting.

Twenty silent minutes later, Alice came upon the exit to Rapid City.

"Mom?"

"Hmm?"

"Is Sheriff Matthews going to be all right?"

Licking her lips, Alice drew a shaky breath. "I hope so."

Lowering her phone, Claire gazed solemnly out the window as they drove past the exit ramp. "Where are we going?"

"We'll know when we get there."

"That's not an answer."

Alice sighed. "I don't know," she said, resting her arm on the side of the door panel. "I was thinking about someplace where it doesn't snow."

"You mean like Florida?" said Claire, her trademark sarcasm shining through.

Alice looked over at her daughter and smiled. "Why not?"

The hardened expression on Claire's face slowly morphed into a grin; it was as big as it was bold — and genuine.

Returning her attention to the road, Alice began to notice that the farther down the highway she got … the freer she felt.

BLACK CLOUDS GATHERED outside the window, further darkening the dimly lit room of the ICU, as Olivia sat next to the bed stroking the side of Liam's face, which — except for the bruising underneath his eyes — was pale and lifeless … just like the rest of him.

The damage from the bullets had caused a massive hemothorax, causing blood to collect between his chest wall and lungs. Dr. Rhodes, the thoracic surgeon on call, had removed the bullets and inserted a tube in his chest in order to drain the blood and re-inflate his lung. He'd continued to bleed, however, and an emergency thoracotomy had to be performed, during which a small portion of the lower lobe of his left lung was removed.

"Aaron stopped by to see you again," Olivia said in a distant voice as her fingers lightly touched upon the five days of stubble running along his jawline. "I think he really, *really* wants to talk to you …"

She swallowed the ache in her throat and rigidly leaned forward, searching his face for the slightest movement or twitch of any kind. Over the past forty-eight hours, Liam's vitals had steadily improved and he'd been taken off the ventilator, but Dr. Rhodes had expressed his concern over the fact that he had not yet regained consciousness.

Wiping at her swollen eyes, Olivia took his hand in hers as it lay limp against his side and held it to her cheek. "Liam," she begged, turning her quivering lips into his palm, "please wake up."

Drops of rain began to hit the window, drowning out her mournful plea.

"I'm sorry for the things I said to you the other day. I didn't mean any of them," she stated, hoping that he could hear her. "Because the truth of the matter is …" An anguished smile found its way between her cheeks as she reached out and brushed his locks from his forehead. "I adore the fact that you always do the right thing. It's just one of a thousand reasons why I love you." Wrapping her fingers around his, she let go of an uneven breath and closed her eyes.

"January fifth …"

Lifting her head, Olivia's blurred gaze met Liam's.

"It was three years ago … at seven twenty-three in the morning."

A joyful sob came tumbling out of Olivia's mouth as she pressed the button above the bed for the nurse. "*What* was three years ago?" she asked, squeezing his hand.

Liam's fingertips closed partly around hers. "That was the exact moment I knew I wanted to marry you," he said in a ragged whisper. "We were lying in bed talking … and I was explaining the difference between *Rocky* and *Rambo* to you … because you had carelessly lumped them together, and as the sun began to rise, you leaned over and kissed me." The blueness behind his eyes wavered as his chest slowly rose and fell. "My heart's never been the same since that moment … because it simply can't beat without you."

Slipping her arms around him, Olivia's tears spilled down her cheeks as she kissed the side of his face. "I love you."

"Everything's going to be all right," he said after a moment, his breath falling tenderly across her neck as he spoke. "And there's something else I want you to know."

"What?" she asked, resting her head upon his shoulder.

"By the end of next summer … whether it's through Loretta Boyd or a miracle from God … we're going to have a beautiful little boy running around."

Olivia drew back to look at him. "How do you know?" she asked, the laugh accompanying her words sounding as broken as her voice.

Brushing away her tears with his thumb, Liam gazed up at her and smiled. "I just know."

## Thank you

Thank you for taking the time to read *Winter's Malice*. If you enjoyed it, please consider telling your friends or posting a short review. Word of mouth is an author's best friend and is very much appreciated.

~ Belinda G. Buchanan

**www.belindagbuchanan.com**

# THE MONSTER OF SILVER CREEK

This small town in Prairie County, Montana has been rocked to its very core with the brutal murders of four women. A serial killer whose calling card is as unusual as it is twisted is on the loose—and troubled Police Chief Nathan Sommers is bent on stopping him at all costs.

While tracking the killer, Nathan must battle his own demons as he struggles to cope with the death of his wife. He feels her dying was a direct result of his actions and is consumed with guilt.

His personal life becomes even more complicated when he meets Katie, the pretty new owner of the bakery. Nathan slowly builds a relationship with her, but still struggles with Jenny's death. As Nathan draws closer to the killer, everything in his life suddenly comes undone. He is forced to deal with his feelings for Katie, as well as his love for his dead wife in this gripping, psychological thriller.

# TRAGEDY AT SILVER CREEK

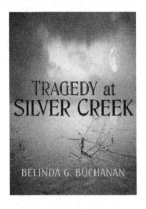

Guilt is a powerful thing, and former deputy Jack Collins is mired in it. Unable to forget the events that have taken place in the town he was sworn to protect, he feels as if he is slowly drowning as he tries to cope with the aftermath of a serial killer's reign of terror, as well as his new — and unwanted — job as chief of police.

When the body of a young woman, having the same puncture wounds as the serial killer's previous victims, is discovered, Jack must determine if this is a copycat crime or the work of a possible accomplice — either of which — could put the killer's only surviving victim in grave danger.

# AFTER ALL IS SAID AND DONE

AFTER ALL IS
SAID AND DONE

A NOVEL
BELINDA G. BUCHANAN

At thirty-four years of age, Ethan Harrington is a brilliant doctor, devoted husband, eager father to be — and borderline alcoholic. He has spent the better part of a year trying to forgive his wife, Jessica, for her infidelity, but her betrayal with a colleague of his has left him hurt beyond words.

That hurt slowly begins to heal with the birth of his son, but it isn't long before he finds out what Jessica has been so desperately trying to keep from him. Ethan's life steadily begins to crumble — and his drinking, fueled by this discovery, slowly engulfs him.

With his marriage now in pieces and his sanity questionable, Ethan struggles to come to terms with his alcoholism and face a past that he has spent a lifetime trying to forget.

# SEASONS OF DARKNESS

Long before Ethan Harrington's turbulent marriage to Jessica, he was just a lonely young man trying to cope with his mother's suicide.

Left alone with his controlling father in an isolated farmhouse, he struggles to live among the shattered remains of a family that was never functional to begin with.

A kindhearted doctor, a beautiful girl, and a caring nanny all love him in different ways, but Ethan, still ravaged by his mother's death, turns to what he has seen his father take comfort in time and time again — thus giving rise to an inner demon that will not turn him loose.

A story of hope, even in the darkest of times, this is a coming-of-age novel that depicts the sometimes difficult, and oftentimes complex, relationship experienced between fathers and sons when tragedy strikes.

To find out more about my novels and myself, you can visit my **website**. I love to talk almost as much as I love to write, so come chat with me on **Facebook** or **Twitter**, and if you're a pinner, come find me on **Pinterest**.

Website: belindagbuchanan.com

facebook.com/Belinda.G.Buchanan.author

twitter.com/BelindaBuchanan

www.pinterest.com/belindabuchanan

## A little bit about me

A native of the bluegrass state, I currently reside there along with my husband and two sons as well as a menagerie of animals that includes two persnickety cats, a hamster, and one dog that thinks he's a person.

Made in the USA
Coppell, TX
21 November 2019